BRINGING IT TO THE TABLE

BRINGING IT TO THE TABLE

ON FARMING AND FOOD

WENDELL BERRY
INTRODUCTION BY MICHAEL POLLAN

COUNTERPOINT

BERKELEY

"Misery" first appeared in *Shenandoah*, Winter 2008.

Library of Congress Cataloging-in-Publication Data

Berry, Wendell, 1934–
Bringing it to the table : on farming and food / Wendell Berry ;
introduction by Michael Pollan.
p. cm.
ISBN 978-1-58243-543-5
1. Agriculture—United States. 2. Family farms—United States. 3. Farmers—
United States—Anecdotes. 4. Local foods—United States.
5. Sustainable agriculture—United States. I. Title.

S441.B472 2009
630.973—dc22

2009024437

Jacket design by Silverander Communications
Interior design by Megan Jones Design
Printed in the United States of America

COUNTERPOINT
2117 Fourth Street
Suite D
Berkeley, CA 94710

www.counterpointpress.com

Distributed by Publishers Group West

10 9 8 7 6 5 4

CONTENTS

INTRODUCTION

by Michael Pollan

A FEW WEEKS AFTER Michelle Obama planted an organic vegetable garden on the South Lawn of the White House in March 2009, the business section of the Sunday *New York Times* published a cover story bearing the headline "Is a Food Revolution Now in Season?" The article, written by the paper's agriculture reporter, said that "after being largely ignored for years by Washington, advocates of organic and locally grown food have found a receptive ear in the White House."

Certainly these are heady days for people who have been working to reform the way Americans grow food and feed themselves—the "food movement" as it is now often called. Markets for alternative kinds of food—local and organic and pastured—are thriving, farmers' markets are popping up like mushrooms, and for the first time in more than a century the number of farmers tallied in the Department of Agriculture's census has gone up rather than down. The new secretary of agriculture has dedicated his department to "sustainability" and holds meetings with the sorts of farmers and activists who not many years ago stood outside the marble walls of the USDA holding signs of protest and snarling traffic with their tractors. Cheap words, you might say, and it is true that, so far at least, there have been more words than deeds, but some of those words are astonishing. Like these: Shortly before his election, Barack Obama told a reporter for *Time* that "our entire agricultural system is built on cheap oil" and went on to connect the dots between the sprawling monocultures of industrial agriculture and, on the one side, the energy crisis and, on the other, the health care crisis.

I have no idea if Barack Obama has ever read Wendell Berry, but Berry's thinking had found its way to his lips.

Americans today are having a national conversation about food and agriculture that it would have been impossible to imagine even a few short years ago. To many Americans it must sound like a brand-new conversation, with its bracing talk about the high price of cheap food, or the links between soil and health, or the impossibility of a society eating well and being in good health unless it also farms well. But to read the essays in this sparkling anthology, many of them dating back to the 1970s and 1980s, is to realize just how little of what we are saying and hearing today Wendell Berry hasn't already said, bracingly, before.

And in that "we" I most definitely, and somewhat abashedly, include myself. I challenge you to find an idea or insight in my own recent writings on food and farming that isn't prefigured (to put it charitably) in Berry's essays on agriculture. There might be one or two in there somewhere, but I must say that reading and rereading these essays has been a deeply humbling experience.

It has also been a powerful reminder that the national conversation now unfolding around the subject of food and farming really began back in the 1970s, with the work of Berry and a small handful of his contemporaries, including Francis Moore Lappé, Barry Commoner, and Joan Gussow. All four of these writers are supreme dot connectors, deeply skeptical of reductive science, and far ahead not only in their grasp of the science of ecology but in their ability to actually *think* ecologically: to draw lines of connection between a hamburger and the price of oil, or between the vibrancy of life in the soil and the health of the plants and animals and people eating from that soil.

I would argue that the conversation got under way in earnest in 1971, when Berry published an article in *The Last Whole Earth Catalogue* introducing Americans to the work of Sir Albert Howard, the British agronomist whose thinking had deeply influenced Berry's own since he first came upon it in 1964. Indeed, much of Berry's thinking about agriculture can be read as an extended elaboration of Howard's master idea that farming should model itself on natural systems such as forests and prairies, and that scientists, farmers, and medical researchers need to reconceive "the whole problem of health in soil, plant, animal and man as one great subject." No single quotation appears more often in Berry's writing than that one, and with good reason: It is manifestly true (as even the most reductive scientists are coming to recognize) and, as a guide to thinking through so many of our problems, it is inexhaustible.

That same year, 1971, Lappé published *Diet for a Small Planet*, which linked modern meat production (and in particular the feeding of grain to cattle) to the problems of world hunger and the environment. Later in the decade, Commoner implicated industrial agriculture in the energy crisis, showing us just how much oil we were eating when we ate from the industrial food chain; and Gussow explained to her nutritionist colleagues that the problem of dietary health could not be understood without reference to the problem of agriculture. Looking back on this remarkably fertile body of work, which told us all we needed to know about the true cost of cheap food and the value of good farming, is to register two pangs of regret, one personal, the other more political: first, that as a young writer coming to these subjects a couple of decades later, I was rather less original than I had thought; and second, that as a society we failed to heed a warning that might have averted or at least mitigated the terrible predicament in which we now find ourselves.

For what would we give today to have back the "environmental crisis" that Berry wrote about so prophetically in the 1970s, a time still innocent of the problem of climate change? Or to have back the comparatively manageable public health problems of that period, before obesity and type 2 diabetes became "epidemic"? (Most experts date the obesity epidemic to the early 1980s.)

But history will show that we failed to take up the invitation to begin thinking ecologically. As soon as oil prices subsided and Jimmy Carter was rusticated to Plains, Georgia (along with his cardigan, thermostat, and solar panels), we went back to business—and agribusiness—as usual, carelessly dropping the thread of the conversation that Berry had helped to start. In the mid-1980s, Ronald Reagan removed Carter's solar panels from the roof of the White House, and the issues that Berry and the others were raising were pushed to the margins of national politics and culture. I worked as an editor at *Harper's Magazine* during the 1980s, and occasionally published Berry's speeches and essays. During the Reagan years Berry was often regarded, at least in the Manhattan media precincts I inhabited, as a "Luddite" and a "crank" and generally as something of a literary and philosophical antique. At a time when everyone else was trading in their typewriters for personal computers, I published his short essay about his refusal to use a typewriter that elicited howls of derision from readers. In those days even the word "agriculture" felt hopelessly out-of-date, something that a culture consumed with the idea of postmodernism had exactly no use for.

In fact when I began writing about agriculture in the late '80s and '90s, I quickly figured out that no editor in Manhattan thought the subject timely or worthy of his or her attention, and that I would be better off avoiding the word entirely and talking instead about food, something people then still had some use for and cared about, yet oddly never thought to connect to the soil or the work of farmers.

It was during this period that I began reading Berry's work closely—avidly, in fact, because I found in it practical answers to questions I was struggling with in my garden. I had begun growing a little of my own food, not on a farm but in the backyard of a second home in the exurbs of New York, and had found myself completely ill-prepared, especially when it came to challenges posed by critters and weeds. An obedient child of Thoreau and Emerson (both of whom mistakenly regarded weeds as emblems of wildness and gardens as declensions from nature), I honored the wild and kept from fencing off my vegetables from the encroaching forest. I don't have to tell you how well that turned out. Thoreau did plant a bean field at Walden, but he couldn't square his love of nature with the need to defend his crop from weeds and birds, and eventually he gave up on agriculture. Thoreau went on to declare that "if it were proposed to me to dwell in the neighborhood of the most beautiful garden that ever human art contrived, or else of a dismal swamp, I should certainly decide for the swamp." With that slightly obnoxious declaration American writing about nature all but turned its back on the domestic landscape. It's not at all surprising that we got better at conserving wilderness than at farming and gardening.

It was Wendell Berry who helped me solve my Thoreau problem, providing a sturdy bridge over the deep American divide between nature and culture. Using the farm rather than the wilderness as his text, Berry taught me I had a legitimate quarrel with nature—a lover's quarrel—and showed me how to conduct it without reaching for the heavy artillery. He relocated wildness from the woods "out there" (beyond the fence) to a handful of garden soil or the shoot of a germinating pea, a necessary quality that could be not just conserved but cultivated. He marked out a path that led us back into nature, no longer as spectators but as full-fledged participants. I battened on every word of his I could find, and to me his words felt anything but antique—indeed, they were fully as alive, and useful, as any writing can be.

Obviously much more is at stake here than a garden fence. My Thoreau problem is another name for the problem of American environmentalism, which historically has had much more to say about leaving nature alone than about how we might use it well. To the extent that we're finally beginning to hear a new, more neighborly conversation between American environmentalists and American farmers, not to mention between urban eaters and rural food producers, Berry deserves much of the credit for getting it started with sentences like these:

> *Why should conservationists have a positive interest in . . . farming? There are lots of reasons, but the plainest is: Conservationists eat. To be interested in food but not in food production is clearly absurd. Urban conservationists may feel entitled to be unconcerned about food production because they are not farmers. But they can't be let off so easily, for they are farming by proxy. They can eat only if land is farmed on their behalf by somebody somewhere in some fashion. If conservationists will attempt to resume responsibility for their need to eat, they will be led back fairly directly to all their previous concerns for the welfare of nature. ("Conservationist and Agrarian," 2002)*

That we are all implicated in farming—that, in his now-famous formulation, "eating is an agricultural act"—is perhaps Berry's signal contribution to the rethinking of food and farming under way today, and in style as well as content this stands as a classically Berry-esque idea: at once perfectly obvious and completely arresting. To read these essays is to feel that way over and over again, to be somehow stopped in your tracks by the plainly self-evident. Here are a few more such ideas that await you in the pages ahead:

> *We have been winning, to our inestimable loss, a competition against our own land and our own people. At present, what we have to show for this "victory" is a surplus of food. But this is a surplus achieved by the ruin of its sources. ("Nature as Measure," 1989)*

"Sustainable agriculture" . . . refers to a way of farming that can be continued indefinitely because it conforms to the terms imposed upon it by the nature of places and the nature of people. ("Stupidity in Concentration," 2002)

Here we come to the heart of the matter—the absolute divorce that the industrial economy has achieved between itself and all ideals and standards outside itself. ("A Defense of the Family Farm," 1986)

This old sun-based agriculture was fundamentally alien to the industrial economy; industrial corporations could make relatively little profit from it. . . . [But] as farmers became more and more dependant on fossil fuel energy, a radical change occurred in their minds. Once focused on biology, the life and health of living things, their thinking now began to focus on technology and economics. Credit, for example, became as pressing an issue as the weather. ("Energy in Agriculture," 1979)

Does the concentration of production in the hands of fewer and fewer big operators really serve the ends of cleanliness and health? Or does it make easier and more lucrative the possibility of collusion between irresponsible producers and corrupt inspectors? ("Sanitation and the Small Farm," 1977)

There is, then, a politics of food that, like any politics, involves our freedom. We still (sometimes) remember that we cannot be free if our minds and voices are controlled by someone else. But we have neglected to understand that we cannot be free if our food and its sources are controlled by someone else. . . . One reason to eat responsibly is to live free. ("The Pleasures of Eating," 1989)

The adjective "prophetic" is often attached to Berry's nonfiction, and while I can understand why people would use the word—he has done an unerring job over the past forty years of showing us precisely where the errors of our ways will lead—his prose never screams or squints in rage. It is always as patient and logical, as plumb and square and scrupulous, as well-planed woodwork. I have learned as much from the construction of his sentences as I have from the construction of his ideas. In my study Berry's books sit on the short shelf I reach for whenever I get tangled in a sentence; reading a few lines at random will often do the trick, break the knot. To enact that unmistakable voice in one's head is to administer a tonic strong enough to freshen thought and expression both and, at its best, to scrub the crud of received opinion from our everyday thoughtless thinking.

Let me leave you with one very recent example of Berry at his best, drawn from an op-ed piece that he published (with his old friend and collaborator Wes Jackson) shortly after the economy crashed in the fall of 2008.

> *For 50 or 60 years, we have let ourselves believe that as long as we have money we will have food. This is a mistake. If we continue our offenses against the land and the labor by which we are fed, the food supply will decline, and we will have a problem far more complex than the failure of our paper economy. The government will bring forth no food by providing hundreds of billions of dollars to the agribusiness corporations.*

I like this passage for its idea—the phrase "paper economy" alone is worth a million words of commentary on the financial crisis—but even more for the very happy news it brings: that this indispensable voice is still out there addressing us in our time of need, and remains as bracing as ever.

PART I
FARMING

Nature as Measure

(1989)

꒳

I LIVE IN A part of the country that at one time a good farmer could take some pleasure in looking at. When I first became aware of it, in the 1940s, the better land, at least, was generally well farmed. The farms were mostly small and were highly diversified, producing cattle, sheep, and hogs, tobacco, corn, and the small grains; nearly all the farmers milked a few cows for home use and to market milk or cream. Nearly every farm household maintained a garden, kept a flock of poultry, and fattened its own meat hogs. There was also an extensive "support system" for agriculture: Every community had its blacksmith shop, shops that repaired harness and machinery, and stores that dealt in farm equipment and supplies.

Now the country is not well farmed, and driving through it has become a depressing experience. Some good small farmers remain, and their farms stand out in the landscape like jewels. But they are few and far between, and they are getting fewer every year. The buildings and other improvements of the old farming are everywhere in decay or have vanished altogether. The produce of the country is increasingly specialized. The small dairies are gone. Most of the sheep flocks are gone, and so are most of the enterprises of the old household economy. There is less livestock and more cash-grain farming. When cash-grain farming comes in, the fences go, the livestock goes, erosion increases, and the fields become weedy.

Like the farmland, the farm communities are declining and eroding. The farmers who are still farming do not farm with as much skill as they did forty years ago, and there are not nearly so many farmers farming as there were forty years ago. As the old have died, they have not been replaced; as the young come of age, they leave farming or leave the community. And as the land and the people deteriorate, so necessarily must the support system. None of the small rural towns is thriving as it did forty years ago. The proprietors of small businesses give up or die and are not replaced. As the farm trade declines, farm equipment franchises are revoked. The remaining farmers must drive longer and longer distances for machines and parts and repairs.

Looking at the country now, one cannot escape the conclusion that there are no longer enough people on the land to farm it well and to take proper care of it. A further and more ominous conclusion is that there is no longer a considerable number of people knowledgeable enough to look at the country and see that it is not properly cared for—though the face of the country is now everywhere marked by the agony of our enterprise of self-destruction.

And suddenly in this wasting countryside there is talk of raising production quotas on Burley tobacco by 24 percent, and tobacco growers are coming under pressure from the manufacturers to decrease their use of chemicals. Everyone I have talked to is doubtful that we have enough people left in farming to meet the increased demand for either quantity or quality, and doubtful that we still have the barnroom to house the increased acreage. In other words, the demand going up has met the culture coming down. No one can be optimistic about the results.

Tobacco, I know, is not a food, but it comes from the same resources of land and people that food comes from, and this emerging dilemma in the production of tobacco can only foreshadow a similar dilemma in the production of food. At every point in our food economy, present conditions remaining, we must expect to come to a time when demand (for quantity or quality) going up will meet the culture coming down. The fact is that we have nearly destroyed American farming, and in the process have nearly destroyed our country.

How has this happened? It has happened because of the application to farming of far too simple a standard. For many years, as a nation, we have asked our land only to produce, and we have asked our farmers only to produce. We have believed that this single economic standard not only guaranteed good performance but also preserved the ultimate truth and rightness of our aims. We have bought unconditionally the economists' line that competition and innovation would solve all problems, and that we would finally accomplish a technological end-run around biological reality and the human condition.

Competition and innovation have indeed solved, for the time being, the problem of production. But the solution has been extravagant, thoughtless, and far too expensive. We have been winning, to our inestimable loss, a competition against our own land and our own people. At present, what we have to show for this "victory" is a surplus of food. But this is a surplus achieved by the ruin of its sources, and it has been used, by apologists for our present economy, to disguise the damage by which it was produced. Food, clearly, is the most important economic product—except when there is a surplus. When there is a surplus, according to our present economic assumptions, food is the *least* important product. The surplus becomes famous as evidence to consumers that they have nothing to worry about, that there is no problem, that present economic assumptions are correct.

But our present economic assumptions are failing in agriculture, and to those having eyes to see the evidence is everywhere, in the cities as well as in the countryside. The singular demand for production has been unable to acknowledge the importance of the sources of production in nature and in human culture. Of course agriculture must be productive; that is a requirement as urgent as it is obvious. But urgent as it is, it is not the *first* requirement; there are two more requirements equally important and equally urgent. One is that if agriculture is to remain productive, it must preserve the land, and the fertility and ecological health of the land; the land, that is, must be used *well*. A further requirement, therefore, is that if the land is to be used well, the people who use it must know it well, must be highly motivated to use it well, must know how to use it well, must have time to use it well, and must be able to afford to use it well. Nothing that has happened in the agricultural revolution of the last fifty years has disproved or invalidated these requirements, though everything that has happened has ignored or defied them.

In light of the necessity that the farmland and the farm people should thrive while producing, we can see that the single standard of productivity has failed.

Now we must learn to replace that standard by one that is more comprehensive: the standard of nature. The effort to do this is not new. It was begun early in this century by Liberty Hyde Bailey of the Cornell University College of Agriculture, by F. H. King of the University of Wisconsin College of Agriculture and the United States Department of Agriculture, by J. Russell Smith, professor of economic geography at Columbia University, by the British agricultural scientist Sir Albert Howard, and by others; and it has continued into our own time in the work of such scientists as John Todd, Wes Jackson, and others. The standard of nature is not so simple or so easy a standard as the standard of productivity. The term "nature" is not so definite or stable a concept as the weights and measures of productivity. But we know what we mean when we say that the first settlers in any American place recognized that place's agricultural potential "by its nature"—that is, by the depth and quality of its soil, the kind and quality of its native vegetation, and so on. And we know what we mean when we say that all too often we have proceeded to ignore the nature of our places in farming them. By returning to "the nature of the place" as standard, we acknowledge the necessary limits of our own intentions. Farming cannot take place except in nature; therefore, if nature does not thrive, farming cannot thrive. But we know too that nature includes us. It is not a place into which we reach from some safe standpoint outside it. We are in it and are a part of it while we use it. If it does not thrive, we cannot thrive. The appropriate measure of farming then is the world's health and our health, and this is inescapably *one* measure.

But the oneness of this measure is far different from the singularity of the standard of productivity that we have been using; it is far more complex. One of its concerns, one of the inevitable natural measures, is productivity; but it is also concerned for the health of all the creatures belonging to a given place, from the creatures of the soil and water to the humans and other creatures of the land surface to the birds of the air. The use of nature as measure proposes an atonement between ourselves and our world, between economy and ecology, between the domestic and the wild. Or it proposes a conscious and careful recognition of the interdependence between ourselves and nature that in fact has always existed and, if we are to live, must always exist.

Industrial agriculture, built according to the single standard of productivity, has dealt with nature, including human nature, in the manner of a monologist or an orator. It has not asked for anything, or waited to hear any response. It has told nature what it wanted, and in various clever ways has taken what it wanted. And since it proposed no limit on its wants, exhaustion has been its inevitable and foreseeable result. This, clearly, is a dictatorial or totalitarian form of behavior, and it is as

7

totalitarian in its use of people as it is in its use of nature. Its connections to the world and to humans and the other creatures become more and more abstract, as its economy, its authority, and its power become more and more centralized.

On the other hand, an agriculture using nature, including human nature, as its measure would approach the world in the manner of a conversationalist. It would not impose its vision and its demands upon a world that it conceives of as a stockpile of raw material, inert and indifferent to any use that may be made of it. It would not proceed directly or soon to some supposedly ideal state of things. It *would* proceed directly and soon to serious thought about our condition and our predicament. On all farms, farmers would undertake to know responsibly where they are and to "consult the genius of the place." They would ask what nature would be doing there if no one were farming there. They would ask what nature would permit them to do there, and what they could do there with the least harm to the place and to their natural and human neighbors. And they would ask what nature would *help* them to do there. And after each asking, knowing that nature will respond, they would attend carefully to her response. The use of the place would necessarily change, and the response of the place to that use would necessarily change the user. The conversation itself would thus assume a kind of creaturely life, binding the place and its inhabitants together, changing and growing to no end, no final accomplishment, that can be conceived or foreseen.

Farming in this way, though it certainly would proceed by desire, is not visionary in the political or utopian sense. In a conversation, you always expect a reply. And if you honor the other party to the conversation, if you honor the *otherness* of the other party, you understand that you must not expect always to receive a reply that you foresee or a reply that you will like. A conversation is immitigably two-sided and always to some degree mysterious; it requires faith.

For a long time now we have understood ourselves as traveling toward some sort of industrial paradise, some new Eden conceived and constructed entirely by human ingenuity. And we have thought ourselves free to use and abuse nature in any way that might further this enterprise. Now we face overwhelming evidence that we are not smart enough to recover Eden by assault, and that nature does not tolerate or excuse our abuses. If, in spite of the evidence against us, we are finding it hard to relinquish our old ambition, we are also seeing more clearly every day how that ambition has reduced and enslaved us. We see how everything—the whole world—is belittled by the idea that all creation is moving or ought to move toward an end that some body, some human body, has thought up. To be free of that end and that ambition would be a delightful and precious thing. Once free of it, we might again go about our work and our lives with a seriousness and pleasure denied to us when we merely submit to a fate already determined by gigantic politics, economics, and technology.

Such freedom is implicit in the adoption of nature as the measure of economic life. The reunion of nature and economy proposes a necessary democracy, for neither economy nor nature can be abstract in practice. When we adopt nature as measure, we require practice that is locally knowledgeable. The particular farm, that is, must not be treated as any farm. And the particular knowledge of particular places is beyond the competence of any centralized power or authority. Farming by the measure of nature, which is to say the nature of the particular place, means that farmers must tend farms that they know and love, farms small enough to know and love, using tools and methods that they know and love, in the company of neighbors that they know and love.

In recent years, our society has been required to think again of the issues of use and abuse of human beings. We understand, for instance, that the inability to distinguish between a particular woman and any woman is a condition predisposing to abuse. It is time that we learn to apply the same understanding to our country. The inability to distinguish between a farm and any farm is a condition predisposing to abuse, and abuse has been the result. Rape, indeed, has been the result, and we have seen that we are not exempt from the damage we have inflicted. Now we must think of marriage.

Stupidity in Concentration

(2002)

༂

I. Confinement, Concentration, Separation

M Y TASK HERE is to show the great stupidity of industrial animal production. Factory farms, like this essay, have the aim of cramming as much as possible into as small a space as possible. To understand these animal factories, we need to keep in mind three principles: confinement, concentration, and separation.

The principle of confinement in so-called animal science is derived from the industrial version of efficiency. The designers of animal factories appear to have had in mind the example of concentration camps or prisons, the aim of which is to house and feed the greatest number in the smallest space at the least expense of money, labor, and attention. To subject innocent creatures to such treatment has long been recognized as heartless. Animal factories make an economic virtue of heartlessness toward domestic animals, to which humans owe instead a large debt of respect and gratitude.

The defenders of animal factories typically assume, or wish others to assume, that these facilities concentrate animals only. But that is not so. They also concentrate the excrement of the animals—which, when properly dispersed, is a valuable source of fertility, but, when concentrated, is at best a waste, at worst a poison.

Perhaps even more dangerous is the inevitability that large concentrations of animals will invite concentrations of disease organisms, which in turn require concentrated and continuous use of antibiotics. And here the issue enlarges beyond the ecological problem to what some scientists think of as an evolutionary problem: The animal factory becomes a breeding ground for treatment-resistant pathogens, exactly as large field monocultures become breeding grounds for pesticide-resistant pests.

To concentrate food-producing animals in large numbers in one place inevitably separates them from the sources of their feed. Pasture and barnyard animals are removed from their old places in the order of a diversified farm, where they roamed about in some freedom, foraging to a significant extent for their own food, grazing in open pastures, or recycling barnyard and household wastes. Confined in the pens of animal factories, they are made dependent almost exclusively upon grains which are grown in large monocultures, at a now generally recognized ecological cost, and which must be transported to the animals sometimes over long distances. Animal factories are energy-wasting enterprises flourishing in a time when we need to be thinking of energy conservation.

The industrialization of agriculture, by concentration and separation, overthrows the restraints inherent in the diversity and balance of healthy ecosystems and good farms. This results in an unprecedented capacity for overproduction, which drives down farm income, which separates yet more farmers from their farms. For the independent farmers of the traditional small family farm, the animal factories substitute hired laborers, who at work are confined in the same unpleasant and unhealthy situation as the animals. Production at such a cost is temporary. The cost finally is diminishment of the human and ecological capacity to produce.

Animal factories ought to have been the subject of much government concern, *if* government is in fact concerned about the welfare of the land and the people. But, instead, the confined animal feeding industry has been the beneficiary of government encouragement and government incentives. This is the result of a political brain disease that causes people in power to think that anything that makes more money or "creates jobs" is good.

We have animal factories, in other words, because of a governmental addiction to short-term economics. Short-term economics is the practice of making as much money as you can as fast as you can by any possible means while ignoring the long-term effects. Short-term economics is the economics of self-interest and greed. People who operate on the basis of short-term economics accumulate large "externalized" costs, which they charge to the future—that is, to the world and to everybody's grandchildren.

People who are concerned about what their grandchildren will have to eat, drink, and breathe tend to be interested in long-term economics. Long-term economics involves a great deal besides the question of how to make a lot of money in a hurry. Long-term economists such as John Ikerd of the University of Missouri believe in applying "the Golden Rule across the generations—doing for future generations as we would have them do for us." Professor Ikerd says: "The three cornerstones of sustainability are ecological soundness, economic viability, and social justice." He thinks that animal factories are deficient by all three measures.

These factories raise issues of public health, of soil and water and air pollution, of the quality of human work, of the humane treatment of animals, of the proper ordering and conduct of agriculture, and of the longevity and healthfulness of food production.

If the people in our state and national governments undertook to evaluate economic enterprises by the standards of long-term economics, they would have to employ their minds in actual thinking. For many of them, this would be a shattering experience, something altogether new, but it would also cause them to learn things and do things that would improve the lives of their constituents.

13

II. FACTORY FARMS VERSUS FARMS

FACTORY FARMS INCREASE and concentrate the ecological risks of food production. This is a well-documented matter of fact. The rivers and estuaries of North Carolina, to use only one example, testify to how quickly a "private" animal factory can become an ecological catastrophe and a public liability.

A farm, on the other hand, disperses the ecological risks involved in food production. A *good* farm not only disperses these risks, but also minimizes them. On a good farm, ecological responsibility is inherent in proper methodologies of land management, and in correct balances between animals and acres, production and carrying capacity. A good farm does not put at risk the healthfulness of the land, the water, and the air.

The ecological differences between a factory farm and a farm may be paramount in a time of rapidly accelerating destruction of the natural world. But there is also an economic difference that, from the standpoint of human communities, is critical.

A factory farm locks the farmer in at the bottom of a corporate hierarchy. In return for the assumption of great economic and other risks, the farmer is permitted to participate minimally in the industry's earnings. In return, moreover, for the security of a contract with the corporation, the farmer gives up the farm's diversity and versatility, reducing it to a specialist operation with one use.

According to one company's projections, a farmer would buy into the broiler business at a cost of $624,275. That would be for four houses that would produce 506,000 birds per year. Under the company's terms, this investment would produce a yearly net income of $23,762. That would be an annual return on investment of 3.8 percent.

I don't know what percentage of annual return this company's shareholders expect to realize from *their* investment. I do know that if it is not substantially better than the farmer's percentage, they would be well advised to sell out and invest elsewhere.

The factory farm, rather than serving the farm family and the local community, is an economic siphon, sucking value out of the local landscape and the local community into distant bank accounts.

To entice them to buy Kentuckians' work and products so cheaply, our state government has given the animal confinement corporations some $200 million in state and federal tax "incentives." In gratitude for these gifts, these corporations now wish to be relieved of any mandated public liability or responsibility for their activities here.

I don't know that the arrogance and impudence of this have been equaled by any other industry. For not only have these people demonstrated, by their contempt for laws and regulations here and elsewhere, their intention to be bad neighbors; they come repeatedly before our elected representatives to ask for special exemptions. But in that very request they acknowledge the great risks and dangers that are involved in their way of doing business. Why should the innocent, why should people with a good conscience, want to be exempt from liability?

It is clear that the advocates of factory farming are not advocates of farming. They do not speak for farmers.

What they support is state-sponsored colonialism—government of, by, and for the corporations.

III. SUSTAINABILITY

THE WORD "SUSTAINABLE" is well on its way to becoming a label, like the word "organic." And so I want to propose a definition of "sustainable agriculture." This phrase, I suggest, refers to a way of farming that can be continued indefinitely because it conforms to the terms imposed upon it by the nature of places and the nature of people.

Our present agriculture, in general, is not ecologically sustainable now, and it is a long way from becoming so. It is too toxic. It is too dependent on fossil fuels. It is too wasteful of soil, of soil fertility, and of water. It is destructive of the health of the natural systems that surround and support our economic life. And it is destructive of genetic diversity, both domestic and wild.

So far, these problems have not received enough attention from the news media or politicians, but the day is coming when they will. A great many people who know about agriculture are worrying about these problems already. It seems likely that the public, increasingly conscious of the issues of personal and ecological health, will sooner or later force the political leadership to pay attention. And a lot of farmers and grassroots farm organizations are now taking seriously the problem of ecological sustainability.

But there is a related issue that is even more neglected, one that has been largely obscured, even for people aware of the requirement of ecological sustainability, by the vogue of the so-called free market and the global economy. I am talking about the issue of the economic sustainability of farms and farmers, farm families and farm communities.

It ought to be obvious that in order to have sustainable agriculture, you have got to make sustainable the lives and livelihoods of the people who do the work. The land cannot thrive if the people who are its users and caretakers do not thrive. Ecological sustainability requires a complex *local* culture as the preserver of the necessary knowledge and skill; and this in turn requires a settled, stable, prosperous local population of farmers and other land users. It ought to be obvious that agriculture cannot be made sustainable by a dwindling population of economically depressed farmers and a growing population of migrant workers.

Why is our farm population dwindling away? Why are the still-surviving farms so frequently in desperate economic circumstances? Why is the suicide rate among farmers three times that of the country as a whole?

There is one reason that is paramount: The present agricultural economy, as designed by the agribusiness corporations (and the politicians, bureaucrats, economists, and experts who do their bidding), uses farmers as expendable "resources" in the process of production, the same way it uses the topsoil, the groundwater, and the ecological integrity of farm landscapes.

From the standpoint of sustainability, either of farmland or farm people, the present agricultural economy is a failure. It is, in fact, a catastrophe. And there is no use in thinking that agriculture can become sustainable by better adapting to the terms imposed by this economy. That is hopeless, because its terms are the wrong terms. The purpose of this economy is rapid, short-term exploitation, not sustainability.

The story we are in now is exactly the same story we have been in for the last hundred years. It is the story of a fundamental conflict between the interests of farmers and farming and the interests of the agribusiness corporations. It is useless to suppose or pretend that this conflict does not exist, or to hope that you can somehow serve both sides at once. The interests are different, they are in conflict, and you have to get on one side or the other.

As a case in point, let us consider the economics of Kentucky's chicken factories, which some are pleased to look upon as a help to farmers. The *Courier-Journal* on May 28, 2000, told the story of a McLean County farmer who raises 1.2 million chickens a year. His borrowed investment of $750,000 brings him an annual income of $20,000 to $30,000. This declares itself immediately as a "deal" tailor-made for desperate farmers. Who besides a desperate farmer would see $20,000 or $30,000 as an acceptable annual return on an investment of $750,000 plus a year's work? In the poultry-processing corporations that sponsor such "farming," how many CEOs would see that as an acceptable return? The fact is that agriculture cannot be made sustainable in this way. The ecological risks are high, and the economic structure is forbidding. How many children of farmers in such an arrangement will want to farm?

Some people would like to claim that this sort of "economic development" is "inevitable." But the only things that seem inevitable about it are the corporate greed that motivates it and the careerism of the academic experts who try to justify it. On May 28, the *Courier-Journal* quoted an agribusiness apologist at the University of Kentucky's experiment station in Princeton, Gary Parker, who said in defense of the animal factories: "Agriculture is a high-volume, high-cost, high-risk type business. You have to borrow a tremendous amount of money. You have to generate a tremendous amount of income just to barely make a living."

The first problem with Mr. Parker's justification is that it amounts to a perfect condemnation of this kind of agriculture. In an editorial on June 4, the *Courier-Journal* quoted Mr. Parker, and then said that such agriculture, though compromising and risky, "can generate great rewards." The *Courier-Journal* did not say who would get those "great rewards." We may be sure, however, that they will not go to the farmers, who, according to Mr. Parker's confession, are just barely making a living.

The second problem with Mr. Parker's statement is that it is not necessarily true. In contrast to the factory farm that realizes a profit of $20,000 or $30,000 on the sale of 1,200,000 chickens, I know a farm family who, last year, as a part of a diversified small farm enterprise, produced 2,000 pastured chickens for a net income of $6,000. This *farm* enterprise involved no large investment for housing or equipment, no large debt, no contract, and no environmental risk. The chickens were of excellent quality. The customers for them were ordinary citizens, about half of whom were from the local rural community. The demand far exceeds the supply. Most of the proceeds for these chickens went to the family that did the work of producing them. A substantial portion of that money will be spent in the local community. Such a possibility has not been noticed by Mr. Parker or the *Courier-Journal* because, I suppose, it is not "tremendous" and it serves the interest of farmers, not corporations.

Agricultural Solutions
for Agricultural Problems

(1978)

⚘

I T MAY TURN out that the most powerful and the most destructive change of modern times has been a change in language: the rise of the image, or metaphor, of the machine. Until the industrial revolution occurred in the minds of most of the people in the so-called developed countries, the dominant images were organic: They had to do with living things; they were biological, pastoral, agricultural, or familial. God was seen as a "shepherd," the faithful as "the sheep of His pasture." One's home country was known as one's "motherland." Certain people were said to have the strength of a lion, the grace of a deer, the speed of a falcon, the cunning of a fox, etc. Jesus spoke of himself as a "bridegroom." People who took good care of the earth were said to practice "husbandry." The ideal relationships among people were "brotherhood" and "sisterhood."

Now we do not flinch to hear men and women referred to as "units" as if they were as uniform and interchangeable as machine parts. It is common, and considered acceptable, to refer to the mind as a computer: one's thoughts are "inputs"; other people's responses are "feedback." And the body is thought of as a machine; it is said, for instance, to use food as "fuel"; and the best workers and athletes are praised by being compared to machines. Work is judged almost exclusively now by its "efficiency," which, as used, is a mechanical standard, or by its profitability, which is our only trusted index of mechanical efficiency. One's country is no longer loved familially and intimately as a "motherland," but rather priced according to its "productivity" of "raw materials" and "natural resources" —valued, that is, strictly according to its ability to keep the machines running. And recently R. Buckminster Fuller asserted that "the universe physically is itself the most incredible technology"—the necessary implication being that God is not father, shepherd, or bridegroom, but a mechanic, operating by principles which, according to Fuller, "can only be expressed mathematically."

In view of this revolution of language, which is in effect the uprooting of the human mind, it is not surprising to realize that farming too has been made to serve under the yoke of this extremely reductive metaphor. Farming, according to most of the most powerful people now concerned with it, is no longer a way of life, no longer husbandry or even agriculture; it is an industry known as "agribusiness," which looks upon a farm as a "factory," and upon farmers, plants, animals, and the land itself as interchangeable parts or "units of production."

This view of farming has been dominant now for a generation, and so it is not too soon to ask: How well does it work? We must answer that it works as any industrial machine works: very "efficiently" according to the terms of an extremely specialized accounting. That is to say that it *apparently* makes it possible for about 4 percent of the population to "feed" the rest. So long as we keep the focus narrowed to the "food factory" itself, we have to be impressed: It is elaborately organized; it is technologically sophisticated; it is, by its own definition of the term, marvelously "efficient."

Only when we widen the focus do we see that this "factory" is in fact a failure. Within itself it has the order of a machine, but, like other enterprises of the industrial vision, it is part of a rapidly widening and deepening disorder. It will be sufficient here to list some of the serious problems that have a demonstrable connection with industrial agriculture: (1) soil erosion, (2) soil compaction, (3) soil and water pollution, (4) pests and diseases resulting from monoculture and ecological deterioration, (5) depopulation of rural communities, and (6) decivilization of the cities.

The most obvious falsehood of "agribusiness" accounting has to do with the alleged "efficiency" of "agribusiness" technology. This is, in the first place, an efficiency calculated in the productivity of workers, not of acres. In the second place the productivity per "man-hour," as given out by "agribusiness" apologists, is dangerously—and, one must assume, intentionally—misleading. For the 4 percent of our population that is left on the farm does not, by any stretch of imagination, feed the rest. That 4 percent is only a small part, and the worst-paid part, of a food production network that includes purchasers, wholesalers, retailers, processors, packagers, transporters, and the manufacturers and salesmen of machines, building materials, feeds, pesticides, herbicides, fertilizers, medicines, and fuel. All these producers are at once in competition with each other and dependent on each other, and all are dependent on the petroleum industry.

As for the farmers themselves, they have long ago lost control of their destiny. They are no longer "independent farmers," subscribing to that ancient and perhaps indispensable ideal, but are agents of their creditors and of the market. They are "units of production" who, or which, must perform "efficiently"—regardless of what they get out of it either as investors or as human beings.

In the larger accounting, then, industrial agriculture is a failure on its way to being a catastrophe. Why is it a failure? There are, I think, two inescapable reasons.

The first is that the industrial vision is perhaps inherently an oversimplifying vision, which proceeds on the assumption that consequence

21

is always singular; industrialists invariably assume that they are solving for X—X being production. In order to solve for X, industrial agriculturists have to reduce any agricultural problem to a problem in mechanics—as, for example, modern confinement-feeding techniques became possible only when animals could be considered as machines.

What this vision excludes, as a matter of course, are biology on the one hand, and human culture on the other. Once vision is enlarged to include these considerations, we see readily that—as wisdom has always counseled us—consequences are invariably multiple, self-multiplying, long-lasting, and unforeseeable in something like geometric proportion to the size or power of the cause. Taking our bearings from traditional wisdom and from the insights of the ecologists—which, so far as I can see, confirm traditional wisdom—we realize that in a country the size of the United States, and economically uniform, the smallest possible agricultural "unit of production" is very large indeed. It consists of all the farmland, plus all the farmers, plus all the farming communities, plus all the knowledge and the technical means of agriculture, plus all the available species of domestic plants and animals, plus the natural systems and cycles that surround farming and support it, plus the knowledge, taste, judgment, kitchen skills, etc. of all the people who buy food. A proper solution to an agricultural problem must preserve and promote the good health of this "unit." Nothing less will do.

The second reason for the failure of industrial agriculture is its wastefulness. In natural or biological systems, waste does not occur. And it is easy to produce examples of nonindustrial human cultures in which waste was or is virtually unknown. All that is sloughed off in the living arc of a natural cycle remains within the cycle; it becomes fertility, the power of life to continue. In nature death and decay are as necessary— are, one may almost say, as lively—as life; and so nothing is wasted. There is really no such thing, then, as natural production; in nature, there is only reproduction.

But waste—so far, at least—has always been intrinsic to industrial production. There have always been unusable "by-products." Because industrial cycles are never complete—because there is no *return*—there are two characteristic results of industrial enterprise: exhaustion and contamination. The energy industry, for instance, is not a cycle, but only a short arc between an empty hole and poisoned air. And farming, which is inherently cyclic, capable of regenerating and reproducing itself indefinitely, becomes similarly destructive and self-exhausting when transformed into an industry. Agricultural pollution is a serious and growing problem. And industrial agriculture is forced by its very character to treat the soil itself as a "raw material," which it proceeds to "use up." It has been estimated, for instance, that at the present rate of cropland erosion Iowa's soil will be exhausted by the year 2050. I have seen no attempt to calculate the *human* cost of such farming—by attrition, displacement, social disruption, etc.—I assume because it is incalculable.

This failure of industrial agriculture is not more obvious, or more noticed, because many of its worst social and economic consequences have collected in the cities, and are erroneously called "urban problems." Also, because the farm population is now so small, most people know nothing of farming, and cannot recognize agricultural problems when they see them.

But if industrial agriculture is a failure, then how does it continue to produce such an enormous volume of food? One reason is that most countries where industrial agriculture is practiced have soils that were originally good, possessing great natural reserves of fertility. (Industrial agriculture is much more quickly destructive in places where the fertility reserves of the soil are not great—as in the Amazon basin.) Another reason is that, as natural fertility has declined, we have so far been able to subsidize food production by large applications of chemical fertilizer. These have effectively disguised the loss of natural fertility, but it is

23

important to emphasize that they *are* a disguise. They delay some of the consequences of failure, but cannot prevent them. Chemical fertilizers are required in vast amounts, they are increasingly expensive, and most of them come from sources that are not renewable. Industrial agriculture is now absolutely dependent on them, and this dependence is one of its fundamental weaknesses.

Another weakness of industrial agriculture is its absolute dependence on an enormous and intricate—hence fragile—economic and industrial organization. Industrial food production can be gravely impaired or stopped by any number of causes, none of which need be agricultural: a trucker's strike, an oil shortage, a credit shortage, a manufacturing "error" such as the PBB catastrophe in Michigan.

A third weakness is the absolute dependence of most of the population on industrial agriculture—and the lack of any "backup system." We have an unprecedentedly large urban population that has no land to grow food on, no knowledge of how to grow it, and less and less knowledge of what to do with it after it is grown. That this population can continue to eat through shortage, strike, embargo, riot, depression, war—or any of the other large-scale afflictions that societies have always been heir to and that industrial societies are uniquely vulnerable to—is not a certainty or even a faith; it is a superstition.

As an example of the unexamined confusions and contradictions that underlie industrial agriculture, consider Agriculture Secretary Bob Bergland's recent remarks on the state of agriculture in China: "From the manpower-production point of view, they're terribly inefficient—700 million people doing the most pedestrian kind of things. But in production per acre, they're enormously successful. They get nine times as many calories per acre as we do in the United States."

This comment is remarkable for its failure to acknowledge any possible connection between China's large agricultural work force and its high per-acre productivity. In many parts of China, according to one recent observer, the agriculture is still much closer to what we call gardening than to what we call farming. Because their farming is done on comparatively small plots, using a lot of hand labor, Chinese farmers have at their disposal such high-production techniques as intercropping and close rotations, which with us are available only to home gardeners. Many Chinese fields have maintained the productivity of gardens for thousands of years, and this is directly attributable to the great numbers of the farming population. Each acre can be intensively used and cared for, maintained for centuries at maximum fertility and yield, because there are enough knowledgeable people to do the necessary handwork.

It is naive to assume, as Mr. Bergland implicitly does, that such an agriculture can be improved by "modernization"—that is, by the introduction of industrial standards, methods, and technology. How can this agriculture be industrialized without destroying its intensive methods, and thus reducing its productivity per acre? How can the so-called pedestrian tasks be taken over by machines without displacing people, increasing unemployment, degrading the quality of land maintenance, increasing slums and other urban blights? How, in other words, can this revolution fail to cause in China the same disorders that it has already caused in the United States? I do not mean to imply that these questions can be answered simply. My point is that before we participate in the industrialization of Chinese agriculture we ought to ask and answer these questions.

Finally, the Secretary's statement is remarkable for its revealing use of the word "pedestrian." This is a usage strictly in keeping with the industrial revolution of our language. The farther industrialization has gone with us, and the more it has influenced our values and behavior, the more contemptuous and belittling has the adjective "pedestrian" become. If you want to know how highly anything "pedestrian" is regarded, try walking along the edge of a busy highway; you will see that you are regarded mainly as an obstruction to the progress of greater power and velocity. The less power and velocity a thing has, the more "pedestrian" it is. A plow with one bottom is, as a matter of course, more "pedestrian" than a plow with eight bottoms; the quality of use is not recognized as an issue. The hand laborers are thus to be eliminated from China's fields for the same reason that we now build housing developments without sidewalks: The pedestrian, not being allowed *for*, is not allowed. By the use of this term, the Secretary ignores the issue of the quality of work on the one hand, and on the other hand the issue of social values and aims. Is field work necessarily improved when done with machines instead of people? And is a worker necessarily improved by being replaced by a machine? Does a worker invariably work better, more ably, with more interest and satisfaction, when his power is mechanically magnified? And is a worker better off working at a "pedestrian" farm task or unemployed in an urban ghetto? In which instance is his country better off?

I have belabored Secretary Bergland's statement at such length not because it is so odd, but because it is so characteristic of the dominant American approach to agriculture. He is using—unconsciously, I suspect—the language of agricultural industrialism, which fails to solve agricultural problems correctly because it cannot understand or define them as agricultural problems.

I WILL NOW try to define an approach to agriculture that is agricultural, that will lead to proper solutions, and that will, in consequence, safeguard and promote the health of the great unit of food production, which includes us all and all of our country. In order to do this I will deal with four problems, which seem to me inherent in the discipline of farming, and which are practical in the sense that their ultimate solutions cannot occur in public places—in organizations, in markets, or in policies—but only *on farms*. These are the problems of scale, of balance, of diversity, of quality. That these problems cannot be separated, and that no one of them can be solved without solving the others, testifies to their authenticity.

1. The Problem of Scale. The identification of scale as a "problem" implies that things can be too big as well as too small, and I believe that this is so. Technology can grow to a size that is first undemocratic and then inhuman. It can grow beyond the control of individual human beings—and so, perhaps, beyond the control of human institutions. How large can a machine be before it ceases to serve people and begins to subjugate them?

The size of landholdings is likewise a *political* fact. In any given region there is a farm size that is democratic, and a farm size that is plutocratic or totalitarian. A great danger to democracy now in the United States is the steep decline in the number of people who own farmland—or landed property of any kind. (According to a just-published report of the General Accounting Office, "Today, it is estimated that less than one-half of all farmland is owned by the operator.") Earl Butz has suggested that this is made up for by the increased numbers of people who own insurance policies. But the value of insurance policies fluctuates with the value of money, whereas the *real* value of land never varies; it is always equal to the value of survival, of life. When this value is controlled by a wealthy or powerful minority, then democracy is reduced to mere governmental *forms*, easy to destroy or ignore.

Moreover, in any given region there is a limit beyond which a farm outgrows the attention, affection, and care of a single owner.

The size of fields is also a matter of agricultural concern. Fields can be too big to permit effective rotation of grazing, or to prevent erosion of land in cultivation. In general, the steeper the ground, the smaller should be the fields. On the steep slopes of the Andes, for instance, agriculture has survived for thousands of years. This survival has obviously depended on holding the soil in place, and the Andean peasants have an extensive

27

methodology of erosion control. Of all their means and methods, none is more important than the smallness of their fields—which is permitted by the smallness of their technology, most of the land still being worked by hand or with oxen.

2. The Problem of Balance. Finding the correct ratio between people and land, so that maintenance always equals production. This is obviously related to the problem of scale. In the correct solution to these problems, such problems as soil erosion and soil compaction will be solved.

But also each farm and each farmer must establish the proper ratio between plants and animals. This is the foundation of agricultural independence. In this balance of plants and animals the fertility cycle is kept complete, or as nearly complete as possible. Ideally, the farm would provide its own fertility. However, in commercial farming, when so many nutrients are shipped off the farm as food, it is necessary to return them to the farm in the form of composted "urban wastes"—sewage, garbage, etc.

By studying the problem of balance, one discovers the carrying capacity of a farm—that is, the amount it can produce without diminishing its ability to produce.

When the problem of balance is solved, a farm's production becomes more or less constant. The farm will no longer be stocked or cultivated according to fluctuations of the market—which is not agriculture but an imitation, on the farm, of industrial economics.

3. The Problem of Diversity. This is the only possible agricultural "backup system." On the farm it means not putting all the eggs in one basket; it means—within the limits of nature, sense, and practicality—having as many kinds, as many species, as possible.

In terms of our country's agriculture as a whole, too, it means the diversity of species. But it also means as many different kinds of *good* agriculture as possible: farms changing in kind, as necessary, from one location to another; but also truck farms and part-time farms near cities,

28

to increase local self-sufficiency and independence; and home gardens everywhere, in the cities as well as in the country.

4. The Problem of Quality. *Quality*, as I shall understand it here, is indistinguishable from *health*—bodily health, coming from good food, but also economic, political, cultural, and spiritual health. All these kinds of health are related. And I hope that my discussion of the other problems has begun to make clear how dependent health is on good work.

INDUSTRIAL AGRICULTURE HAS tended to look on the farmer as a "worker"—a sort of obsolete but not yet dispensable machine—acting on the advice of scientists and economists. We have neglected the truth that a *good* farmer is a craftsman of the highest order, a kind of artist. It is the good work of good farmers—nothing else—that ensures a sufficiency of food over the long term.

Ignoring that, industrial economics has encouraged poor work on the farm. I believe that it has done so because poor work can be easily priced. Since poor work lasts only a short time, the money value of its whole life can be readily calculated. Good work, which in fact or influence endures beyond the foresight of economists, can be valued but not priced, because its worth is incalculable. I am talking about the difference, say, between a wire fence and a stone wall, or between any gasoline engine and any good breed of livestock.

I am more and more convinced that the only guarantee of quality in practice lies in the subsistence principle—that is, in the use of the product by the producer—a principle depreciated virtually out of existence by industrial agriculture. Indeed, it is sometimes offered as one of the benefits of industrial agriculture that farm families now patronize the supermarkets just like city people. On the other hand, it can be well argued that people who use their own products will be as concerned for quality as for quantity, whereas people who produce exclusively for the market will be mainly interested in quantity.

It will be noticed that production is not on my list of problems. The reason is that if the four problems I have dealt with are properly solved, production will not be a problem. Good production is merely the result of good farming.

A Defense of the Family Farm

(1986)

꒦

D EFENDING THE FAMILY farm is like defending the Bill of Rights or
the Sermon on the Mount or Shakespeare's plays. One is amazed
at the necessity for defense, and yet one agrees gladly, knowing that the
family farm is both eminently defensible and a part of the definition of
one's own humanity. But having agreed to this defense, one remembers
uneasily that there has been a public clamor in defense of the family farm
throughout all the years of its decline—that, in fact, "the family farm"
has become a political catchword, like democracy and Christianity, and
much evil has been done in its name.

Several careful distinctions are therefore necessary. What I shall
mean by the term "family farm" is a farm small enough to be farmed by a
family and one that *is* farmed by a family, perhaps with a small amount of
hired help. I shall *not* mean a farm that is owned by a family and worked
by other people. The family farm is both the home and the workplace of
the family that owns it.

By the verb "farm," I do not mean just the production of marketable
crops but also the responsible maintenance of the health and usability of

the place while it is in production. A family farm is one that is properly cared for by its family.

Furthermore, the term "family farm" implies longevity in the connection between family and farm. A family farm is not a farm that a family has bought on speculation and is only occupying and using until it can be profitably sold. Neither, strictly speaking, is it a farm that a family has newly bought, though, depending on the intentions of the family, we may be able to say that such a farm is *potentially* a family farm. This suggests that we may have to think in terms of ranks or degrees of family farms. A farm that has been in the same family for three generations may rank higher as a family farm than a farm that has been in a family only one generation; it may have a higher degree of familiness or familiarity than the one-generation farm. Such distinctions have a practical usefulness to the understanding of agriculture, and, as I hope to show, there are rewards of longevity that do not accrue only to the family farm.

I mentioned the possibility that a family farm might use a small amount of hired help. This greatly complicates matters, and I wish it were possible to say, simply, that a family farm is farmed with family labor. But it seems important to allow for the possibility of supplementing family labor with wagework or some form of sharecropping. Not only may family labor become insufficient as a result, say, of age or debility but also an equitable system of wage earning or sharecropping would permit unpropertied families to earn their way to farm ownership. The critical points, in defining "family farm," are that the amount of nonfamily labor should be small and that it should supplement, not replace, family labor. On a family farm, the family members are workers, not overseers. If a family on a family farm does require supplementary labor, it seems desirable that the hired help should live on the place and work year-round; the idea of a family farm is jeopardized by supposing that the farm family might be simply the guardians or maintainers of crops planted and harvested by seasonal workers. These requirements, of course, imply both small scale and diversity.

Finally, I think we must allow for the possibility that a family farm might be very small or marginal and that it might not entirely support its family. In such cases, though the economic return might be reduced, the *values* of the family-owned and family-worked small farm are still available both to the family and to the nation.

THE IDEA OF the family farm, as I have just defined it, is conformable in every way to the idea of good farming—that is, farming that does not destroy either farmland or farm people. The two ideas may, in fact, be inseparable. If family farming and good farming are as nearly synonymous as I suspect they are, that is because of a law that is well understood, still, by most farmers but that has been ignored in the colleges, offices, and corporations of agriculture for thirty-five or forty years. The law reads something like this: Land that is in human use must be lovingly used; it requires intimate knowledge, attention, and care.

The practical meaning of this law (to borrow an insight from Wes Jackson[1]) is that there is a ratio between eyes and acres, between farm size and farm hands, that is correct. We know that this law is unrelenting—that, for example, one of the meanings of our current high rates of soil erosion is that we do not have enough farmers; we have enough farmers to use the land but not enough to use it and protect it at the same time.

In this law, which is not subject to human repeal, is the justification of the small, family-owned, family-worked farm, for this law gives a preeminent and irrevocable value to *familiarity*, the family life that alone can properly connect a people to a land. This connection, admittedly, is easy to sentimentalize, and we must be careful not to do so. We all know that small family farms can be abused because we know that sometimes they have been; nevertheless, it is true that familiarity tends to mitigate and to correct abuse. A family that has farmed land through two or three

33

generations will possess not just the land but a remembered history of its own mistakes and of the remedies of those mistakes. It will know not just what it *can* do, what is technologically possible, but also what it *must* do and what it must *not* do; the family will have understood the ways in which it and the farm empower and limit one another. This is the value of longevity in landholding: In the long term, knowledge and affection accumulate, and, in the long term, knowledge and affection pay. They do not just pay the family in goods and money; they also pay the family and the whole country in health and satisfaction.

But the justifications of the family farm are not merely agricultural; they are political and cultural as well. The question of the survival of the family farm and the farm family is one version of the question of who will own the country, which is, ultimately, the question of who will own the people. Shall the usable property of our country be democratically divided, or not? Shall the power of property be a democratic power, or not? If many people do not own the usable property, then they must submit to the few who do own it. They cannot eat or be sheltered or clothed except in submission. They will find themselves entirely dependent on money; they will find costs always higher, and money always harder to get. To renounce the principle of democratic property, which is the only basis of democratic liberty, in exchange for specious notions of efficiency or the economics of the so-called free market is a tragic folly.

There is one more justification, among many, that I want to talk about—namely, that the small farm of a good farmer, like the small shop of a good craftsman or craftswoman, gives work a quality and a dignity that it is dangerous, both to the worker and the nation, for human work to go without. If using ten workers to make one pin results in the production of many more pins than the ten workers could produce individually, that is undeniably an improvement in production, and perhaps uniformity is a virtue in pins. But, in the process, ten workers have been demeaned; they have been denied the economic use of their minds;

their work has become thoughtless and skill-less. Robert Heilbroner says that such "division of labor reduces the activity of labor to dismembered gestures."[2]

Eric Gill sees in this industrial dismemberment of labor a crucial distinction between *making* and *doing*, and he describes "the degradation of the mind" that is the result of the shift from making to doing.[3] This degradation of the mind cannot, of course, be without consequences. One obvious consequence is the degradation of products. When workers' minds are degraded by loss of responsibility for what is being made, they cannot use judgment; they have no use for their critical faculties; they have no occasions for the exercise of workmanship, of workmanly pride. And the consumer is degraded by loss of the opportunity for qualitative choice. This is why we must now buy our clothes and immediately resew the buttons; it is why our expensive purchases quickly become junk.

With industrialization has come a general depreciation of work. As the price of work has gone up, the value of it has gone down, until it is now so depressed that people simply do not want to do it anymore. We can say without exaggeration that the present national ambition of the United States is unemployment. People live for quitting time, for weekends, for vacations, and for retirement; moreover, this ambition seems to be classless, as true in the executive suites as on the assembly lines. One works not because the work is necessary, valuable, useful to a desirable end, or because one loves to do it, but only to be able to quit—a condition that a saner time would regard as infernal, a condemnation. This is explained, of course, by the dullness of the work, by the loss of responsibility for, or credit for, or knowledge of the thing made. What can be the status of the working small farmer in a nation whose motto is a sigh of relief: "Thank God it's Friday"?

But there is an even more important consequence: By the dismemberment of work, by the degradation of our minds as workers, we are denied our highest calling, for, as Gill says, "every man is called to give

35

love to the work of his hands. Every man is called to be an artist."[4] The small family farm is one of the last places—they are getting rarer every day—where men and women (and girls and boys, too) can answer that call to be an artist, to learn to give love to the work of their hands. It is one of the last places where the maker—and some farmers still do talk about "making the crops"—is responsible, from start to finish, for the thing made. This certainly is a spiritual value, but it is not for that reason an impractical or uneconomic one. In fact, from the exercise of this responsibility, this giving of love to the work of the hands, the farmer, the farm, the consumer, and the nation all stand to gain in the most practical ways: They gain the means of life, the goodness of food, and the longevity and dependability of the sources of food, both natural and cultural. The proper answer to the spiritual calling becomes, in turn, the proper fulfillment of physical need.

THE FAMILY FARM, then, is good, and to show that it is good is easy. Those who have done most to destroy it have, I think, found no evil in it. But, if a good thing is failing among us, pretty much without being argued against and pretty much without professed enemies, then we must ask *why* it should fail. I have spent years trying to answer this question, and, while I am sure of some answers, I am also sure that the complete answer will be hard to come by because the complete answer has to do with who and what we are as a people; the fault lies in our identity and therefore will be hard for us to see.

However, we must *try* to see, and the best place to begin may be with the fact that the family farm is not the only good thing that is failing among us. The family farm is failing because it belongs to an order of values and a kind of life that are failing. We can only find it wonderful, when we put our minds to it, that many people now seem willing to mount an emergency effort to "save the family farm" who have not yet thought to save the family or the community, the neighborhood schools or the small local businesses, the domestic arts of household and homestead, or cultural and moral tradition—all of which are also failing, and on all of which the survival of the family farm depends.

The family farm is failing because the pattern it belongs to is failing, and the principal reason for this failure is the universal adoption, by our people and our leaders alike, of industrial values, which are based on three assumptions:

1. That value equals price—that the value of a farm, for example, is whatever it would bring on sale, because both a place and its price are "assets." There is no essential difference between farming and selling a farm.

2. That all relations are mechanical. That a farm, for example, can be used like a factory, because there is no essential difference between a farm and a factory.

3. That the sufficient and definitive human motive is competitiveness— that a community, for example, can be treated like a resource or a market, because there is no difference between a community and a resource or a market.

The industrial mind is a mind without compunction; it simply accepts that people, ultimately, will be treated as things and that things, ultimately, will be treated as garbage.

Such a mind is indifferent to the connections, which are necessarily both practical and cultural, between people and land; which is to say that it is indifferent to the fundamental economy and economics of human life. Our economy is increasingly abstract, increasingly a thing of paper, unable either to describe or to serve the real economy that determines whether or not people will eat and be clothed and sheltered. And it is this increasingly false or fantastical economy that is invoked as a standard of national health and happiness by our political leaders.

That this so-called economy can be used as a universal standard can only mean that it is itself without standards. Industrial economists cannot measure the economy by the health of nature, for they regard nature as simply a source of "raw materials." They cannot measure it by the health of people, for they regard people as "labor" (that is, as tools or machine parts) or as "consumers." They can measure the health of the economy only in sums of money.

Here we come to the heart of the matter—the absolute divorce that the industrial economy has achieved between itself and all ideals and standards outside itself. It does this, of course, by arrogating to itself the status of primary reality. Once that is established, all its ties to principles of morality, religion, or government necessarily fall slack.

But a culture disintegrates when its economy disconnects from its government, morality, and religion. If we are dismembered in our economic life, how can we be members in our communal and spiritual life? We assume that we can have an exploitive, ruthlessly competitive, profit-for-profit's-sake economy, and yet remain a decent and a democratic nation, as we still apparently wish to think ourselves. This simply means that our highest principles and standards have no practical force or influence and are reduced merely to talk.

That this is true was acknowledged by William Safire in a recent column, in which he declared that our economy is driven by greed and that greed, therefore, should no longer count as one of the seven deadly sins. "Greed," he said, "is finally being recognized as a virtue . . . the best engine of betterment known to man." It is, moreover, an agricultural virtue: "The cure for world hunger is the driving force of Greed." Such statements would be possible only to someone who sees the industrial economy as the ultimate reality. Mr. Safire attempts a disclaimer, perhaps to maintain his status as a conservative: "I hold no brief for Anger, Envy, Lust, Gluttony, Pride or Sloth."[5] But this is not a cat that can be let only partly out of the bag. In fact, all seven of the deadly sins are "driving forces" of this economy, as its advertisements and commercials plainly show.

As a nation, then, we are not very religious and not very democratic, and *that* is why we have been destroying the family farm for the last forty years—along with other small local economic enterprises of all kinds. We have been willing for millions of people to be condemned to failure and dispossession by the workings of an economy utterly indifferent to any claims they may have had either as children of God or as citizens of a democracy. "That's the way a dynamic economy works," we have said. We have said, "Get big or get out." We have said, "Adapt or die." And we have washed our hands of them.

THROUGHOUT THIS PERIOD of drastic attrition on the farm, we supposedly have been "subsidizing agriculture," but, as Wes Jackson has pointed out,[6] this is a misstatement. What we have actually been doing is using the farmers to launder money for the agribusiness corporations, which have controlled both their supplies and their markets, while the farmers have overproduced and been at the mercy of the markets. The result has been that the farmers have failed by the millions, and the agribusiness corporations have prospered—or they prospered until the present farm depression, when some of them have finally realized that, after all, they are dependent on their customers, the farmers.

Throughout this same desperate time, the colleges of agriculture, the experiment stations, and the extension services have been working under their old mandate to promote "a sound and prosperous agriculture and rural life," to "aid in maintaining an equitable balance between agriculture and other segments of the economy," to contribute "to the establishment and maintenance of a permanent and effective agricultural industry," and to help "the development and improvement of the rural home and rural life."[7]

That the land-grant system has failed this commission is, by now, obvious. I am aware that there are many individual professors, scientists, and extension workers whose lives have been dedicated to the fulfill-ment of this commission and whose work has genuinely served the rural home and rural life. But, in general, it can no longer be denied that the system as a whole has failed. One hundred and twenty-four years af-ter the Morrill Act, ninety-nine years after the Hatch Act, seventy-two years after the Smith-Lever Act, the "industrial classes" are not liberally educated, agriculture and rural life are not sound or prosperous or per-manent, and there is no equitable balance between agriculture and other segments of the economy. Anybody's statistics on the reduction of the farm population, on the decay of rural communities, on soil erosion, soil and water pollution, water shortages, and farm bankruptcies tell indis-putably a story of failure.

This failure cannot be understood apart from the complex alle-giances between the land-grant system and the aims, ambitions, and values of the agribusiness corporations. The willingness of land-grant professors, scientists, and extension experts to serve as state-paid re-searchers and traveling salesmen for those corporations has been well documented and is widely known.

The reasons for this state of affairs, again, are complex. I have already given some of them; I don't pretend to know them all. But I would like to mention one that I think is probably the most telling: that the offices of the land-grant complex, like the offices of the agricultural bureaucracy, have been looked upon by their aspirants and their occupants as a means not to serve farmers, but to escape farming. Over and over again, one hears the specialists and experts of agriculture introduced as "old farm boys" who have gone on (as is invariably implied) to better things. The reason for this is plain enough: The life of a farmer has characteristically been a fairly hard one, and the life of a college professor or professional expert has charac-teristically been fairly easy. Farmers—working family farmers—do not have tenure, business hours, free weekends, paid vacations, sabbaticals, and retirement funds; they do not have professional status.

The direction of the career of agricultural professionals is, typically, not toward farming or toward association with farmers. It is "upward" through the hierarchy of a university, a bureau, or an agribusiness corporation. They do not, like Cincinnatus, leave the plow to serve their people and return to the plow. They leave the plow, simply, for the sake of leaving the plow.

This means that there has been for several decades a radical disconnection between the land-grant institutions and the farms, and this disconnection has left the land-grant professionals free to give bad advice; indeed, if they can get this advice published in the right place, from the standpoint of their careers it does not matter whether their advice is good or not.

For example, after years of milk glut, when dairy farmers are everywhere threatened by their surplus production, university experts are still working to increase milk production and still advising farmers to cull their least productive cows—apparently oblivious both of the possible existence of other standards of judgment and of the fact that this culling of the least productive cows is, ultimately, the culling of the smaller farmers.

Perhaps this could be dismissed as human frailty or inevitable bureaucratic blundering—except that the result is damage, caused by people who probably would not have given such advice if they were themselves in a position to suffer from it. Serious responsibilities are undertaken by public givers of advice, and serious wrong is done when the advice is bad. Surely a kind of monstrosity is involved when tenured professors with protected incomes recommend or even tolerate Darwinian economic policies for farmers, or announce (as one university economist after another has done) that the failure of so-called inefficient farmers is good for agriculture and good for the country. They see no inconsistency, apparently, between their own protectionist economy and the "free market" economy that they recommend to their supposed constituents, to whom the "free market" has proved, time and again, to be fatal. Nor do they see any inconsistency, apparently, between the economy of a university, whose sources, like those of any tax-supported institution, are highly diversified, and the extremely specialized economies that they have recommended to their farmer-constituents. These inconsistencies nevertheless exist, and they explain why, so far, there has been no epidemic of bankruptcies among professors of agricultural economics.

These, of course, are simply instances of the notorious discrepancy between theory and practice. But this discrepancy need not exist, or it need not be so extreme, in the colleges of agriculture. The answer to the problem is simply that those who profess should practice. Or at least a significant percentage of them should. This is, in fact, the rule in other colleges and departments of the university. A professor of medicine who was no doctor would readily be seen as an oddity; so would a law professor who could not try a case; so would a professor of architecture who could not design a building. What, then, would be so strange about an agriculture professor who would be, and who would be expected to be, a proven farmer?

BUT IT WOULD be wrong, I think, to imply that the farmers are merely the victims of their predicament and share none of the blame. In fact, they, along with all the rest of us, do share the blame, and their first hope of survival is in understanding that they do.

Farmers, as much as any other group, have subscribed to the industrial fantasies that I listed earlier: that value equals price, that all relations are mechanical, and that competitiveness is a proper and sufficient motive. Farmers, like the rest of us, have assumed, under the tutelage of people with things to sell, that selfishness and extravagance are merely normal. Like the rest of us, farmers have believed that they might safely live a life prescribed by the advertisers of products, rather than the life required by fundamental human necessities and responsibilities.

42

One could argue that the great breakthrough of industrial agriculture occurred when most farmers became convinced that it would be better to own a neighbor's farm than to have a neighbor, and when they became willing, necessarily at the same time, to borrow extravagant amounts of money. They thus violated the two fundamental laws of domestic or community economy: You must be thrifty and you must be generous; or, to put it in a more practical way, you must be (within reason) independent, and you must be neighborly. With that violation, farmers became vulnerable to everything that has intended their ruin.

An economic program that encourages the unlimited growth of individual holdings not only anticipates but actively proposes the failure of many people. Indeed, as our antimonopoly laws testify, it proposes the failure, ultimately, of all but one. It is a fact, I believe, that many people have now lost their farms and are out of farming who would still be in place had they been willing for their neighbors to survive along with themselves. In light of this, we see that the machines, chemicals, and credit that farmers have been persuaded to use as "labor savers" have, in fact, performed as neighbor replacers. And whereas neighborhood tends to work as a service free to its members, the machines, chemicals, and credit have come at a cost set by people who were *not* neighbors.

THAT IS A description of the problem of the family farm, as I see it. It is a dangerous problem, but I do not think it is hopeless. On the contrary, a number of solutions to the problem are implied in my description of it.

What, then, can be done?

The most obvious, the most desirable, solution would be to secure that "equitable balance between agriculture and other segments of the economy" that is one of the stated goals of the Hatch Act. To avoid the intricacies of the idea of "parity," which we inevitably think of here, I will just say that the price of farm products, as they leave the farm, should be on a par with the price of those products that the farmer must buy.

In order to achieve this with minimal public expense, we must control agricultural production; supply must be adjusted to demand. Obviously this is something that individual farmers, or individual states, cannot do for themselves; it is a job that belongs appropriately to the federal government. As a governmental function, it is perfectly in keeping with the ideal, everywhere implicit in the originating documents of our government, that the small have a right to certain protections from the great. We have, within limits that are obvious and reasonable, the *right* to be small farmers or small businessmen or -women, just as, or perhaps insofar as, we have a right to life, liberty, and prosperity. The individual citizen is not to be victimized by the rich any more than by the powerful. When Marty Strange writes, "To the extent that only the exceptional succeed, the system fails,"[8] he is economically and agriculturally sound, but he is also speaking directly from American political tradition.

The plight of the family farm would be improved also by other governmental changes—for example, in policies having to do with taxation and credit.

Our political problem, of course, is that farmers are neither numerous enough nor rich enough to be optimistic about government help. The government tends, rather, to find their surplus production useful and their economic failure ideologically desirable. Thus, it seems to me that we must concentrate on those things that farmers and farming communities can do for themselves—striving in the meantime for policies that would be desirable.

It may be that the gravest danger to farmers is their inclination to look to the government for help, after the agribusiness corporations and the universities (to which they have already looked) have failed them. In the process, they have forgotten how to look to themselves, to their farms, to their families, to their neighbors, and to their tradition.

Marty Strange has written also of his belief "that commercial agriculture can survive within pluralistic American society, as we know it—*if* [my emphasis] the farm is rebuilt on some of the values with which it is popularly associated: conservation, independence, self-reliance, family, and community. To sustain itself, commercial agriculture will have to reorganize its social and economic structure as well as its technological base and production methods in a way that reinforces these values."[9] I agree. Those are the values that offer us survival, not just as farmers, but as human beings. And I would point out that the transformation that Marty is proposing cannot be accomplished by the governments, the corporations, or the universities; if it is to be done, the farmers themselves, their families, and their neighbors will have to do it.

What I am proposing, in short, is that farmers find their way out of the gyp joint known as the industrial economy.

The first item on the agenda, I suggest, is the remaking of the rural neighborhoods and communities. The decay or loss of these has demonstrated their value; we find, as we try to get along without them, that they are worth something to us—spiritually, socially, and economically. And we hear again the voices out of our cultural tradition telling us that to have community, people don't need a "community center" or "recreational facilities" or any of the rest of the paraphernalia of "community improvement" that is always for sale. Instead, they need to love each other, trust each other, and help each other. That is hard. All of us know that no community is going to do those things easily or perfectly, and yet we know that there is more hope in that difficulty and imperfection than in all the neat instructions for getting big and getting rich that have come out of the universities and the agribusiness corporations in the past fifty years.

Second, the farmers must look to their farms and consider the losses, human and economic, that may be implicit in the way those farms are structured and used. If they do that, many of them will understand how they have been cheated by the industrial orthodoxy of competition—how specialization has thrown them into competition with other farmer-specialists, how bigness of scale has thrown them into competition with

45

neighbors and friends and family, how the consumer economy has thrown them into competition with themselves.

If it is a fact that for any given farm there is a ratio between people and acres that is correct, there are also correct ratios between dependence and independence and between consumption and production. For a farm family, a certain degree of independence is possible and is desirable, but no farmer and no family can be entirely independent. A certain degree of dependence is inescapable; whether or not it is desirable is a question of who is helped by it. If a family removes its dependence from its neighbors—if, indeed, farmers remove their dependence from their families—and give it to the agribusiness corporations (and to moneylenders), the chances are, as we have seen, that the farmers and their families will not be greatly helped. This suggests that dependence on family and neighbors may constitute a very desirable kind of independence.

It is clear, in the same way, that a farm and its family cannot be *only* productive; there must be some degree of consumption. This, also, is inescapable; whether or not it is desirable depends on the ratio. If the farm consumes too much in relation to what it produces, then the farm family is at the mercy of its suppliers and is exposed to dangers to which it need not be exposed. When, for instance, farmers farm on so large a scale that they cannot sell their labor without enormous consumption of equipment and supplies, then they are vulnerable. I talked to an Ohio farmer recently who cultivated his corn crop with a team of horses. He explained that, when he was plowing his corn, he was *selling* his labor and that of his team (labor fueled by the farm itself and, therefore, very cheap) rather than *buying* herbicides. His point was simply that there is a critical difference between buying and selling and that the name of this difference at the year's end ought to be net gain.

Similarly, when farmers let themselves be persuaded to buy their food instead of grow it, they become consumers instead of producers and lose a considerable income from their farms. This is simply to say that there is a domestic economy that is proper to the farming life and that it is different from the domestic economy of the industrial suburbs.

FINALLY, I WANT to say that I have not been talking from speculation but from proof. I have had in mind throughout this essay the one example known to me of an American community of small family farmers who have not only survived but thrived during some very difficult years: I mean the Amish. I do not recommend, of course, that all farmers should become Amish, nor do I want to suggest that the Amish are perfect people or that their way of life is perfect. What I want to recommend are some Amish principles:

1. They have preserved their families and communities.

2. They have maintained the practices of neighborhood.

3. They have maintained the domestic arts of kitchen and garden, household and homestead.

4. They have limited their use of technology so as not to displace or alienate available human labor or available free sources of power (the sun, wind, water, and so on).

5. They have limited their farms to a scale that is compatible both with the practice of neighborhood and with the optimum use of low-power technology.

6. By the practices and limits already mentioned, they have limited their costs.

7. They have educated their children to live at home and serve their communities.

8. They esteem farming as both a practical art and a spiritual discipline.

These principles define a world to be lived in by human beings, not a world to be exploited by managers, stockholders, and experts.

NOTES

1. In conversation.

2. Robert Heilbroner, "The Art of Work," Occasional Paper of the Council of Scholars (Washington, D.C.: Library of Congress, 1984), p. 20.

3. Eric Gill, *A Holy Tradition of Working* (Suffolk, England: Golgonooza Press, 1983), p. 61.

4. Ibid., p. 65.

5. William Safire, "Make That *Six* Deadly Sins—A Re-examination Shows Greed to Be a Virtue," *Courier-Journal* (Louisville, Ky.), 7 Jan. 1986.

6. In conversation.

7. Hatch Act, United States Code, Section 361b.

8. Marty Strange, "The Economic Structure of a Sustainable Agriculture," in *Meeting the Expectations of the Land*, ed. Wes Jackson, Wendell Berry, and Bruce Colman (San Francisco: North Point Press, 1984), p. 118.

9. Ibid., p. 116.

Let the Farm Judge

(1997)

༈

TO ME, ONE of the most informative books on agriculture is *British Sheep*, published by the National Sheep Association of Britain. This book contains photographs and descriptions of sixty-five British sheep breeds and "recognized half-breds." I have spent a good deal of time looking at the pictures in this book and reading its breed descriptions, for I think that it represents one of the great accomplishments of agriculture. It makes a most impressive case for the intelligence and the judgment of British farmers over many centuries.

What does it mean that an island not much bigger than Kansas or not much more than twice the size of Kentucky should have developed sixty or so breeds of sheep? It means that many thousands of farmers were paying the most discriminating attention, not only to their sheep, but also to the nature of their local landscapes and economies, for a long time. They were responding intelligently to the requirement of local adaptation. The result, when such an effort is carried on by enough intelligent farmers in the same region for a long time, is the development of a distinct breed that fits regional needs. Such local adaptation is the most important requirement for agriculture, wherever it occurs. If you are going to adapt your farming to a variety of landscapes, you are going to need a variety of livestock breeds, and a variety of types within breeds.

The great diversity of livestock breeds, along with the great diversity of domestic plant varieties, can be thought of as a sort of vocabulary with which we may make appropriate responses to the demands of a great diversity of localities. The goal of intelligent farmers, who desire the long-term success of farming, is to adapt their work to their places. Local adaptation always requires reasonably correct answers to *two* questions: What is the nature—the need and the opportunity—of the local economy? and, What is the nature of the place? For example, it is a mistake to answer the economic question by plowing too steep a hillside, just as it is a mistake to answer the geographic or ecological question in a way that denies the farmer a living.

Intelligent livestock breeders may find that, in practice, the two questions become one: How can I produce the best meat at the lowest economic and ecological cost? This question cannot be satisfactorily answered by the market, by the meatpacking industry, by breed societies, or by show ring judges. It cannot be answered satisfactorily by "animal science" experts, or by genetic engineers. It can only be answered satisfactorily by the farmer, and only if the farm, the place itself, is allowed to play a part in the process of selection.

It goes without saying that the animal finally produced by any farm will be a product to some extent of the judgment of the farmer, the meatpacker, the breed society, and the show ring judge. But the farm too must be permitted to make and enforce its judgment. If it is not permitted to do so, then there can be no local adaptation. And where there is no local adaptation, the farmer and the farm must pay significant penalties.

In our era, because of commercial demand and the allure of the show ring, livestock breeding has tended to concentrate on the production of outstanding individual animals as determined by the ideal breed characteristics or the ideal carcass. In other words, a good brood cow or ewe is one that produces offspring that fit the prevailing show or commercial standards. We don't worry enough about the *cost* of production, which would lead us directly to the issue of local adaptation. This sort of negligence, I think, could have been possible only in our time, when "cheap" fossil fuel has set the pattern in agriculture. Suffice it to say that much thoughtlessness in livestock breeding has been subsidized by large checks paid to veterinarians and drug companies, and covered over by fat made of allegedly cheap corn.

Allegedly cheap fossil fuel, allegedly cheap transportation, and allegedly cheap corn and other feed grains have pushed agriculture toward uniformity, obscuring regional differences and, with them, the usefulness of locally adapted breeds, especially those that do well on forages. This is why there are now only a few dominant breeds, and why those breeds are large and grain-dependent. Now, for example, nearly all dairy cows are Holsteins, and the modern sheep is more than likely to have a black face and to be "big and tall."

My friend Maury Telleen has pointed out to me that fifty years ago the Ayrshire was a popular dairy cow in New England and Kansas. The reason was her ability to make milk on the feed that was locally available; she did not require the optimal conditions and feedstuffs of Iowa or Illinois. She was, Maury says, "a cow that could 'get along.' " It is dangerous to assume that we have got beyond the need for farm animals that can "get along."

If we assume that the inescapable goal of the farmer, especially in the present economy, must be to reduce costs, and, further, that costs are reduced by local adaptation, then we can begin to think about the problems of livestock breeding by noting that corn, whatever its market price, is not cheap. What is cheap is grass—*grazed* grass—and where the grass grows determines the kind of animal needed to graze it.

Our farm, in the lower Kentucky River valley, is mostly on hillsides. Heavy animals tend to damage hillsides, especially in winter. Our experience with brood cows showed us that our farm needs sheep. It needs, in addition, sheep that can make their living by grazing coarse pasture on hillsides. And so in the fall of 1978 we bought six Border Cheviot ewes and a buck. At present we have about thirty ewes, and eventually we will have more.

Our choice of breed was a good one. The Border Cheviot is a hill sheep, developed to make good use of such rough pasture as we have. Moreover, it can make good use of a little corn, and our farm is capable of producing a little corn. There have been problems, of course. Some of them have had to do with adapting ourselves to our breed. These have been important, but just as important have been the problems of adapting our flock to our farm. And those are the problems I want to discuss.

There are now probably more Cheviots in the Midwest than elsewhere in the United States. For us, at any rate, the inevitable source of breeding stock has been the Midwest, and many of our problems have been traceable to that fact. What I am going to say implies no fault in the midwestern breeders, to whom we and our breed have an enormous debt. It is nevertheless true that, for a flock of sheep, living is easier in the prairie lands than on a Kentucky hillside. Just walking around on a hillside farm involves more strain and requires more energy, and the less fertile the land the farther a ewe will have to walk to fill her belly. Knees that might have remained sound on the gentle topography of Ohio or Iowa may become arthritic at our place. Also a ewe that would have twin lambs on a prairie farm may have only one on a hill farm. Similarly, a lamb will grow to slaughter weight more slowly where he has to allocate more energy to getting around. We once sold five yearling ewes to our friend Bob Willerton in Danvers, Illinois, where on their first lambing they produced eleven lambs. On our farm, they *might* have produced seven or eight. We have noticed the same difference with cull ewes that we have sent to our son's farm, which is less steep and more fertile than ours.

Our farm, then, is asking for a ewe that can stay healthy, live long, breed successfully, have two lambs without assistance, and feed them well, in comparatively demanding circumstances. Experience has shown us that the Border Cheviot breed is capable of producing a ewe of this kind, but that it does not do so inevitably. In eighteen years, and out of a good many ewes bought or raised, we have identified so far only two ewe families (the female descendants of two ewes) that fairly dependably perform as we and our place require.

The results of identifying and keeping the daughters of these ewe families have been very satisfactory. This year they made up more than half of our bred ewes. Presumably because of that, our lambing percentage, which previously hovered around 150 percent, increased to 172 percent. This year also we reduced our winter hay-feeding by one month, not beginning until the first of February. Next year, we hope to feed no hay until we bring the ewes to the barn for lambing, which will be about the first of March.[1] In livestock breeding it is always too early to brag, but of course we are encouraged.

In the language of Phillip Sponenberg and Carolyn Christman's excellent *Conservation Breeding Handbook*, we have employed "extensive" or "land-race" husbandry in managing a standardized breed. From the first, our flock has been "challenged by the environment"—required to live on what the place can most cheaply and sustainably provide, mainly pasture, with a minimum of attention and virtually no professional veterinary care. We give selenium injections to ewes and lambs and use a prudent amount of medication for parasites. We give no inoculations except for tetanus to the newborn lambs, and we have never trimmed a hoof.

Until recently, and even now with ewes, our practice has been to buy bargains, animals that for one reason or another fell below the standards of the show ring. But I don't believe that our flock would have developed to our standards and requirements any faster if we had bought the champions out of the best shows every year. Some of the qualities we were after simply are not visible to show ring judges.

I am not trying to argue that there is no good in livestock shows. The show ring is a useful tool; it is obviously instructive when good breeders bring good animals together for comparison. I am saying only that the show ring alone cannot establish and maintain adequate standards for livestock breeders. You could not develop locally adapted strains if your only standards came from the show ring or from breed societies.

The point is that, especially now when grain-feeding and confinement-feeding are so common, no American breeder should expect any *breed* to be locally adapted. Breeders should recognize that from the standpoint of local adaptation and cheap production, every purchase of a breeding animal is a gamble. A newly purchased ewe or buck may improve the performance of your flock on your farm or it may not. Good breeders will know, or they will soon find out, that theirs is not the only judgment that is involved. While the breeder is judging, the breeder's farm also is judging, enforcing its demands, and making selections. And this is as it should be. The judgment of the farm serves the breed, helping to preserve its genetic diversity.

Because of the necessity of purchasing sires from time to time, the continuity of the locally adapted flock must reside in the female lineages. Studying and preserving the most long-lived, thrifty, and productive ewe families are paramount. But this need not be laborious, for your farm will be selecting along with you. You pick the individuals that look good. This always implies that they have done well; and sooner or later you will know the look of "your kind," the kind that is apt to do well on your place. Your farm, however, will pick the ones that last. Even if you do not select at all, or if you select wrongly, a ewe that is not fitted to your farm will not contribute as many breeding animals to your flock as will a ewe that *is* fitted to your farm.

It is generally acknowledged that a shepherd should know what he or she is doing. It is not so generally understood that the flock should know what *it* is doing—that is, how to live, thrive, and reproduce successfully on its home farm. But this knowledge, bred into the flock, is critical; it means meat from grass, at the lowest cost.

NOTE

1. We did so the next year, and have continued to do so, except in times of deep or crusted snow. We winter our ewes on a hillside that is ungrazed from early August until about Christmas.

Energy in Agriculture

(1979)

۲

I HAVE JUST BEEN rereading Donald Hall's lovely memoir, *String Too
Short to Be Saved*. It is about the summers of his boyhood that the
author spent on his grandparents' New Hampshire farm, from the late
1930s until the early 1950s. There are many good things in this book, but
one of the best is its description of the life and economy of an old-time
New England small farm.

The farm of Kate and Wesley Wells, as their grandson knew it, was
already a relic. It was what would now be called a "marginal farm" in
mountainous country, in an agricultural community that had been dying
since the Civil War. The farm produced food for the household and made
a cash income from a small hand-milked herd of Holsteins and a flock of
sheep. It furnished trees for firewood and maple syrup. The Wellses sent
their daughters to school by the sale of timber from a woodlot. The farm
and its household were "poor" by our present standards, taking in very
little money—but spending very little too, and that is the most important thing about it. Its principle was thrift. Its needs were kept within the
limits of its resources.

This farm was ordered according to an old agrarian pattern which made it far more independent than modern farms built upon the pattern of industrial capitalism. And its energy economy was as independent as its money economy. The working energy of this farm came mainly from its people and from one horse.

Mr. Hall's memories inform us, more powerfully than any argument, that the life of Wesley and Kate Wells was a life worth living, decent though not easy; not adventurous or affluent, either—or not in our sense—but sociable, neighborly, and humane. They were intelligent, morally competent, upright, kind to people and animals, full of generous memories and good humor. From all that their grandson says of them, it is clear that his acquaintance with them and their place was profoundly enabling to his mind and his feelings.

One cannot read this book—or I, anyhow, cannot—without asking how that sort of life escaped us, how it depreciated as a possibility so that we were able to give it up in order, as we thought, to "improve" ourselves. Mr. Hall makes it plain that farms like his grandparents' did not die out in New England necessarily because of bad farming, or because they did not provide a viable way of life. They died for want of people with the motivation, the skill, the character, and the culture to keep them alive. They died, in other words, by a change in cultural value. Though it survived fairly intact until the middle of this century, Mr. Hall remembers that his grandparents' farm was surrounded by people and farms that had dwindled away because the human succession had been broken. It was no longer a place to come to, but a place to leave.

At the time Mr. Hall writes about, something was gaining speed in our country that I think will seem more and more strange as time goes on. This was a curious set of assumptions, both personal and public, about "progress." If you could get into a profession, it was assumed, then of course you must not be a farmer; if you could move to the city, then you must not stay in the country; if you could farm more profitably in the corn belt than on the mountainsides of New England, then the mountainsides of New England must not be farmed. For years this set of assumptions was rarely spoken and more rarely questioned, and yet it has been one of the most powerful social forces at work in this country in modern times.

But these assumptions could not accomplish much on their own. What gave them power, and made them able finally to dominate and re-shape our society, was the growth of technology for the production and use of fossil fuel energy. This energy could be made available to empower such unprecedented social change because it was "cheap." But we were able to consider it "cheap" only by a kind of moral simplicity: the assumption that we had a "right" to as much of it as we could use. This was a "right" made solely by might. Because fossil fuels, however abundant they once were, were nevertheless limited in quantity and not renewable, they obviously did not "belong" to one generation more than another. We ignored the claims of posterity simply because we could, the living being stronger than the unborn, and so worked the "miracle" of industrial progress by the theft of energy from (among others) our children.

That is the real foundation of our progress and our affluence. The reason that we are a rich nation is not that we have earned so much wealth—you cannot, by any honest means, earn or deserve so much. The reason is simply that we have learned, and become willing, to market and use up in our own time the birthright and livelihood of posterity.

And so it is too simple to say that the "marginal" farms of New England were abandoned because of progress or because they were no longer productive or desirable as living places. They were given up for one very "practical" reason: They did not lend themselves readily to exploitation by fossil fuel technology. Their decline began with the rise of steam power and the industrial economy after the Civil War; the coming of industrial agriculture after World War II finished them off. Industrial agriculture needs large holdings and large level fields. As the scale of technology grows, the small farms with small or steep fields are pushed farther and farther toward the economic margins and are finally abandoned. And so industrial agriculture sticks itself deeper and deeper into a curious paradox: The larger its technology grows in order "to feed the world," the more potentially productive "marginal" land it either ruins or causes to be abandoned. If the sweeping landscapes of Nebraska now have to be reshaped by computer and bulldozer to allow the more efficient operation of big farm machines, then thousands of acres of the smaller-featured hill country of the eastern states must obviously be considered "unfarmable." Or so the industrialists of agriculture have ruled.

And so energy is not just fuel. It is a powerful social and cultural influence. The kind and quantity of the energy we use determine the kind and quality of the life we live. Our conversion to fossil fuel energy subjected society to a sort of technological determinism, shifting population and values according to the new patterns and values of industrialization. Rural wealth and materials and rural people were caught within the gravitational field of the industrial economy and flowed to the cities, from which comparatively little flowed back in return. And so the human life of farmsteads and rural communities dwindled everywhere, and in some places perished.

IF THE SHIFT to fossil fuel energy radically changed the life and the values of farm communities, it should be no surprise that it also radically changed our understanding of agriculture. Some figures from an article by Professor Mark D. Shaw help to show the nature of this change. The "food system," according to Professor Shaw, now uses 16.5 percent of all energy used in the United States. This 16.5 percent is used in the following ways:

On-farm production ⌐ 3.0%
Manufacturing ⌐ 4.9%

Wholesale marketing ↗ 0.5%

Retail marketing ↗ 0.8%

Food preparation (in home) ↗ 4.4%

Food preparation (commercial) ↗ 2.9%

Apologists for industrial agriculture frequently stop with that first figure—showing that agriculture uses only a small amount of energy, relatively speaking, and that people hunting a cause of the "energy crisis" should therefore point their fingers elsewhere. The other figures, amounting to 13.5 percent of national energy consumption, are more interesting, for they suggest the way the food system has been expanded to make room for industrial enterprise. Between farm and home, producer and consumer, we have interposed manufacturers, a complex marketing structure, and food preparation. I am not sure how this last category differs from "manufacturing." And I would like to know what percentage of the energy budget goes for transportation, and whether or not Professor Shaw figured in the miles that people now drive to shop. The gist is nevertheless plain enough: The industrial economy grows and thrives by lengthening and complicating the essential connection between producer and consumer. In a *local* food economy, dealing in fresh produce to be prepared in the home (thus eliminating transporters, manufacturers, packagers, preparers, etc.), the energy budget would be substantially lower, and we might have both cheaper food and higher earnings on the farm.

But Professor Shaw provides another set of figures that is even more telling. These have to do with the "sources of energy for Pennsylvania agriculture" (I don't think the significance would vary much from one state to another):

Nuclear ↗ 1%

Coal ↗ 5%

Natural gas ⌐ 27%

Petroleum ⌐ 67%

And so we see that, though our agriculture may use relatively little fossil fuel energy, it is almost totally dependent on what it does use. It uses fossil fuel energy almost exclusively and uses it in competition with other users. And the sources of this energy are not renewable.

This critical dependence on nonrenewable energy sources is the direct result of the industrialization of agriculture. Before industrialization, agriculture depended almost exclusively on solar energy. Solar energy not only grew the plants, as it still does, but also provided the productive power of farms in the form of the work of humans and animals. This energy is derived and made available biologically, and it is recyclable. It is inexhaustible in the topsoil so long as good husbandry keeps the life cycle intact.

This old sun-based agriculture was fundamentally alien to the industrial economy; industrial corporations could make relatively little profit from it. In order to make agriculture fully exploitable by industry it was necessary (in Barry Commoner's terms) to weaken "the farm's link to the sun" and to make the farmland a "colony" of the industrial corporations. The farmers had to be persuaded to give up the free energy of the sun in order to pay dearly for the machine-derived energy of the fossil fuels.

Thus we have another example of a system artificially expanded for profit. The farm's originally organic, coherent, independent production system was expanded into a complex dependence on remote sources and on manufactured supplies.

What happened, from a cultural point of view, was that machines were substituted for farmers, and energy took the place of skill. As farmers became more and more dependent on fossil fuel energy, a radical change occurred in their minds. Once focused on biology, the life and health of living things, their thinking now began to focus on technology and economics. Credit, for example, became as pressing an issue as the weather, for farmers had begun to climb the one-way ladder of survival by debt. Bigger machines required more land, and more land required yet bigger machines, which required yet more land, and on and on—the survivors climbing to precarious and often temporary success by way of machines and mortgages and the ruin of their neighbors. And so the farm became a "factory," where speed, "efficiency," and profitability were the main standards of performance. These standards, of course, are industrial, not agricultural.

The old solar agriculture, moreover, was time oriented. Timeliness was its virtue. One took pride in having the knowledge to do things at the right time. Industrial agriculture is space oriented. Its virtue is speed. One takes pride in being first. The right time, by contrast, could be late as well as early; the proof of the work was in its quality.

THE MOST IMPORTANT point I have to make is that once agriculture shifted its dependence from solar, biologically derived energy to machine-derived fossil fuel energy, it committed itself, as a matter of course, to several kinds of waste:

1. The waste of solar energy, not just as motive power, but even as growing power. As landholdings become larger and the number of farmers smaller, more and more fields must go without cover crops, which means that for many days in the fall and early spring the sunlight on these fields is not captured in green leaves and so made useful to the soil and to people. It goes to waste.

2. The waste of human energy and ability. Industrial agriculture replaces people with machines; the ability of millions of people to become skillful and to do work therefore comes to nothing. We now have millions on some kind of government support, grown useless and helpless, while our country becomes unhealthy and ugly for want of human work and care. And we have additional millions not on welfare who have grown almost equally useless and helpless for want of

health. How much potentially useful energy do we now have stored in human belly fat? And what is it costing us, not only in medical bills, but in money spent on diets, drugs, and exercise machines?

3. The waste of animal energy. I mean not just the abandonment of live horsepower, but the waste involved in confinement-feeding. Why use fossil fuel energy to bring food to grazing animals that are admirably designed to go get it themselves?

4. The waste of soil and soil health. Because the number of farmers has now grown so small in proportion to the number of acres that must be farmed, it has been necessary to resort to all sorts of mechanical shortcuts. But shortcuts never have resulted in good work, and there is no reason to believe that they ever will. When a farmer must cover an enormous acreage within the strict limits of the seasons of planting and harvest, speed necessarily becomes the first consideration. And so the machinery, not the land, becomes the focus of attention and the standard of the work. Consequently, the fields get larger so as to require less turning, waterways are plowed out, and one sees less and less terracing and contour or strip plowing. And, as I mentioned above, less and less land is sowed in a cover crop; when such large acreages must be harvested, there is no time for a fall seeding. The result is catastrophic soil erosion even in such "flat" states as Iowa.

A problem related to soil waste is that of soil compaction. Part of the reason for this is that industrial agriculture reduces the humus in the soil, which becomes more cohesive and less porous as a result. Another reason is the use of heavier equipment, which becomes necessary, in the first place, because of soil compaction. But the main reason, I think, is again that we don't have enough farmers to farm the land properly. The industrial farmer has so much land that he cannot afford to wait for "the right time" to work his fields. As long as the ground will support his equipment, he plows and harrows; the time is right for the work whenever the work is mechanically possible. It is commonplace now, wherever I have traveled in farm country, to see fields cut to pieces by deep wheel tracks.

The final irony is that we are abusing our land in this way partly in order to correct our "balance of payments"—that is, in order to buy foreign petroleum. In the language of some "agribusiness" experts we are using "agridollars" to offset the drain of "petrodollars." We are, in effect, exporting our topsoil in order to keep our tractors running.

There is no question that you can cover a lot of ground with the big machines now on the market. A lot of people seem entranced by the power and speed of those machines, which the manufacturers love to refer to as "monsters" and "acre eaters." But the result is not farming; it is a process closely akin to mining. In what is left of the country communities, in earshot of the monster acre eaters of the "agribusinessmen," a lot of old farmers must be turning over in their graves.

Conservationist and Agrarian

(2002)

࿐

I AM A CONSERVATIONIST and a farmer, a wilderness advocate and an agrarian. I am in favor of the world's wildness, not only because I like it, but also because I think it is necessary to the world's life and to our own. For the same reason, I want to preserve the natural health and integrity of the world's economic landscapes, which is to say that I want the world's farmers, ranchers, and foresters to live in stable, locally adapted, resource-preserving communities, and I want them to thrive.

One thing that this means is that I have spent my life on two losing sides. As long as I have been conscious, the great causes of agrarianism and conservation, despite local victories, have suffered an accumulation of losses, some of them probably irreparable—while the third side, that of the land-exploiting corporations, has appeared to grow ever richer. I say "appeared" because I think their wealth is illusory. Their capitalism is based, finally, not on the resources of nature, which it is recklessly destroying, but on fantasy. Not long ago I heard an economist say, "If the consumer ever stops living beyond his means, we'll have a recession." And so the two sides of nature and the rural communities are being defeated by a third side that will eventually be found to have defeated itself.

Perhaps in order to survive its inherent absurdity, the third side is asserting its power as never before: by its control of politics, of public education, and of the news media; by its dominance of science; and by biotechnology, which it is commercializing with unprecedented haste and aggression in order to control totally the world's land-using economies and its food supply. This massive ascendancy of corporate power over democratic process is probably the most ominous development since the end of World War II, and for the most part "the free world" seems to be regarding it as merely normal.

My sorrow in having been for so long on two losing sides has been compounded by knowing that those two sides have been in conflict, not only with their common enemy, the third side, but also, and by now almost conventionally, with each other. And I am further aggrieved in understanding that everybody on my two sides is deeply implicated in the sins and in the fate of the self-destructive third side.

As a part of my own effort to think better, I decided not long ago that I would not endorse any more wilderness preservation projects that do not seek also to improve the health of the surrounding economic landscapes and human communities. One of my reasons is that I don't think we can preserve either wildness or wilderness areas if we can't preserve the economic landscapes and the people who use them. This has put me into discomfort with some of my conservation friends, but that discomfort only balances the discomfort I feel when farmers or ranchers identify me as an "environmentalist," both because I dislike the term and because I sympathize with farmers and ranchers.

Whatever its difficulties, my decision to cooperate no longer in the separation of the wild and the domestic has helped me to see more clearly the compatibility and even the coherence of my two allegiances. The dualism of domestic and wild is, after all, mostly false, and it is misleading. It has obscured for us the domesticity of the wild creatures. More important, it has obscured the absolute dependence of human

68

domesticity upon the wildness that supports it and in fact permeates it. In suffering the now-common accusation that humans are "anthropocentric" (ugly word), we forget that the wild sheep and the wild wolves are respectively ovicentric and lupocentric. The world, we may say, is wild, and all the creatures are homemakers within it, practicing domesticity: mating, raising young, seeking food and comfort. Likewise, though the wild sheep and the farm-bred sheep are in some ways unlike in their domesticities, we forget too easily that if the "domestic" sheep become too unwild, as some occasionally do, they become uneconomic and useless: They have reproductive problems, conformation problems, and so on. Domesticity and wildness are in fact intimately connected. What is utterly alien to both is corporate industrialism—a displaced economic life that is without affection for the places where it is lived and without respect for the materials it uses.

The question we must deal with is not whether the domestic and the wild are separate or can be separated; it is how, in the human economy, their indissoluble and necessary connection can be properly maintained.

But to say that wildness and domesticity are not separate, and that we humans are to a large extent responsible for the proper maintenance of their relationship, is to come under a heavy responsibility to be practical. I have two thoroughly practical questions on my mind.

THE FIRST IS: Why should conservationists have a positive interest in, for example, farming? There are lots of reasons, but the plainest is: Conservationists eat. To be interested in food but not in food production is clearly absurd. Urban conservationists may feel entitled to be unconcerned about food production because they are not farmers. But they can't be let off so easily, for they all are farming by proxy. They can eat only if land is farmed on their behalf by somebody somewhere in some fashion. If conservationists will attempt to resume responsibility for their need to eat, they will be led back fairly directly to all their previous concerns for the welfare of nature.

Do conservationists, then, wish to eat well or poorly? Would they like their food supply to be secure from one year to the next? Would they like their food to be free of poisons, antibiotics, alien genes, and other contaminants? Would they like a significant portion of it to be fresh? Would they like it to come to them at the lowest possible ecological cost? The answers, if responsibly given, will influence production, will influence land use, will determine the configuration and the health of landscapes.

If conservationists merely eat whatever the supermarket provides and the government allows, they are giving economic support to all-out industrial food production: to animal factories; to the depletion of soil, rivers, and aquifers; to crop monocultures and the consequent losses of biological and genetic diversity; to the pollution, toxicity, and overmedication that are the inevitable accompaniments of all-out industrial food production; to a food system based on long-distance transportation and the consequent waste of petroleum and the spread of pests and diseases; and to the division of the countryside into ever larger farms and ever larger fields receiving always less human affection and human care.

If, on the other hand, conservationists are willing to insist on having the best food, produced in the best way, as close to their homes as possible, and if they are willing to learn to judge the quality of food and food production, then they are going to give economic support to an entirely different kind of land use in an entirely different landscape. This landscape will have a higher ratio of caretakers to acres, of care to use. It will be at once more domestic and more wild than the industrial landscape. Can increasing the number of farms and farmers in an agricultural landscape enhance the quality of that landscape as wildlife habitat? Can it increase what we might call the wilderness value of that landscape? It *can* do so, and the determining factor would be diversity. Don't forget that we are talking about a landscape that is changing in response to an increase in local consumer demand for local food. Imagine a modern agricultural landscape devoted mainly to corn and soybeans and to animal factories. And then imagine its neighboring city developing a demand for good, locally grown food. To meet that demand, local farming would have to diversify.

If that demand is serious, if it is taken seriously, if it comes from informed and permanently committed consumers, if it promises the necessary economic support, then that radically oversimplified landscape will change. The crop monocultures and animal factories will give way to the mixed farming of plants and animals. Pastured flocks and herds of meat animals, dairy herds, and poultry flocks will return, requiring, of course, pastures and hayfields. If the urban consumers would extend their competent concern for the farming economy to include the forest economy and its diversity of products, that would improve the quality and care, and increase the acreage, of farm woodlands. And we should not forget the possibility that good farmers might, for their own instruction and pleasure, preserve patches of woodland unused. As the meadows and woodlands flourished in the landscape, so would the wild birds and animals. The acreages devoted to corn and soybeans, grown principally as livestock feed or as raw materials for industry, would diminish in favor of the fruits and vegetables required by human dinner tables.

As the acreage under perennial cover increased, soil erosion would decrease and the water-holding capacity of the soil would increase. Creeks and rivers would grow cleaner and their flow more constant. As farms diversified, they would tend to become smaller because complexity and work increase with diversity, and so the landscape would acquire more owners. As the number of farmers and the diversity of their farms increased, the toxicity of agriculture would decrease—insofar as agricultural chemicals are used to replace labor and to defray the biological costs of monoculture. As food production became decentralized, animal

71

wastes would be dispersed, and would be absorbed and retained in the soil as nutrients rather than flowing away as waste and as pollutants. The details of such a transformation could be elaborated almost endlessly. To make short work of it here, we could just say that a dangerously oversimplified landscape would become healthfully complex, both economically and ecologically.

Moreover, since we are talking about a city that would be living in large measure from its local fields and forests, we are talking also about a local economy of decentralized, small, nonpolluting value-adding factories and shops that would be scaled to fit into the landscape with the least ecological or social disruption. And thus we can also credit to this economy an increase in independent small businesses, in self-employment, and a decrease in the combustible fuel needed for transportation and (I believe) for production.

Such an economy is technically possible, there can be no doubt of that; we have the necessary methods and equipment. The capacity of nature to accommodate, and even to cooperate in, such an economy is also undoubtable; we have the necessary historical examples. This is not, from nature's point of view, a pipe dream.

What *is* doubtable, or at least unproven, is the capacity of modern humans to choose, make, and maintain such an economy. For at least half a century we have taken for granted that the methods of farming could safely be determined by the mechanisms of industry, and that the economies of farming could safely be determined by the economic interests of industrial corporations. We are now running rapidly to the end of the possibility of that assumption. The social, ecological, and even the economic costs have become too great, and the costs are still increasing, all over the world.

Now we must try to envision an agriculture founded not on mechanical principles, but on the principles of biology and ecology. Sir Albert Howard and Wes Jackson have argued at length for such a change of standards. If you want to farm sustainably, they have told us, then you have got to make your farming conform to the natural laws that govern the local ecosystem. You have got to farm with both plants and animals in as great a diversity as possible, you have got to conserve fertility, recycle wastes, keep the ground covered, and so on. Or, as J. Russell Smith put it seventy years ago, you have got to "fit the farming to the land"—not to the available technology or the market, as important as those considerations are, but to the land. It is necessary, in short, to maintain a proper connection between the domestic and the wild. The paramount standard by which the work is to be judged is the health of the place where the work is done.

But this is not a transformation that we can just drift into, as we drift in and out of fashions, and it is not one that we should wait to be forced into by large-scale ecological breakdown. It won't happen if a lot of people—consumers and producers, city people and country people, conservationists and land users—don't get together deliberately to make it happen.

Those are some of the reasons why conservationists should take an interest in farming and make common cause with good farmers. Now I must get on to the second of my practical questions.

WHY SHOULD FARMERS be conservationists? Or maybe I had better ask why *are* good farmers conservationists? The farmer lives and works in the meeting place of nature and the human economy, the place where the need for conservation is most obvious and most urgent. Farmers either fit their farming to their farms, conform to the laws of nature, and keep the natural powers and services intact—or they do not. If they do not, then they increase the ecological deficit that is being charged to the future. (I had better admit that some farmers do increase the ecological deficit, but they are not the farmers I am talking about. I am not asking conservationists to support destructive ways of farming.)

Good farmers, who take seriously their duties as stewards of Creation and of their land's inheritors, contribute to the welfare of society in more ways than society usually acknowledges, or even knows. These farmers produce valuable goods, of course; but they also conserve soil, they conserve water, they conserve wildlife, they conserve open space, they conserve scenery.

All that is merely what farmers *ought* to do. But since our present society's first standard in all things is profit and it loves to dwell on "economic reality," I can't resist a glance at these good farmers in their economic circumstances, for these farmers will be poorly paid for the goods they produce, and for the services they render to conservation they will not be paid at all. Good farmers today may market products of high quality and perform well all the services I have listed, and *still* be unable to afford health insurance, and *still* find themselves mercilessly caricatured in the public media as rural simpletons, hicks, or rednecks. And then they hear the voices of the "economic realists": "Get big or get out. Sell out and go to town. Adapt or die." We have had fifty years of such realism in agriculture, and the result has been more and more large-scale monocultures and factory farms, with their ever larger social and ecological—and ultimately economic—costs.

Why do good farmers farm well for poor pay and work as good stewards of nature for no pay, many of them, moreover, having no hope that their farms will be farmed by their children (for the reasons given) or that they will be farmed by anybody?

Well, I was raised by farmers, have farmed myself, and have in turn raised two farmers—which suggests to me that I may know something about farmers, and also that I don't know very much. But over the years I along with a lot of other people have wondered, "Why do they do it?" Why do farmers farm, given their economic adversities on top of the many frustrations and difficulties normal to farming? And always the answer is: "Love. They must do it for love." Farmers farm for the love of farming. They love to watch and nurture the growth of plants. They love to live in the presence of animals. They love to work outdoors. They love the weather, maybe even when it is making them miserable. They love to live where they work and to work where they live. If the scale of their farming is small enough, they like to work in the company of their children and with the help of their children. They love the measure of independence that farm life can still provide. I have an idea that a lot of farmers have gone to a lot of trouble merely to be self-employed, to live at least a part of their lives without a boss.

And so the first thing farmers as conservationists must try to conserve is their love of farming and their love of independence. Of course they can conserve these things only by handing them down, by passing them on to their children, or to *somebody's* children. Perhaps the most urgent task for all of us who want to eat well and to keep eating is to encourage farm-raised children to take up farming. And we must recognize that this only can be done economically. Farm children are not encouraged by watching their parents take their products to market only to have them stolen at prices less than the cost of production.

But farmers obviously are responsible for conserving much more than agrarian skills and attitudes. I have already told why farmers should be, as much as any conservationists, conservers of the wildness of the world—and that is their inescapable dependence on nature. Good farmers, I believe, recognize a difference that is fundamental between what is natural and what is man-made. They know that if you treat a farm as a factory and living creatures as machines, or if you tolerate the idea of "engineering" organisms, then you are on your way to something destructive and, sooner or later, too expensive. To treat creatures as machines is an error with large practical implications.

Good farmers know too that nature can be an economic ally. Natural fertility is cheaper, often in the short run, always in the long run, than purchased fertility. Natural health, inbred and nurtured, is cheaper than

75

pharmaceuticals and chemicals. Solar energy—if you know how to cap-
ture and use it: in grass, say, and the bodies of animals—is cheaper than
petroleum. The highly industrialized factory farm is entirely dependent
on "purchased inputs." The agrarian farm, well integrated into the natural systems that support it, runs to an economically significant extent on
resources and supplies that are free.

It is now commonly assumed that when humans took to agriculture they gave up hunting and gathering. But hunting and gathering
remained until recently an integral and lively part of my own region's
traditional farming life. People hunted for wild game; they fished the
ponds and streams; they gathered wild greens in the spring, hickory
nuts and walnuts in the fall; they picked wild berries and other fruits;
they prospected for wild honey. Some of the most memorable, and least
regrettable, nights of my own youth were spent in coon hunting with
farmers. There is no denying that these activities contributed to the
economy of farm households, but a further fact is that they were pleasures; they were wilderness pleasures, not greatly different from the
pleasures pursued by conservationists and wilderness lovers. As I was
always aware, my friends the coon hunters were not motivated just by
the wish to tree coons and listen to hounds and listen to each other, all
of which were sufficiently attractive; they were coon hunters also because they wanted to be afoot in the woods at night. Most of the farmers I have known, and certainly the most interesting ones, have had the
capacity to ramble about outdoors for the mere happiness of it, alert to
the doings of the creatures, amused by the sight of a fox catching grass-
hoppers, or by the puzzle of wild tracks in the snow.

As the countryside has depopulated and the remaining farmers have
come under greater stress, these wilderness pleasures have fallen away.
But they have not yet been altogether abandoned; they represent something probably essential to the character of the best farming, and they
should be remembered and revived.

Those, then, are some reasons why good farmers are conservationists, and why all farmers ought to be.

WHAT I HAVE been trying to do is to define a congruity or community of interest between farmers and conservationists who are not farmers. To name the interests that these two groups have in common, and to observe, as I did at the beginning, that they also have common enemies, is to raise a question that is becoming increasingly urgent: Why don't the two groups publicly and forcefully agree on the things they agree on, and make an effort to cooperate? I don't mean to belittle their disagreements, which I acknowledge to be important. Nevertheless, cooperation is now necessary, and it is possible. If Kentucky tobacco farmers can meet with antismoking groups, draw up a set of "core principles" to which they all agree, and then support those principles, something of the sort surely could happen between conservationists and certain land-using enterprises: family farms and ranches, small-scale, locally owned forestry and forest products industries, and perhaps others. Something of the sort, in fact, is beginning to happen, but so far the efforts are too small and too scattered. The larger organizations on both sides need to take an interest and get involved.

If these two sides, which need to cooperate, have so far been at odds, what is the problem? The problem, I think, is economic. The small land users, on the one hand, are struggling so hard to survive in an economy controlled by the corporations that they are distracted from their own economy's actual basis in nature. They also have not paid enough attention to the difference between their always threatened local economies and the apparently thriving corporate economy that is exploiting them.

On the other hand, the mostly urban conservationists, who mostly are ignorant of the economic adversities of, say, family-scale farming or ranching, have paid far too little attention to the connection between

their economic life and the despoliation of nature. They have trouble seeing that the bad farming and forestry practices that they oppose as conservationists are done on their behalf, and with their consent implied in
the economic proxies they have given as consumers.

These clearly are serious problems. Both of them indicate that the
industrial economy is not a true description of economic reality, and
moreover that this economy has been wonderfully successful in getting its falsehoods believed. Too many land users and too many conservationists seem to have accepted the doctrine that the availability
of goods is determined by the availability of cash, or credit, and by the
market. In other words, they have accepted the idea always implicit
in the arguments of the land-exploiting corporations: that there can
be, and that there is, a safe disconnection between economy and ecology, between human domesticity and the wild world. Industrializing
farmers have too readily assumed that the nature of their land could
safely be subordinated to the capability of their technology, and that
conservation could safely be left to conservationists. Conservationists
have too readily assumed that the integrity of the natural world could
be preserved mainly by preserving tracts of wilderness, and that the
nature and nurture of the economic landscapes could safely be left to
agribusiness, the timber industry, debt-ridden farmers and ranchers,
and migrant laborers.

To me, it appears that these two sides are as divided as they are
because each is clinging to its own version of a common economic error. How can this be corrected? I don't think it can be, so long as each
of the two sides remains closed up in its own conversation. I think the
two sides need to enter into *one* conversation. They have got to talk to
one another. Conservationists have got to know and deal competently
with the methods and economics of land use. Land users have got to
recognize the urgency, even the economic urgency, of the requirements
of conservation.

Failing this, these two sides will simply concede an easy victory to their common enemy, the third side, the corporate totalitarianism which is now rapidly consolidating as "the global economy" and which will utterly dominate both the natural world and its human communities.

Sanitation and the Small Farm

(1971)

౩౨

I N THE TIME when my memories begin—the late 1930s—people in
the country did not go around empty-handed as much as they do
now. As I remember them from that time, farm people on the way somewhere characteristically had buckets or kettles or baskets in their hands,
sometimes sacks on their shoulders.

Those were hard times—not unusual in our agricultural history—
and so a lot of the fetching and carrying had to do with foraging, search-
ing the fields and woods for nature's free provisions: greens in the spring-
time, fruits and berries in the summer, nuts in the fall. There was fishing
in warm weather and hunting in cold weather; people did these things
for food and for pleasure, not for "sport." The economies of many households were small and thorough, and people took these seasonal opportunities seriously.

For the same reason, they practiced household husbandry. They
raised gardens, fattened meat hogs, milked cows, kept flocks of chickens and other poultry. These enterprises were marginal to the farm, but
central to the household. In a sense, they comprised the direct bond between farm and household. These enterprises produced surpluses which,

81

in those days, were marketable. And so when one saw farm people in town they would be laden with buckets of cream or baskets of eggs. Or maybe you would see a woman going into the grocery store, carrying two or three old hens with their legs tied together. Sometimes this surplus paid for what the family had to buy at the store. Sometimes after they "bought" their groceries in this way, they had money to take home. These households were places of production, at least some of the time operating at a net economic *gain*. The idea of "consumption" was alien to them. I am not talking about practices of exceptional families, but about what was ordinarily done on virtually all farms.

That economy was in the truest sense democratic. Everybody could participate in it—even little children. An important source of instruction and pleasure to a child growing up on a farm was participation in the family economy. Children learned about the adult world by participating in it in a small way, by doing a little work and making a little money—a much more effective, because pleasurable, and a much cheaper method than the present one of requiring the adult world to be learned in the abstract in school. One's elders in those days were always admonishing one to save nickels and dimes, and there was tangible purpose in their advice: With enough nickels and dimes, one could buy a cow or a sow; with the income from a cow or a sow, one could begin to save to buy a farm. This scheme was plausible enough, evidently, for it seemed that all grown-ups had meditated on it. Now, according to the savants of agriculture—and most grown-ups now believe them—one does not start in farming with a sow or a cow; one must start with a quarter of a million dollars. What are the political implications of *that* economy?

I have so far mentioned only the most common small items of trade, but it was also possible to sell prepared foods: pies, bread, butter, beaten biscuits, cured hams, etc. And among the most attractive enterprises of that time were the small dairies that were added without much expense or trouble to the small, diversified farms. There would usually

82

be a milking room or stall partitioned off in a barn, with homemade wooden stanchions to accommodate perhaps three to half a dozen cows. The cows were milked by hand. The milk was cooled in cans in a tub of well water. For a minimal expenditure and an hour or so of effort night and morning, the farm gained a steady, dependable income. All this conformed to the ideal of my grandfather's generation of farmers, which was to "sell something every week"—a maxim of diversity, stability, and small scale.

Both the foraging in fields and woods and the small husbandries of household and barn have now been almost entirely replaced by the "consumer economy," which assumes that it is better to buy whatever one needs than to find it or make it or grow it. Advertisements and other forms of propaganda suggest that people should congratulate themselves on the quantity and variety of their purchases. Shopping, in spite of traffic and crowds, is held to be "easy" and "convenient." Spending money gives one status. And physical exertion for any useful purpose is looked down upon; it is permissible to work hard for "sport" or "recreation," but to make any practical use of the body is considered beneath dignity.

Aside from the fashions of leisure and affluence—so valuable to corporations, so destructive of values—the greatest destroyer of the small economies of the small farms has been the doctrine of sanitation. I have no argument against cleanliness and healthfulness; I am for them as much as anyone. I do, however, question the validity and the honesty of the sanitation laws that have come to rule over farm production in the last thirty or forty years. Why have new sanitation laws always required more, and more expensive, equipment? Why have they always worked against the survival of the small producer? Is it impossible to be inexpensively healthful and clean?

I am not a scientist or a sanitation expert, and cannot give conclusive answers to those questions; I can only say what I have observed and what I think. In a remarkably short time I have seen the demise of all the small dairy operations in my part of the country, the shutting down of all local creameries and of all the small local dealers in milk and milk products. I have seen the grocers forced to quit dealing in eggs produced by local farmers, and have seen the closing of all markets for small quantities of poultry.

Recently, in continuation of the "trend," the local slaughterhouses in Kentucky were required to make expensive alterations or go out of business. Most of them went out of business. These were not offering meat for sale in the wholesale or retail trade. They did custom work mainly for local farmers who brought their animals in for slaughter and took the meat home or to a locker plant for processing. They were essential to the effort of many people to live self-sufficiently from their own produce— and these people had raised *no* objections to the way their meat was being handled. The few establishments that managed to survive this "improvement" found it necessary, of course, to charge higher prices for their work. Who benefited from this? Not the customers, who were put to considerable expense and inconvenience, if they were not forced to quit producing their own meat altogether. Not, certainly, the slaughterhouses or the local economies. Not, so far as I can see, the public's health. The only conceivable beneficiaries were the meatpacking corporations, and for this questionable gain local life was weakened at its economic roots.

This sort of thing is always justified as "consumer protection." But we need to ask a few questions about that. How are consumers protected by a system that puts more and more miles, middlemen, agencies, and inspectors between them and the producers? How, over all these obstacles, can consumers make producers aware of their tastes and needs? How are consumers protected by a system that apparently cannot "improve" except by eliminating the small producer, increasing the cost of production, and increasing the retail price of the product?

Does the concentration of production in the hands of fewer and fewer big operators really serve the ends of cleanliness and health? Or does it make easier and more lucrative the possibility of collusion between irresponsible producers and corrupt inspectors?

In so strenuously and expensively protecting food from contamination by germs, how much have we increased the possibility of its contamination by antibiotics, preservatives, and various industrial poisons? The notorious PBB disaster in Michigan could probably not have happened in a decentralized system of small local suppliers and producers.

And, finally, what do we do to our people, our communities, our economy, and our political system when we allow our necessities to be produced by a centralized system of large operators, dependent on expensive technology, and regulated by expensive bureaucracy? The modern food industry is said to be a "miracle of technology." But it is well to remember that this technology, in addition to so-called miracles, produces economic and political consequences that are not favorable to democracy.

The connections among farming, technology, economics, and politics are important for many reasons, one of the most obvious being their influence on food production. Probably the worst fault of our present system is that it simply eliminates from production the land that is not suitable for, as well as the people who cannot afford, large-scale technology. And it ignores the potential productivity of these "marginal" acres and people.

It is possible to raise these issues because our leaders have been telling us for years that our agriculture needs to become more and more productive. If they mean what they say, they will have to revise production standards and open the necessary markets to provide a livelihood for small farmers. Only small farmers can keep the so-called marginal land in production, for only they can give the intensive care necessary to keep it productive.

Renewing Husbandry

(2004)

༄

I REMEMBER WELL A summer morning in about 1950 when my father sent a hired man with a McCormick High Gear No. 9 mowing
machine and a team of mules to the field I was mowing with our nearly
new Farmall A. That memory is a landmark in my mind and my history.
I had been born into the way of farming represented by the mule team,
and I loved it. I knew irresistibly that the mules were good ones. They
were stepping along beautifully at a rate of speed in fact only a little
slower than mine. But now I saw them suddenly from the vantage point
of the tractor, and I remember how fiercely I resented their slowness. I
saw them as "in my way." For those who have had no similar experience,
I was feeling exactly the outrage and the low-grade superiority of a hot-
rodder caught behind an aged dawdler in urban traffic. It is undoubtedly
significant that in the summer of 1950 I passed my sixteenth birthday and
became eligible to solve all my problems by driving an automobile.

This is not an exceptional or a remarkably dramatic bit of history.
I recite it here to confirm that the industrialization of agriculture is a
part of my familiar experience. I don't have the privilege of looking
at it as an outsider. It is not incomprehensible to me. The burden of

this essay, on the contrary, is that the industrialization of agriculture is a grand oversimplification, too readily comprehensible, to me and to everybody else.

We were mowing that morning, the teamster with his mules and I with the tractor, in the field behind the barn on my father's home place, where he and before him his father had been born, and where his father had died in February of 1946. The old way of farming was intact in my grandfather's mind until the day he died at eighty-two. He had worked mules all his life, understood them thoroughly, and loved the good ones passionately. He knew tractors only from a distance, he had seen only a few of them, and he rejected them out of hand because he thought, correctly, that they compacted the soil.

Even so, four years after his death his grandson's sudden resentment of the "slow" mule team foretold what history would bear out: The tractor would stay and the mules would go. Year after year, agriculture would be adapted more and more to the technology and the processes of industry and to the rule of industrial economics. This transformation occurred with astonishing speed because, by the measures it set for itself, it was wonderfully successful. It "saved labor," it conferred the prestige of modernity, and it was highly productive.

THOUGH I NEVER entirely departed from farming or at least from thoughts of farming, and my affection for my homeland remained strong, during the fourteen years after 1950 I was much away from home and was not giving to farming the close and continuous attention I have given to it in the forty years since.

In 1964 my family and I returned to Kentucky, and in a year were settled on a hillside farm in my native community, where we have continued to live. Perhaps because I was a returned traveler intending to stay, I now saw the place more clearly than before. I saw it critically, too, for it was evident at once that the human life of the place, the life of the farms and the farming community, was in decline. The old self-sufficient way of farming was passing away. The economic prosperity that had visited the farmers briefly during World War II and for a few years afterward had ended. The little towns that once had been social and economic centers, thronged with country people on Saturdays and Saturday nights, were losing out to the bigger towns and the cities. The rural neighborhoods, once held together by common memories, common work, and the sharing of help, had begun to dissolve. There were no longer local markets for chickens or eggs or cream. The spring lamb industry, once a staple of the region, was gone. The tractors and other mechanical devices certainly were saving the labor of the farmers and farm hands who had moved away, but those who had stayed were working harder and longer than ever.

Because I remembered with affection and respect my grandparents and other country people of their generation, and because I had admirable friends and neighbors with whom I was again farming, I began to ask what was happening, and why. I began to ask what would be the effects on the land, on the community, on the natural world, and on the art of farming. And these questions have occupied me steadily ever since.

The effects of this process of industrialization have become so apparent, so numerous, so favorable to the agribusiness corporations, and so unfavorable to everything else that by now the questions troubling me and a few others in the 1960s and 1970s are being asked everywhere.

There are no doubt many ways of accounting for this change, but for convenience and brevity I am going to attribute it to the emergence of context as an issue. It has become increasingly clear that the way we farm affects the local community, and that the economy of the local community affects the way we farm; that the way we farm affects the health and integrity of the local ecosystem, and that the farm is intricately dependent, even economically, upon the health of the local ecosystem. We can no longer pretend that agriculture is a sort of economic machine with interchangeable parts, the same everywhere, determined by "market forces" and independent of everything else. We are not farming in a specialist capsule or a professionalist department; we are farming in the world, in a webwork of dependences and influences more intricate than we will ever understand. It has become clear, in short, that we have been running our fundamental economic enterprise by the wrong rules. We were wrong to assume that agriculture could be adequately defined by reductionist science and determinist economics.

If you can keep the context narrow enough (and the accounting period short enough), then the industrial criteria of labor saving and high productivity seem to work well. But the old rules of ecological coherence and of community life have remained in effect. The costs of ignoring them have accumulated, until now the boundaries of our reductive and mechanical explanations have collapsed. Their collapse reveals, plainly for all to see, the ecological and social damages that they were meant to conceal. It will seem paradoxical to some that the national and global corporate economies have narrowed the context for thinking about agriculture, but it is merely the truth. Those large economies, in their understanding and in their accounting, have excluded any concern for the land and the people. Now, in the midst of much unnecessary human and ecological damage, we are facing the necessity of a new start in agriculture.

AND SO IT is not possible to look back at the tableau of team and tractor on that morning in 1950 and see it as I saw it then. That is not because I have changed, though obviously I have; it is because, in the fifty-four years since then, history and the law of consequence have widened the context of the scene as circles widen on water around a thrown stone.

My impatience at the slowness of the mules, I think, was a fairly representative emotion. I thought I was witnessing a contest of machine against organism, which the machine was bound to win. I did not see that the team arrived at the field that morning from the history of farming

90

and from the farm itself, whereas the tractor arrived from almost an opposite history, and by means of a process reaching a long way beyond that farm or any farm. It took me a long time to understand that the team belonged to the farm and was directly supportable by it, whereas the tractor belonged to an economy that would remain alien to agriculture, functioning entirely by means of distant supplies and long supply lines. The tractor's arrival had signaled, among other things, agriculture's shift from an almost exclusive dependence on free solar energy to a total dependence on costly fossil fuel. But in 1950, like most people at that time, I was years away from the first inkling of the limits of the supply of cheap fuel.

We had entered an era of limitlessness, or the illusion thereof, and this in itself is a sort of wonder. My grandfather lived a life of limits, both suffered and strictly observed, in a world of limits. I learned much of that world from him and others, and then I changed; I entered the world of labor-saving machines and of limitless cheap fossil fuel. It would take me years of reading, thought, and experience to learn again that in this world limits are not only inescapable but indispensable.

My purpose here is not to disturb the question of the use of draft animals in agriculture—though I doubt that it will sleep indefinitely. I want instead to talk about the tractor as an influence. The means we use to do our work almost certainly affect the way we look at the world. If the fragment of autobiography I began with means anything, it means that my transformation from a boy who had so far grown up driving a team to a boy driving a tractor was a sight-changing experience.

Brought up as a teamster but now driving a tractor, a boy almost suddenly, almost perforce, sees the farm in a different way: as ground to be got over by a means entirely different, at an entirely different cost. The team, like the boy, would grow weary, but that weariness has all at once been subtracted, and the boy is now divided from the ground by the absence of a living connection that enforced sympathy as a practical

91

good. The tractor can work at maximum speed hour after hour without tiring. There is no longer a reason to remember the shady spots where it was good to stop and rest. Tirelessness and speed enforce a second, more perilous change in the way the boy sees the farm: Seeing it as ground to be got over as fast as possible and, ideally, without stopping, he has taken on the psychology of a traveler by interstate highway or by air. The focus of his attention has shifted from the place to the technology.

I now suspect that if we work with machines the world will seem to us to be a machine, but if we work with living creatures the world will appear to us as a living creature. Be that as it may, mechanical farming certainly makes it easy to think mechanically about the land and its creatures. It makes it easy to think mechanically even about oneself, and the tirelessness of tractors brought a new depth of weariness into human experience, at a cost to health and family life that has not been fully accounted.

Once one's farm and one's thoughts have been sufficiently mechanized, industrial agriculture's focus on production, as opposed to maintenance or stewardship, becomes merely logical. And here the trouble completes itself. The almost exclusive emphasis on production permits the way of working to be determined, not by the nature and character of the farm in its ecosystem and in its human community, but rather by the national or the global economy and the available or affordable technology. The farm and all concerns not immediately associated with production have in effect disappeared from sight. The farmer too in effect has vanished. He is no longer working as an independent and loyal agent of his place, his family, and his community, but instead as the agent of an economy that is fundamentally adverse to him and to all that he ought to stand for.

After mechanization it is certainly possible for a farmer to maintain a proper creaturely and stewardly awareness of the lives in her keeping. If you look, you can still find farmers who are farming well on mechanized farms. After mechanization, however, to maintain this kind of awareness requires a distinct effort of will. And if we ask what are the cultural resources that can inform and sustain such an effort of will, I believe that we will find them gathered under the heading of *husbandry*, and here my essay arrives finally at its subject.

THE WORD *husbandry* is the name of a connection. In its original sense, it is the name of the work of a domestic man, a man who has accepted a bondage to the household. We have no cause here, I think, to raise the issue of "sexual roles." We need only to say that our earthly life requires both husbandry and housewifery, and that nobody, certainly no household, is excused from a proper attendance to both.

Husbandry pertains first to the household; it connects the farm to the household. It is an art wedded to the art of housewifery. To husband is to use with care, to keep, to save, to make last, to conserve. Old usage tells us that there is a husbandry also of the land, of the soil, of the domestic plants and animals—obviously because of the importance of these things to the household. And there have been times, one of which is now, when some people have tried to practice a proper human husbandry of the nondomestic creatures in recognition of the dependence of our households and domestic life upon the wild world. Husbandry is the name of all the practices that sustain life by connecting us conservingly to our places and our world; it is the art of keeping tied all the strands in the living network that sustains us.

And so it appears that most and perhaps all of industrial agriculture's manifest failures are the result of an attempt to make the land produce without husbandry. The attempt to remake agriculture as a science and an industry has excluded from it the age-old husbandry that was central and essential to it, and that denoted always the fundamental domestic connections and demanded a restorative care in the use of the land and its creatures.

This effort had its initial and probably its most radical success in separating farming from the economy of subsistence. Through World War II, farm life in my region (and, I think, nearly everywhere) rested solidly upon the garden, dairy, poultry flock, and meat animals that fed the farm's family. Especially in hard times these farm families, and their farms too, survived by means of their subsistence economy. This was the husbandry and the housewifery by which the farm lived. The industrial program, on the contrary, suggested that it was "uneconomic" for a farm family to produce its own food; the effort and the land would be better applied to commercial production. The result is utterly strange in human experience: farm families who buy everything they eat at the store.

AN INTENTION TO replace husbandry with science was made explicit in the renaming of disciplines in the colleges of agriculture. "Soil husbandry" became "soil science," and "animal husbandry" became "animal science." This change is worth lingering over because of what it tells us about our susceptibility to poppycock. When any discipline is made or is called a science, it is thought by some to be much increased in preciseness, complexity, and prestige. When "husbandry" becomes "science," the lowly has been exalted and the rustic has become urbane. Purporting to increase the sophistication of the humble art of farming, this change in fact brutally oversimplifies it.

"Soil science," as practiced by soil scientists, and even more as it has been handed down to farmers, has tended to treat the soil as a lifeless matrix in which "soil chemistry" takes place and "nutrients" are "made available." And this, in turn, has made farming increasingly shallow—literally so—in its understanding of the soil. The modern farm is understood as a surface on which various mechanical operations are performed, and to which various chemicals are applied. The under-surface reality of organisms and roots is mostly ignored.

"Soil husbandry" is a different kind of study, involving a different kind of mind. Soil husbandry leads, in the words of Sir Albert Howard, to understanding "health in soil, plant, animal, and man as one great subject." We apply the word "health" only to living creatures, and to soil husbandry a healthy soil is a wilderness, mostly unstudied and unknown, but teemingly alive. The soil is at once a living community of creatures and their habitat. The farm's husband, its family, its crops and animals, all are members of the soil community; all belong to the character and identity of the place. To rate the farm family merely as "labor" and its domestic plants and animals merely as "production" is thus an oversimplification, both radical and destructive.

"Science" is too simple a word to name the complex of relationships and connections that compose a healthy farm—a farm that is a full membership of the soil community. If we propose not the reductive science we generally have, but a science of complexity, that too will be inadequate, for any complexity that science can comprehend is going to be necessarily a human construct, and therefore too simple.

The husbandry of mere humans of course cannot be complex enough either. But husbandry always has understood that what is husbanded is ultimately a mystery. A farmer, as one of his farmer correspondents once wrote to Liberty Hyde Bailey, is "a dispenser of the 'Mysteries of God.'" The mothering instinct of animals, for example, is a mystery that husbandry must use and trust mostly without understanding. The husband, unlike the "manager" or the would-be objective scientist, belongs inherently to the complexity and the mystery that is to be husbanded, and so the husbanding mind is both careful and humble. Husbandry originates precautionary sayings like "Don't put all your eggs into one basket" and "Don't count your chickens before they hatch." It does not boast of technological feats that will "feed the world."

Husbandry, which is not replaceable by science, nevertheless uses science, and corrects it too. It is the more comprehensive discipline. To reduce husbandry to science, in practice, is to transform agricultural "wastes" into pollutants, and to subtract perennials and grazing animals from the rotation of crops. Without husbandry, the agriculture of science and industry has served too well the purpose of the industrial economy in reducing the number of landowners and the self-employed. It has transformed the United States from a country of many owners to a country of many employees.

WITHOUT HUSBANDRY, "SOIL science" too easily ignores the community of creatures that live in and from, that make and are made by, the soil. Similarly, "animal science" without husbandry forgets, almost as a requirement, the sympathy by which we recognize ourselves as fellow creatures of the animals. It forgets that animals are so called because we once believed them to be endowed with souls. Animal science has led us away from that belief or any such belief in the sanctity of animals. It has led us instead to the animal factory, which, like the concentration camp, is a vision of Hell. Animal husbandry, on the contrary, comes from and again leads to the psalmist's vision of good grass, good water, and the husbandry of God.

(It is only a little off my subject to notice also that the high and essential art of housewifery, later known as "home economics," has now become "family and consumer science." This presumably elevates the intellectual standing of the faculty by removing family life and consumption from the context—and the economy—of a home or household.)

Agriculture must mediate between nature and the human community, with ties and obligations in both directions. To farm well requires an elaborate courtesy toward all creatures, animate and inanimate. It is sympathy that most appropriately enlarges the context of human work. Contexts become wrong by being too small—too small, that is, to contain the scientist or the farmer or the farm family or the local ecosystem or the local community—and this is crucial. "Out of context," as Wes Jackson has said, "the best minds do the worst damage."

Looking for a way to give an exact sense of this necessary sympathy, the *feeling* of husbandry at work, I found it in a book entitled *Feed My Sheep* by Terry Cummins. Mr. Cummins is a man of about my age, who grew up farming with his grandfather in Pendleton County, Kentucky, in the 1940s and early '50s. In the following sentences he is remembering himself at the age of thirteen, in about 1947:

> *When you see that you're making the other things feel good, it gives you a good feeling, too.*
>
> *The feeling inside sort of just happens, and you can't say this did it or that did it. It's the many little things. It doesn't seem that taking sweat-soaked harnesses off tired, hot horses would be something that would make you notice. Opening a barn door for the sheep standing out in a cold rain, or throwing a few grains of corn to the chickens are small things, but these little things begin to add up in you, and you can begin to understand that you're important. You may not be real important like people who do great things that you read about in the newspaper, but you begin to feel that you're important to all the life around you. Nobody else knows or cares too much about what you do, but if you get a good feeling inside about what you do, then it doesn't matter if nobody else knows. I do think about myself a lot when I'm alone way back on the place bringing in the cows or sitting on a mowing machine all day. But when I start thinking about how our animals and crops and fields and woods and gardens sort of all fit together, then I get that good feeling inside and don't worry much about what will happen to me.*

This passage goes to the heart of what I am trying to say, because it goes to the heart of farming as I have known it. Mr. Cummins's sentences describe an experience regrettably and perhaps dangerously missing now from the childhood of most children. They also describe the communion between the farmer as husband and the well-husbanded farm. This communion is a cultural force that can exist only by becoming personal.

To see it so described is to understand at once how necessary and how threatened it now is.

I HAVE TRIED to say what husbandry is, how it works, and why it is necessary. Now I want to speak of two paramount accomplishments of husbandry to which I think we will have to pay more deliberate attention, in our present circumstances, than we ever have before. These are local adaptation and local coherence of form. It is strange that a science of agriculture founded on evolutionary biology, with its practical emphasis on survival, would exempt the human species from these concerns.

True husbandry, as its first strategy of survival, has always striven to fit the farming to the farm and to the field, to the needs and abilities of the farm's family, and to the local economy. Every wild creature is the product of such an adaptive process. The same process once was a dominant influence on agriculture, for the cost of ignoring it was hunger. One striking and well-known example of local adaptation in agriculture is the number and diversity of British sheep breeds, most of which are named for the localities in which they were developed. But local adaptation must be even more refined than this example suggests, for it involves consideration of the individuality of every farm and every field.

Our recent focus upon productivity, genetic and technological uniformity, and global trade—all supported by supposedly limitless supplies of fuel, water, and soil—has obscured the necessity for local adaptation. But our circumstances are changing rapidly now, and this requirement will be forced upon us again by terrorism and other kinds of political violence, by chemical pollution, by increasing energy costs, by depleted soils, aquifers, and streams, and by the spread of exotic weeds, pests, and diseases. We are going to have to return to the old questions about local nature, local carrying capacities, and local needs. And we are going to have to resume the breeding of plants and animals to fit the region and the farm.

98

The same obsessions and extravagances that have caused us to ignore the issue of local adaptation have at the same time caused us to ignore the issue of form. These two issues are so closely related that it is difficult to talk about one without talking about the other. During the half century and more of our neglect of local adaptation, we have subjected our farms to a radical oversimplification of form. The diversified and reasonably self-sufficient farms of my region and of many other regions have been conglomerated into larger farms with larger fields, increasingly specialized, and subjected increasingly to the strict, unnatural linearity of the production line.

But the first requirement of a form is that it must be comprehensive; it must not leave out something that essentially belongs within it. The farm that Terry Cummins remembers was remarkably comprehensive, and it was not any one of its several enterprises alone that made him feel good, but rather "how our animals and crops and fields and woods and gardens sort of all fit together."

The form of the farm must answer to the farmer's feeling for the place, its creatures, and its work. It is a never-ending effort of fitting together many diverse things. It must incorporate the life cycle and the fertility cycles of animals. It must bring crops and livestock into balance and mutual support. It must be a pattern on the ground and in the mind. It must be at once ecological, agricultural, economic, familial, and neighborly. It must be inclusive enough, complex enough, coherent, intelligible, and durable. It must have within its limits the completeness of an organism or an ecosystem, or of any other good work of art.

The making of a form begins in the recognition and acceptance of limits. The farm is limited by its topography, its climate, its ecosystem, its human neighborhood and local economy, and of course by the larger economies, and by the preferences and abilities of the farmer. The true husbandman shapes the farm within an assured sense of what it cannot

99

be and what it should not be. And thus the problem of form returns us to that of local adaptation.

THE TASK BEFORE us, now as always before, is to renew and husband the means, both natural and human, of agriculture. But to talk now about renewing husbandry is to talk about unsimplifying what is in reality an extremely complex subject. This will require us to accept again, and more competently than before, the health of the ecosystem, the farm, and the human community as the ultimate standard of agricultural performance.

Unsimplification is difficult, I imagine, in any circumstances; our present circumstances will make it especially so. Soon the majority of the world's people will be living in cities. We are now obliged to think of so many people demanding the means of life from the land, to which they will no longer have a practical connection, and of which they will have little knowledge. We are obliged also to think of the consequences of any attempt to meet this demand by large-scale, expensive, petroleum-dependent technological schemes that will ignore local conditions and local needs. The problem of renewing husbandry, and the need to promote a general awareness of everybody's agricultural responsibilities, thus become urgent.

How are we to do this? How can we restore a competent husbandry to the minds of the world's producers and consumers?

For a start of course we must recognize that this effort is already in progress on many farms and in many urban consumer groups scattered across our country and the world. But we must recognize too that this effort needs an authorizing focus and force that would grant it a new legitimacy, intellectual rigor, scientific respectability, and responsible teaching. There are many reasons to hope that this might be supplied by our colleges of agriculture, and there are some reasons to think that this hope is not fantastical.

With that hope in mind, I want to return to the precaution that I mentioned earlier. The effort of husbandry is partly scientific, but it is entirely cultural, and a cultural initiative can exist only by becoming personal. It will become increasingly clear, I believe, that agricultural scientists, and the rest of us as well, are going to have to be less specialized, or less isolated by our specialization. Agricultural scientists will need to work as indwelling members of agricultural communities or of consumer communities. Their scientific work will need to accept the limits and the influence of that membership. It is not irrational to propose that a significant number of these scientists should be farmers, and so subject their scientific work, and that of their colleagues, to the influence of a farmer's practical circumstances. Along with the rest of us, they will need to accept all the imperatives of husbandry as the context of their work. We cannot keep things from falling apart in our society if they do not cohere in our minds and in our lives.

PART II
FARMERS

Seven Amish Farms

(1981)

⌇

IN TYPICAL MIDWESTERN farming country the distances between
inhabited houses are stretching out as bigger farmers buy out their
smaller neighbors in order to "stay in." The signs of this "movement"
and its consequent specialization are everywhere: good houses standing
empty, going to ruin; good stock barns going to ruin; pasture fences
fallen down or gone; machines too large for available doorways left in
the weather; windbreaks and woodlots gone down before the bulldozers;
small schoolhouses and churches deserted or filled with grain.

In the latter part of March this country shows little life. Field after
field lies under the dead stalks of last year's corn and soybeans, or lies
broken for the next crop; one may drive many miles between fields that
are either sodded or planted in winter grain. If the weather is wet, the
country will seem virtually deserted. If the ground is dry enough to support their wheels, there will be tractors at work, huge machines with
glassed cabs, rolling into the distances of fields larger than whole farms
used to be, as solitary as seaborne ships.

The difference between such country and the Amish farmlands in
northeast Indiana seems almost as great as that between a desert and an

oasis. And it is the *same* difference. In the Amish country there is a great deal more life: more natural life, more agricultural life, more human life. Because the farms are small—most of them containing well under a hundred acres—the Amish neighborhoods are more thickly populated than most rural areas, and you see more people at work. And because the Amish are diversified farmers, their plowed croplands are interspersed with pastures and hayfields and often with woodlots. It is a varied, interesting, healthy-looking farm country, pleasant to drive through. When we were there, on the twentieth and twenty-first of last March, the spring plowing had just started, and so you could still see everywhere the annual covering of stable manure on the fields, and the teams of Belgians or Percherons still coming out from the barns with loaded spreaders.

Our host, those days, was William J. Yoder, a widely respected breeder of Belgian horses, an able farmer and carpenter, and a most generous and enjoyable companion. He is a vigorous man, strenuously involved in the work of his farm and in the life of his family and community. From the look of him and the look of his place, you know that he has not just done a lot of work in his time, but has done it well, learned from it, mastered the necessary disciplines. He speaks with heavy stress on certain words—the emphasis of conviction, but also of pleasure, for he enjoys the talk that goes on among people interested in horses and in farming. But unlike many people who enjoy talking, he speaks with care. Bill was born in this community, has lived there all his life, and he has grandchildren who will probably live there all their lives. He belongs there, then, root and branch, and he knows the history and the quality of many of the farms. On the two days, we visited farms belonging to Bill himself, four of his sons, and two of his sons-in-law.

The Amish farms tend to divide up between established ones, which are prosperous-looking and well maintained, and run-down, abused, or neglected ones, on which young farmers are getting started. Young Amish farmers *are* still getting started, in spite of inflation, speculators' prices, and usurious interest rates. My impression is that the proportion of young farmers buying farms is significantly greater among the Amish than among conventional farmers.

Bill Yoder's own eighty-acre farm is among the established ones. I had been there in the fall of 1975 and had not forgotten its aspect of cleanness and good order, its well-kept white buildings, neat lawns, and garden plots. Bill has owned the place for twenty-six years. Before he bought it, it had been rented and row cropped, with the usual result: It was nearly played out. "The buildings," he says, "were nothing," and there were no fences. The first year, the place produced five loads (maybe five tons) of hay, "and that was mostly sorrel." The only healthy plants on it were the spurts of grass and clover that grew out of the previous year's manure piles. The corn crop that first year "might have been thirty bushels an acre," all nubbins. The sandy soil blew in every strong wind, and when he plowed the fields his horses' feet sank into "quicksand potholes" that the share uncovered.

The remedy has been a set of farming practices traditional among the Amish since the seventeenth century: diversification, rotation of crops, use of manure, seeding of legumes. These practices began when the Anabaptist sects were disfranchised in their European homelands and forced to the use of poor soil. We saw them still working to restore farmed-out soils in Indiana. One thing these practices do is build humus in the soil, and humus does several things: increases fertility, improves soil structure, improves both water-holding capacity and drainage. "No humus, you're in trouble," Bill says.

After his rotations were established and the land had begun to be properly manured, the potholes disappeared, and the soil quit blowing. "There's something in it now—there's some substance there." Now the farm produces abundant crops of corn, oats, wheat, and alfalfa. Oats now yield 90–100 bushels per acre. The corn averages 100–125 bushels per acre, and the ears are long, thick, and well filled.

Bill's rotation begins and ends with alfalfa. Every fall he puts in a new seeding of alfalfa with his wheat; every spring he plows down an old stand of alfalfa, "no matter how good it is." From alfalfa he goes to corn for two years, planting thirty acres, twenty-five for ear corn and five for silage. After the second year of corn, he sows oats in the spring, wheat and alfalfa in the fall. In the fourth year the wheat is harvested; the alfalfa then comes on and remains through the fifth and sixth years. Two cuttings of alfalfa are taken each year. After curing in the field, the hay is hauled to the barn, chopped, and blown into the loft. The third cutting is pastured.

Unlike cow manure, which is heavy and chunky, horse manure is light and breaks up well coming out of the spreader; it interferes less with the growth of small seedlings and is less likely to be picked up by a hay rake. On Bill's place, horse manure is used on the fall seedings of wheat and alfalfa, on the young alfalfa after the wheat harvest, and both years on the established alfalfa stands. The cow manure goes on the corn ground both years. He usually has about 350 eighty-bushel spreader loads of manure, and each year he covers the whole farm—cropland, hayland, and pasture.

With such an abundance of manure there obviously is no *dependence* on chemical fertilizers, but Bill uses some as a "starter" on his corn and oats. On corn he applies 125 pounds of nitrogen in the row. On oats he uses 200–250 pounds of 16-16-16, 20-20-20, or 24-24-24. He routinely spreads two tons of lime to the acre on the ground being prepared for wheat.

His out-of-pocket costs per acre of corn last year were as follows:

Seed (planted at a rate of seven acres per bushel) ⸰ $7.00
Fertilizer ⸰ $7.75
Herbicide (custom applied, first year only) ⸰ $16.40

That comes to a total of $31.15 per acre—or, if the corn makes only a hundred bushels per acre, a little over $0.31 per bushel. In the second year his per-acre cost is $14.75, less than $0.15 per bushel, bringing the two-year average to $22.95 per acre or about $0.23 per bushel.

The herbicide is used because, extra horses being on the farm during the winter, Bill has to buy eighty to a hundred tons of hay, and in that way brings in weed seed. He had no weed problem until he started buying hay. Even though he uses the herbicide, he still cultivates his corn three times.

His cost per acre of oats came to $33.00 ($12.00 for seed and $21.00 for fertilizer)—or, at ninety bushels per acre, about $0.37 per bushel.

Of Bill's eighty acres, sixty-two are tillable. He has ten acres of permanent pasture, and seven or eight of woodland, which produced the lumber for all the building he has done on the place. In addition, for $500 a year he rents an adjoining eighty acres of "hill and woods pasture" which provides summer grazing for twenty heifers; and on another neighboring farm he rents varying amounts of cropland.

All the field work is done with horses, and this, of course, comes virtually free—a by-product of the horse-breeding enterprise. Bill has an ancient Model D John Deere tractor that he uses for belt power.

At the time of our visit, there were twenty-two head of horses on the place. But that number was unusually low, for Bill aims to keep "around thirty head." He has a band of excellent brood mares and three stallions, plus young stock of assorted ages. Since October 1 of last year, he had sold eighteen head of registered Belgian horses. In the winters he operates a "urine line," collecting "pregnant mare urine," which is sold to a pharmaceutical company for the extraction of various hormones. For this purpose he boards a good many mares belonging to neighbors; that is why he must buy the extra hay that causes his weed problem. (Horses are so numerous on this farm because they are one of its money-making enterprises. If horses were used only for work on this farm, four good geldings would be enough.)

One bad result of the dramatic rise in draft horse prices over the last eight or ten years is that it has tended to focus attention on such characteristics as size and color to the neglect of less obvious qualities such as good feet. To me, foot quality seems a critical issue. A good horse with bad feet is good for nothing but decoration, and at sales and shows there are far too many flawed feet disguised by plastic wood and black shoe polish. And so I was pleased to see that every horse on Bill Yoder's place had sound, strong-walled, correctly shaped feet. They were good horses all around, but their other qualities were well-founded; they stood on good feet, and this speaks of the thoroughness of his judgment and also of his honesty.

Though he is a master horseman, and the draft horse business is more lucrative now than ever in its history, Bill does not specialize in horses, and that is perhaps the clearest indication of his integrity as a farmer. Whatever may be the dependability of the horse economy, on this farm it rests upon a diversified agricultural economy that is sound.

He was milking five Holstein cows; he had fifteen Holstein heifers that he had raised to sell; and he had just marketed thirty finished hogs, which is the number that he usually has on hand. All the animals had been well wintered—Bill quotes his father approvingly: "Well wintered is half summered"—and were in excellent condition. Another saying of his father's that Bill likes to quote—"Keep the horses on the side of the fence the feed is on"—has obviously been obeyed here. The feeding is careful, the feed is good, and it is abundant. Though it was almost spring, there were ample surpluses in the hayloft and in the corn cribs.

Other signs of the farm's good health were three sizable garden plots, and newly pruned grapevines and raspberry canes. The gardener of the family is Mrs. Yoder. Though most of the children are now gone from home, Bill says that she still grows as much garden stuff as she ever did.

ALL SEVEN OF the Yoders' sons live in the community. Floyd, the youngest, is still at home. Harley has a house on nearly three acres, works in town, and returns in the afternoons to his own shop where he works as a farrier. Henry, who also works in town, lives with Harley and his wife. The other four sons are now settled on farms that they are in the process of paying for. Richard has eighty acres, Orla eighty, Mel fifty-seven, and Wilbur eighty. Two sons-in-law also living in the community are Perry Bontrager, who owns ninety-five acres, and Ervin Mast, who owns sixty-five. Counting Bill's eighty acres, the seven families are living on 537 acres. Of the seven farms, only Mel's is entirely tillable, the acreages in woods or permanent pasture varying from five to twenty-six.

These young men have all taken over run-down farms, on which they are establishing rotations and soil husbandry practices that, being traditional, more or less resemble Bill's. It seemed generally agreed that after three years of this treatment the land would grow corn, as Perry Bontrager said, "like anywhere else."

These are good farmers, capable of the intelligent planning, sound judgment, and hard work that good farming requires. Abused land heals and flourishes in their care. None of them expressed a wish to own more land; all, I believe, feel that what they have will be enough—when it is paid for. The big problems are high land prices and high interest rates, the latter apparently being the worst.

The answer, for Bill's sons so far, has been town work. All of them, after leaving home, have worked for Redman Industries, a manufacturer of mobile homes in Topeka. They do piecework, starting at seven in the morning and quitting at two in the afternoon, using the rest of the day for farming or other work. This, Bill thinks, is now "the only way" to get started farming. Even so, there is "a lot of debt" in the community— "more than ever."

With a start in factory work, with family help, with government and bank loans, with extraordinary industry and perseverance, with highly developed farming skills, it is still possible for young Amish families to own a small farm that will eventually support them. But there is more strain in that effort now than there used to be, and more than there should be. When the burden of usurious interest becomes too great, these young men are finding it necessary to make temporary returns to their town jobs.

The only one who spoke of his income was Mel, who owns fifty-seven acres, which, he says, *will be* enough. He and his family milk six Holsteins. He had nine mares on the urine line last winter, seven of which belonged to him. And he had twelve brood sows. Last year his gross income was $43,000. Of this, $12,000 came from hogs, $7,000 from his milk cows, the rest from his horses and the sale of his wheat. After his production costs, but *before* payment of interest, he netted $22,000. In order to cope with the interest payments, Mel was preparing to return to work in town.

These little Amish farms thus become the measure both of "conventional" American agriculture and of the cultural meaning of the national industrial economy.

To begin with, these farms give the lie directly to that false god of "agribusiness": the so-called economy of scale. The small farm is not an anachronism, is not unproductive, is not unprofitable. Among the Amish, it is still thriving, and is still the economic foundation of what John A. Hostetler (in *Amish Society*, third edition) rightly calls "a healthy culture." Though they do not produce the "record-breaking yields" so touted by the "agribusiness" establishment, these farms are nevertheless highly productive. And if they are not likely to make their owners rich (never an Amish goal), they can certainly be said to be sufficiently profitable. The economy of scale has helped corporations and banks, not farmers and farm communities. It has been an economy of dispossession and waste—plutocratic, if not in aim, then certainly in result.

What these Amish farms suggest, on the contrary, is that in farming there is inevitably a scale that is suitable both to the productive capacity of the land and to the abilities of the farmer; and that agricultural problems are to be properly solved, not in expansion, but in management, diversity, balance, order, responsible maintenance, good character, and in the sensible limitation of investment and overhead. (Bill makes a careful distinction between "healthy" and "unhealthy" debt, a "healthy debt" being "one you can hope to pay off in a reasonable way.")

Most significant, perhaps, is that while conventional agriculture, blindly following the tendency of any industry to exhaust its sources, has made soil erosion a national catastrophe, these Amish farms conserve the land and improve it in use.

And what is one to think of a national economy that drives such obviously able and valuable farmers to factory work? What value does such an economy impose upon thrift, effort, skill, good husbandry, family and community health?

In spite of the unrelenting destructiveness of the larger economy, the Amish—as Hostetler points out with acknowledged surprise and respect—have almost doubled in population in the last twenty years. The doubling of a population is, of course, no significant achievement. What is significant is that these agricultural communities have doubled their population *and yet remained agricultural communities* during a time when conventional farmers have failed by the millions. This alone would seem to call for a careful look at Amish ways of farming. That those ways have, during the same time, been ignored by the colleges and the agencies of agriculture must rank as a prime intellectual wonder.

Amish farming has been so ignored, I think, because it involves a complicated structure that is at once biological and cultural, rather than industrial or economic. I suspect that anyone who might attempt an accounting of the economy of an Amish farm would soon find himself dealing with virtually unaccountable values, expenses, and benefits. He would be dealing with biological forces and processes not always measurable, with spiritual and community values not quantifiable; at certain points he would be dealing with mysteries—and he would be finding that these unaccountables and inscrutables have results, among others, that are economic. Hardly an appropriate study for the "science" of agricultural economics.

The economy of conventional agriculture or "agribusiness" is remarkable for the simplicity of its arithmetic. It involves a manipulation of quantities that are all entirely accountable. List your costs (land, equipment, fuel, fertilizer, pesticides, herbicides, wages), add them up, subtract them from your earnings, or subtract your earnings from them, and you have the result.

Suppose, on the other hand, that you have an eighty-acre farm that is not a "food factory" but your home, your given portion of Creation which you are morally and spiritually obliged "to dress and to keep." Suppose you farm, not for wealth, but to maintain the integrity and the practical supports of your family and community. Suppose that, the farm being small enough, you farm it with family work and work exchanged with neighbors. Suppose you have six Belgian brood mares that you use for field work. Suppose that you also have milk cows and hogs, and that you raise a variety of grain and hay crops in rotation. What happens to your accounting then?

To start with, several of the costs of conventional farming are greatly diminished or done away with. Equipment, fertilizer, chemicals all cost much less. Fuel becomes feed, but you have the mares and are feeding them anyway; the work ration for a brood mare is not a lot more costly than a maintenance ration. And the horses, like the rest of the livestock, are making manure. Figure that in, and figure, if you can, the value of the difference between manure and chemical fertilizer. You can probably get an estimate of the value of the nitrogen fixed by your alfalfa, but how will you quantify the value to the soil of its residues and deep roots? Try to compute the value of humus in the soil—in improved drainage, improved drought resistance, improved tilth, improved health. Wages, if you pay your children, will still be among your costs. But compute the difference between paying your children and paying "labor." Work exchanged with neighbors can be reduced to "man-hours" and assigned a dollar value. But compute the difference between a neighbor and "labor." Compute the value of a family or a community to any one of its members. We may, as we must, grant that among the values of family and community there is economic value—but what is it?

In the Louisville *Courier-Journal* of April 5, 1981, the Mobil Oil Corporation ran an advertisement which was yet another celebration of "scientific agriculture." American farming, the Mobile people are of course happy to say, "requires more petroleum products than almost any other industry. A gallon of gasoline to produce a single bushel of corn, for example. . . ." This, they say, enables "each American farmer to feed sixty-seven people." And they say that this is "a-maizing."

Well, it certainly is! And the chances are good that an agriculture totally dependent on the petroleum industry is not yet as amazing as it is going to be. But one thing that is already sufficiently amazing is that a bushel of corn produced by the burning of one gallon of gasoline has already cost more than *six times* as much as a bushel of corn grown by Bill Yoder. How does Bill Yoder escape what may justly be called the petroleum tax on agriculture? He does so by a series of substitutions: of horses for tractors, of feed for fuel, of manure for fertilizer, of sound agricultural methods and patterns for the exploitive methods and patterns of industry. But he has done more than that—or, rather, he and his people and their tradition have done more. They have substituted themselves, their families, and their communities for petroleum. The Amish use little petroleum—and need little—because they have those other things.

I do not think that we can make sense of Amish farming until we see it, until we become willing to see it, as belonging essentially to the Amish practice of Christianity, which instructs that one's neighbors are to be loved as oneself. To farmers who give priority to the maintenance of their community, the economy of scale (that is, the economy of *large* scale, of "growth") can make no sense, for it requires the ruination and displacement of neighbors. A farm cannot be increased except by the decrease of a neighborhood. What the interest of the community proposes is invariably an economy of *proper* scale. A whole set of agricultural proprieties must be observed: of farm size, of methods, of tools, of energy sources, of plant and animal species. Community interest also requires charity, neighborliness, the care and instruction of the young, respect for the old; thus it ensures its integrity and survival. Above all, it requires good stewardship of the land, for the community, as the Amish have always understood, is no better than its land. "If treated violently or exploited selfishly," John Hostetler writes, the land "will yield poorly." There could be no better statement of the meaning of the *practice* and the practicality of charity. Except to the insane narrow-mindedness of industrial economics, selfishness does not pay.

The Amish have steadfastly subordinated economic value to the values of religion and community. What is too readily overlooked by a secular, exploitive society is that their ways of doing this are not "empty gestures" and are not "backward." In the first place, these ways have kept the communities intact through many varieties of hard times. In the second place, they conserve the land. In the third place, they yield economic benefits. The community, the religious fellowship, has many kinds of value, and among them is economic value. It is the result of the practice of neighborliness, and of the practice of stewardship. What moved me most, what I liked best, in those days we spent with Bill Yoder was the sense of the continuity of the community in his dealings with his children and in their dealings with their children.

Bill has helped his sons financially so far as he has been able. He has helped them with his work. He has helped them by sharing what he has—lending a stallion, say, at breeding time, or lending a team. And he helps them by buying good pieces of equipment that come up for sale. "If he ever gets any money," he says of one of the boys, for whom he has bought an implement, "he'll pay me for it. If he don't, he'll just use it." He has been their teacher, and he remains their advisor. But he does not stand before them as a domineering patriarch or "authority figure." He seems to speak, rather, as a representative of family and community experience. In their respect for him, his sons respect their tradition. They are glad for his help, advice, and example, but there is nothing servile in this. It seems to be given and taken in a kind of familial friendship, respect going both ways.

Everywhere we went, when school was not in session, the children were at the barns, helping with the work, watching, listening, learning to farm in the way it is best learned. Wilbur told us that his eleven-year-old son had cultivated twenty-three acres of corn last year with a team and a riding cultivator. That reminded Bill of the way he taught Wilbur to do the same job.

Wilbur was little then, and he loved to sit in his father's lap and drive the team while Bill worked the cultivator. If Wilbur could drive, Bill thought, he could do the rest of it. So he got off and shortened the stirrups so the boy could reach them with his feet. Wilbur started the team, and within a few steps began plowing up the corn.

"Whoa!" he said.

And Bill, who was walking behind him, said, "Come up!"

And it went that way for a little bit:

"Whoa!"

"Come up!"

And then Wilbur started to cry, and Bill said:

"Don't cry! Go ahead!"

A Good Farmer of the Old School

(1985)

⨍

AT THE 1982 Draft Horse Sale in Columbus, Ohio, Maury Telleen summoned me over to the group of horsemen with whom he was talking: "Come here," he said, "I want you to hear this." One of those horsemen was Lancie Clippinger, and what Maury wanted me to hear was the story of Lancie's corn crop of the year before.

The story, which Lancie obligingly told again, was as interesting to me as Maury had expected it to be. Lancie, that year, had planted forty acres of corn; he had also bred forty gilts that he had raised so that their pigs would be ready to feed when the corn would be ripe. The gilts produced 360 pigs, an average of nine per head. When the corn was ready for harvest, Lancie divided off a strip of the field with an electric fence and turned in the 360 shoats. After the shoats had fed on that strip for a while, Lancie opened a new strip for them. He then picked the strip where they had just fed. In that way, he fattened his 360 shoats and also harvested all the corn he needed for his other stock.

The shoats brought $40,000. Lancie's expenses had been for seed corn, 275 pounds of fertilizer per acre, and one quart per acre of herbicide. He did not say what the total costs amounted to, but it was clear enough that his net income from the forty acres of corn had been high, in a year when the corn itself would have brought perhaps two dollars a bushel.

At the end of the story, I remember, Lancie and Maury had a conversation that went about like this:

"Do you farrow your sows in a farrowing house?"

"No."

"Oh, you do it in huts, then?"

"No, I have a field I turn them out in. It has plenty of shade and water. And I see them every day."

Here was an intelligent man, obviously, who knew the value of doing his own thinking and paying attention, who understood clearly that the profit is in the difference between costs and earnings, and who proceeded directly to minimize his costs. In a time when hog farmers often spend many thousands of dollars on highly specialized housing and equipment, Lancie's "hog operation" consisted almost entirely of hogs. His principal outlays otherwise were for the farm itself and for fencing. But what struck me most, I think, was the way he had employed nature and the hogs themselves to his own advantage. The bred sows needed plenty of shade, water, and room for exercise; Lancie provided those things, and nature did the rest. He also supplied his own care and attention, which came free; they did not have to be purchased at an inflated cost from an industrial supplier. And then, instead of harvesting his corn mechanically, hauling it, storing it, grinding it, and hauling it to his shoats, he let the shoats harvest and grind it for themselves. He had the use of the whole hog, whereas in a "confinement operation," the hog's feet, teeth, and eyes have virtually no use and produce no profit.

At the next Columbus Sale, I hunted Lancie up, and again we spent a long time talking. We talked about draft horses, of course, but also about milk cows and dairying. And that part of our conversation interested me about as much as the hog story had the year before. What so impressed me was Lancie's belief that there is a limit to the number of cows that a dairy farmer can manage well; he thought the maximum number to be about twenty-five: "If a fellow milks twenty-five cows, he'll *see* them all." If he milks more than that, Lancie said, even though he may touch them all, he will not *see* them all. As in Lancie's account of his corn crop and the 360 shoats, the emphasis here was on the importance of seeing, of paying attention. That this is important economically, he made clear in something he said to me later: "You can take care of twenty or twenty-five cows and do it right. More, you're overlooking things that cost you money." It is necessary, Lancie thinks, to limit the scale of operation, not only in dairying, but in all other enterprises on the farm because proper scale permits a correct balance between work and care. The distinction he was making, it seemed to me, was between work, as it has been understood traditionally on the farm, and processing, as it is understood in industry.

Those two conversations stayed in my mind, proving useful many times in my effort to understand the troubles developing in our agricultural economy. I knew that Lancie Clippinger was one of the best farmers of the old school, and I promised myself that I would visit him at his farm, which I was finally able to do in October 1985.

The farm is on somewhat rolling land, surrounded by woodlots and brushy fencerows, so that it has a little of the feeling of a large forest clearing. There are 175 acres, of which about 135 are cropped; the rest are in permanent pasture and woods. Although conveniently close to the state road, the farm is at the end of a lane, set off to itself. It is pretty and quiet, a pleasant place to live and to farm, as well as to visit. Lancie and his wife, Verna Bell, bought the place and moved there in the fall of 1971.

When my wife and I drove into the yard, Kathy, one of Lancie's granddaughters, who had evidently been watching for us, came out of the house to meet us. She took us out through the barn lot to a granary where Lancie, his son Keith, and Sherri, another granddaughter, were sacking some oats. We waited, talking with Kathy, while they finished the job, and then we went with Lancie and Keith to look at the horses.

Lancie keeps only geldings, buying them at sales as weanlings, raising and breaking them, selling them, and then replacing them with new colts. When we were there, he had nine head: a pair of black Percherons, a handsome crossbred bay with black mane and tail, and six Belgians. Though he prefers Percherons, he does not specialize; at the sales, his only aim is to buy "colts that look like they'll grow into good big horses." He wants them big because the big ones bring the best prices, but, like nearly all draft horse people who use their horses, he would rather have smaller ones—fifteen hundred pounds or so—if he were keeping them only to work.

The horses he led out for us were in prime condition, and he had been right about them: They had, sure enough, grown into good big ones. These horses may be destined for pulling contests and show hitches, but while they are at Lancie's they put in a lot of time at farm work—they work their way through school, you might say. Like so many farmers of his time, Lancie once made the change from horses to tractors, but with him this did not last long. He was without horses "for a little while" in the seventies, and after that he began to use them again. Now he uses the horses for "just about everything" except cutting and baling his hay and picking his corn. Last spring he used his big tractor only two days. The last time he went to use it, it wouldn't start, and he left it sitting in the shed; it was still sitting there at the time of our visit.

Part of the justification for the return to the use of horses is economic. When he was doing all his work with tractors, Lancie's fuel bill was $6,000 a year; now it is about $2,000. Since the horses themselves are a profit-making enterprise on this farm, the $4,000 they save on fuel is money in the bank. But the economic reason is not the only one: "Pleasure," Lancie says, "is a big part of it." At the year's end, his bank account will show a difference that the horses have made, but day by day his reason for working them is that he *likes* to.

He does not need nine horses in order to do his farming. He has so many because he needs to keep replacements on hand for the horses he sells. He aims, he says, to sell "two or three or four horses every year." To farm his 175 acres, he needs only four good geldings, although he would probably like to keep five, in case he needed a spare. With four horses on his grain drill, he can plant fifteen or twenty acres in a day. He uses four horses also on an eight-foot tandem disk and a springtooth harrow, and he can plant twelve or fifteen acres of corn a day "and not half try."

In plowing, he goes by the old rule of thumb that you can plow an acre per horse per day, provided the horses are in hard condition. "If you start at seven in the morning and stay there the way you ought to," he says, "you can plow three acres a day with three horses." That is what he does, and he does it with a walking plow because, he says, it is easier to walk than to ride. That, of course, is hardly a popular opinion, and Lancie is amused by the surprise it sometimes causes.

One spring, he says, after he had started plowing, he ordered some lime. When the trucker brought the first load, he stopped by the house to ask where to spread it. Mrs. Clippinger told him that Lancie was plowing, and pointed out to the field where Lancie could be seen walking in the furrow behind his plow and team. The trucker was astonished: "Even the *Amish* ride!"

In 1936, Lancie remembers, he plowed a hundred acres, sixty of them in sod, with two horses, Bob and Joe. Together, that team weighed about thirty-five hundred pounds. They were blacks. Lancie had been logging with them before he started plowing, and they were in good shape, ready to go. They plowed two acres a day, six days a week, for nearly nine weeks. It is the sort of thing, one guesses, that could have been done only because all the conditions were right: a strong young man, a tough team, a good season. "Looked like, back then, there wasn't any bad weather," Lancie says, laughing. "You could work all the time."

This farmer's extensive use of live horsepower is possible because his farm is the right size for it and because a sensible rotation of crops both reduces the acreage to be plowed each year and distributes the other field work so that not too much needs to be done at any one time. Of the farm's 135 arable acres, approximately fifty-five will be in corn, forty in oats, and forty in alfalfa. Each of the crops will be grown on the same land two years in order to avoid buying alfalfa seed every year.

The two-year-old alfalfa, turned under, supplies enough nitrogen for the first year of corn. In the second year, the corn crop receives a little commercial nitrogen. The routine application of fertilizer on the corn is 275 pounds per acre of 10-10-20, drilled into the row with the planter. The oats are fertilized at the same rate as the corn, while the alfalfa field, because Lancie sells quite a bit of hay, receives 600 pounds per acre of 3-14-42 in two applications every year. The land is limed at a rate of two tons per acre every time it is plowed. Otherwise, for fertilization Lancie depends on manure from his cattle and horses. "That's what counts," he says. It counts because it pays but does not cost. He usually has enough manure to cover his corn ground every year.

This system of management has not only maintained the productive capacity of the farm but has greatly improved it. Fourteen years ago, when Lancie began on it, the place was farmed out. The previous farmer had plowed it all and planted it all in corn year after year. When the farm sold in the fall of 1971, the corn crop, which was still standing, was bought by a neighboring farmer, who found it not worth picking. Lancie plowed it under the next spring. In order to have a corn crop that first year, he used 900 pounds of fertilizer to the acre—300 pounds of nitrogen and 600 of "straight analysis." After that, when his rotations and other restorative practices had been established, he went to his present rate of 275 pounds of 10-10-20. The resulting rates of production speak well for good care: The corn has made 150 bushels per acre, Lancie says, "for a long time"; this year his oats made 109 bushels per acre, and he also harvested 11,000 fifty-pound bales of alfalfa hay from a forty-acre field (a per-acre yield of about seven tons) and sold 4,800 bales for $12,000.

In addition to seed and fertilizer, Lancie purchases some insecticide and herbicide. This year his alfalfa was sprayed once for weevils, and he used a half-pint of 2-4-D per acre on his corn. The 2-4-D, he says, would not have been necessary if he had cultivated four times instead of twice. Using the chemical saved two cultivations that would have interfered with hay harvest.

What is most significant about Lancie's management of his crops is that it gives his farm a degree of independence that is unusual in these times. The farm, first of all, is ordered and used according to its own nature and carrying capacity, not according to the dictates of farm policy, expert advice, or fluctuations of the economy. The possibility of solving one's economic problems by production alone is not, in Lancie's opinion, a good possibility. If you are losing money on the corn you produce, he points out, the more you produce the more you lose. That so many farmers continue to compensate for low grain prices by increasing production, at great cost to their farms and to themselves, is a sort of wonder to him. "The cheaper it is, the more they plow," he says. "I don't know what they mean." His own farm, by contrast, grows approximately the same acreages of the same crops every year, not because that is what the economy supposedly demands, but because that is what the land can produce at the least cost for the longest time.

Since the farm itself is so much the source of its own fertility and operating energy, Lancie's use of purchased supplies can be minimal, selective, and nonaddictive. Because his cropping pattern and system of management are sound, Lancie can buy these things to suit his convenience. His total expense for 2-4-D for his corn this year, for example, was $56—a very small price to pay in order to have his hands and his mind free at haying time. The point, I think, is that he had a choice: He could choose to do what made the most sense. A further point is that he can quit using chemicals and purchased fertilizer if it ever makes economic sense to do so. As a farmer, he is not addicted to these things.

The conventional industrial farmer, on the other hand, is too often the prisoner of his own technology and methods and has no choice but to continue to do as he has done, whatever the disadvantages. A farmer who has no fences cannot turn hogs in to harvest his corn when prices are low. A farmer who has invested heavily in a farrowing house and all the equipment that goes with it is stuck with that investment. If, for some reason, it ceases to be profitable for him to produce feeder pigs, he still has the farrowing house, which is good for little else, and perhaps a debt on it as well. Thus, mental paralysis and economic slavery can be instituted on a farm by the farmer's technological choices.

One of the main results of Lancie Clippinger's independence is versatility, enabling him to take advantage quickly of opportunities as they appear. Because he has invested in no expensive specialized equipment, he can change his ways to suit his wishes or his circumstances. That he did well raising and finishing shoats one year does not mean that he must continue to raise them. Last year, for instance, he thought there was money to be made on skinny sows. He bought sixty-two at $100 a head, turned them into his cornfield, and, while they ate, he picked. "We all worked together," he says. The sows did a nearly perfect job of gleaning the field, and they brought $200 a head when he sold them.

There is a direct economic payoff in this freedom of choice: It pays to be able to choose to substitute a team of horses for a tractor, or manure for fertilizer, or cultivation for herbicides. When you cultivate a field of corn, as Lancie says, "you're selling your labor"; in other words, you ensure a relation between production and consumption that is proper because it makes sound economic sense. If the farmer does not achieve that proper relation on his farm, he will be a victim. When Lancie prepares his ground with plow and harrow and cultivates his crop instead of buying chemicals, he is a producer, not a consumer; he is selling his labor, not buying an expensive substitute for labor. Moreover, when he does this with a team of horses instead of buying fuel, he is selling his team's labor, not paying for an expensive substitute. When he uses his own corn, oats, and hay to replace petroleum, he is selling those feeds for a far higher return than he could get on the market. He and his horses are functioning, in effect, as solar converters, making usable and profitable the free sunlight that falls onto the farm. They are producing at home the energy, weed control, and fertility that other farmers are going broke trying to pay for.

The industrial farmer consumes more than he produces and is a captive consumer of the suppliers who have prospered by the ruination of such farmers. So far as the national economy is concerned, this kind of farmer exists only to provide cheap food and to enrich the agribusiness corporations, at his own expense.

Sometimes Lancie's intelligent methods and his habit of paying attention yield unexpected dividends. The year after he hogged down the forty acres of corn with the 360 shoats, the field was covered with an excellent stand of alsike clover. "It was pretty," Lancie says, but he didn't know where it came from. He asked around in the neighborhood and discovered that the field had been in alsike seventeen years before. The seed had lain in the ground all that time, waiting for conditions to be right, and somehow the hogs had made them right. Thus, that year's very profitable corn harvest, which had been so well planned, resulted in a valuable gift that nobody had planned—or could have planned. There is no recipe, so far as I know, for making such a thing happen. Obviously, though, a certain eligibility is required. It happened on Lancie's farm undoubtedly because he is the kind of farmer he is. If he had been plowing the whole farm every year and planting it all in corn, as his predecessor had, such a thing would not have happened.

127

It is care, obviously, that makes the difference. The farm gives gifts because it is given a chance to do so; it is not overcropped or overused. One of Lancie's kindnesses to his farm is his regular rotation of his crops; another is his keeping of livestock, which gives him not only the advantages I have already described but also permits him to make appropriate use of land not suited to row cropping. Like many farms in the allegedly flat corn belt, Lancie's farm includes some land that should be kept permanently grassed, and on his farm, unlike many, it *is* kept permanently grassed. He can afford this because he can make good use of it that way, without damaging it, for these thirty or so acres give him five hundred bales of bluegrass hay early in the year and, after that, months of pasture, at the cost only of a second clipping. The crop on that land does not need to be planted or cultivated, and it is harvested by the animals; it is therefore the cheapest feed on the place.

Lancie Clippinger is as much in the business of growing crops and making money on them as any other farmer. But he is also in the business of making sense—making sense, that is, for himself, not for the oil, chemical, and equipment companies, or for the banks. He is taking his own advice, and his advice comes from his experience and the experience of farmers like him, not from experts who are not farmers. For those reasons, Lancie Clippinger is doing all right. He is farming well and earning a living by it in a time when many farmers are farming poorly and making money for everybody but themselves.

"I don't know what they mean," he says. "You'd think some in the bunch would use their heads a *little* bit."

Charlie Fisher

(1996)

॰ॐ

I DON'T IMAGINE CHARLIE Fisher told me everything he has done, but in the day and a half I spent with him I did find out that he was raised on a truck farm, that for a while he rode bulls and exhibited a trick horse on the rodeo circuit, that as a young man he worked for a dairy-man, and that later he had a dairy farm of his own. His interest in logging and in working horses began while he was a hired hand in the dairy. In the winter, between milkings, he and his elderly employer spent their time in the woods at opposite ends of a crosscut saw—which, Charlie says, made him tireder than it made the old dairyman. They cut some big timber and dragged out the logs with horses. The old dairyman saw that Charlie liked working horses and was good at it. And so it was that he became both a teamster and a logger.

Though he tried other employment, those two early interests stayed with him, and he has spent many years logging with horses. There were times when he worked alone, cutting and skidding out the logs by himself. Later, his son David began to work with him, skidding out the logs while Charlie cut. David, who is now twenty-two, virtually grew up in the woods. He started skidding logs with a team when he was nine, and he is still working with his father, as both teamster and log cutter.

Nine years ago, near Andover in northeast Ohio, Charlie Fisher and Jeff Green formed a company, Valley Veneer, which involves both a logging operation and a sawmill. Charlie buys the standing timber, marks the trees that are to be cut, and supervises the logging crews, while Jeff keeps things going at the mill and markets the lumber.

The mill employs eight or nine hands, and it saws three million board feet a year. It provides a local market for local timber. This obviously is good for the economy of the Andover neighborhood, but it also is good for the forest. By establishing the mill, Charlie and Jeff have invested in the neighborhood and formed a permanent connection to it, and so they have an inescapable interest in preserving the productivity of the local forest. Thus a local forest economy, if it is complex enough, will tend almost naturally to act as a conserver of the local forest ecosystem. Valley Veneer, according to Charlie and Jeff, has been warmly received into the neighborhood. The company deals with the only locally owned bank in the area. The bankers have been not only cooperative but also friendly, at times offering more help than Charlie and Jeff asked for.

The mill yard is the neatest I have ever seen. The logs are sorted and ricked according to species. Veneer logs are laid down separately with one end resting on a pole, so that they can be readily examined by buyers. The mill crew is skillful in salvaging good lumber from damaged or inferior trees. This is extremely important, as is Jeff's marketing of lumber from inferior species such as soft maple, for it means that the cutting in the woods is never limited to the best trees. Charlie marks the trees, knowing that whatever the woodland can properly yield—soft maple or fine furniture-quality cherry or trees damaged by disease or wind—can be sawed into boards and sold. The mill seemed to me an extraordinarily efficient place, where nothing of value is wasted. Twenty percent of the slabs are sold for firewood; the rest go to the chipper and are used for pulp. The sawdust is sold to farmers, who use it as bedding for animals.

The woods operation—Charlie's end of the business—consists of three logging crews, each made up of one faller and two teamsters. Each of the teamsters works two horses on a logging cart or "logging arch." And so Charlie routinely employs nine men and twelve horses. At times, the cutter also will do some skidding, and this increases the number of teams in use. The three crews will usually be at work at three different sites.

Mostly they log small, privately owned woodlots within a radius of forty or fifty miles. Charlie recently counted up and found that he had logged 366 different tracts of timber in the last three years. And there are certain advantages to working on this scale. In a horse logging operation, it is best to limit the skidding distance to five or six hundred feet, though Charlie says they sometimes increase it to a thousand, and they can go somewhat farther in winter when snow or freezing weather reduces the friction. Big tracts, however, involve longer distances, and eventually it becomes necessary either to build a road for the truck or to use a bulldozer to move the logs from where the teamsters yard them in the woods to a second yarding place accessible from the highway. For this purpose, in addition to a log truck equipped with a hydraulic loading boom, Valley Veneer owns two bulldozers, one equipped with a fork, one with a blade, and both with winches. Even so, about 98 percent of the logs are moved with horses.

The logging crews work the year round and in all weather except pouring rain. The teamsters, who furnish their own teams and equipment, receive forty dollars per thousand board feet. Two of his teamsters, Charlie says, make more than thirty thousand dollars a year each.

The logging arch, in comparison to a mechanical skidder, is a very forthright piece of equipment. Like the forecart that is widely used for field work, it is simply a way to provide a drawbar for a team of horses.

There are a number of differences in design, but the major difference is that the logging arch's drawbar is welded on edge-up and has slots instead of holes. The slots are made so as to catch and hold the links of a log chain. Each cart carries an eighteen-foot chain with a grab hook at each end. Four metal hooks (which Charlie calls "log grabs," but which are also called "J-hooks" or "logging dogs") are linked to rings and strung on the chain, thus permitting the cart to draw as many as four logs at a time. The chain can also be used at full length if necessary to reach a hard-to-get-to log. Larger logs require the use of tongs, which the teamsters also carry with them, or two grabs driven into the log on opposite sides. The carts are equipped also with a cant hook and a "skipper" with which to drive the grabs into the log and knock them out again.

The slotted drawbar permits the chain to be handily readjusted as the horses work a log into position for skidding. When the log is ready to go, it is chained as closely as possible to the drawbar, so that when the horses tighten the fore end of the log is raised off the ground. This is the major efficiency of the logging arch: By thus raising the log, the arch both keeps it from digging and reduces its friction against the ground by more than half.

We watched a team drag out a twelve-foot log containing about 330 board feet. They were well loaded but were not straining. Charlie says that a team can handle up to five or six hundred board feet. For bigger logs, they use an additional team or a bulldozer. A good teamster can skid 3,000 to 3,500 board feet a day in small logs. The trick, Charlie says, is to know what your horses can do, and then see that they do that much on every pull. Overload, and you're resting too much. Underload, and you're wasting energy and time. The important thing is to keep loaded and keep moving.

Charlie Fisher is a man of long experience in the woods and extensive knowledge of the timber business and of logging technology. He has no prejudice against mechanical equipment as such, but uses it readily according to need; for a time, during his thirties, he used mechanical skidders. That this man greatly prefers horses for use in the woods is therefore of considerable interest. I asked him to explain.

His first reason, and the most important, is one I'd heard before from draft horsemen: "I've always liked horses." Charlie and David are clearly the sort of men who can't quite live without horses. Between them, they own six excellent, very large Belgian geldings and two Belgian mares. Charlie, as he explained, owns three and a half horses, and David four and a half. The two halves, fortunately, belong to the same horse, which Charlie and David own in partnership. Charlie has long been an enthusiastic participant in pulling contests, and David has followed in his father's footsteps in the arena as in the woods. Last season, David participated in twenty-three contests and Charlie in five, which for him was many fewer than usual. Charlie and his wife, Becky, showed us several shelves crowded with trophies, many of which were David's. It looked to me like they are going to need more shelves. Charlie and Becky are very proud of David, who is an accomplished logger and horseman. David, Charlie says, is an exceptionally quiet hand with a team—unlike Charlie, who confessed, "I holler." Since they would have the horses anyhow, Charlie said, they might as well put them to work in the woods, which keeps them fit and allows them to earn their keep.

Charlie's second reason for using horses in the woods, almost as important as the first, is that he likes the woods, and horses leave the woods in better condition than a skidder. A team and a logging arch require a much narrower roadway than a skidder; unlike a skidder, they don't bark trees; and they leave their skidding trails far less deeply rutted. "The horse," Charlie says, "will always be the answer to good logging in a woods."

A third attractive feature of the horse economy in the woods is that the horse logger both earns and spends his money in the local community, whereas the mechanical skidder siphons money away from the community and into the hands of large corporate suppliers. Moreover, the horse logger's kinder treatment of the woods will, in the long run, yield an economic benefit.

And, finally, horses work far more cheaply and cost far less than a skidder, thus requiring fewer trees to be cut per acre, and so permitting the horse logger to be more selective and conservative.

(Another issue involved in the use of horses for work is that of energy efficiency. Legs are more efficient than wheels over rough ground—something that will quickly be apparent to you if you try riding a bicycle over a plowed field.)

Well ahead of the logging crews, Charlie goes into the woods to mark the trees that are to be cut. Except when he is working for a "developer" who is going to clear the land, Charlie never buys or marks trees with the idea of taking every one that is marketable. His purpose is to select a number of trees, often those that need cutting because they are diseased or damaged or otherwise inferior, which will provide a reasonable income to landowner and logger alike, without destroying the wood-making capacity of the forest. The point can best be understood by considering the difference between a year's growth added to a tree fourteen inches in diameter and that added to a tree four inches in diameter. Clear-cutting or any other kind of cutting that removes all the trees of any appreciable size radically reduces the wood-making capacity of the forest. After such a cutting, in Charlie's part of the country, it will be sixty to a hundred years before another cutting can be made. Of a clear-cut woodland that adjoined one of his own tracts, Charlie said, "In fifty years there still won't be a decent log in it."

Charlie does not believe that such practices are good for the forest or the people—or, ultimately, for the timber business. He stated his interest forthrightly in economic terms, but his is the right kind of economics: "I hope maybe there'll be trees here for my son to cut in ten or twenty years." If you don't overdo the cutting, he says, a woodland can yield a cash crop every ten to fifteen years. We looked at one tract of twenty acres on which Charlie had marked about 160 trees and written the owner a check for $23,000. Charlie described this as "a young piece of timber," and he said that it "definitely" could be logged again in ten years—at which time he could both take more and leave more good trees than he will take and leave at this cutting.

Owners of wooded land should consider carefully the economics of this twenty-acre tract. If it is selectively and carefully logged every ten years, as Charlie says it can be, then every acre will earn $1,150 every ten years, or $115 per year. And this comes to the landowner without expense or effort. (These particular figures, of course, apply only to this particular woodlot. Some tracts might be more productive, others less.)

We looked at marked woodlands, at woodlands presently being logged, and finally, at the end of the second day of our visit, at a woodland that one of Charlie's crews had logged three years ago. The last, a stand predominantly of hard and soft maples, provided convincing evidence of the good sense of Charlie's kind of forestry. Very few of the remaining trees had been damaged by trees felled during the logging. I saw not a single tree that had been barked by a skidded log. The skid trails had completely healed over; there was no sign of erosion. And, most striking, the woodland was still ecologically intact. It was still a diverse, uneven-aged stand of trees, many of which were over sixteen inches in diameter. We made a photograph of three trees, standing fairly close together, which varied in diameter from seventeen to twenty-one inches. After logging, the forest is still a forest, and it will go on making wood virtually without interruption or diminishment. It seems perfectly reasonable to think that, if several generations of owners were so inclined, this sort of forestry could eventually result in an "old growth" forest that would have produced a steady income for two hundred years.

I was impressed by a good many things during my visit with Charlie Fisher, but what impressed me most is the way that Charlie's kind of logging achieves a complex fairness or justice to the several interests that are involved: the woods, the landowner, the timber company, the woods crews and their horses.

Charlie buys standing trees, and he marks every tree he buys. Within a fairly narrow margin of error, Charlie knows what he is buying, and the landowner knows what he is getting paid for. When Charlie goes in to mark the trees, he is thinking not just about what he will take, but also about what he will leave. He sees the forest as it is, and he sees the forest as it will be when the logging job is finished. I think he sees it too as it will be in ten or fifteen or twenty years, when David or another logger will return to it. By this long-term care, he serves the forest and the landowner as well as himself. As he marks the trees he is thinking also of the logging crew that will soon be there. He marks each tree that is to be cut with a slash of red paint. Sometimes, where he has seen a leaning deadfall or a dead limb or a flaw in the trunk, he paints an arrow above the slash, and this means "Look up!" The horses, like the men, are carefully borne in mind. Everywhere, the aim is to do the work in the best and the safest way.

Moreover, these are not competing interests, but seem rather to merge into one another. Thus one of Charlie's economic standards—"I hope maybe there'll be trees here for my son to cut in ten or twenty years"—becomes, in application, an ecological standard. And the ecological standard becomes, again, an economic standard as it proves to be good for business.

Most landowners, Charlie says, care how their woodlands are logged. Though they may need the income from their trees, they don't want to sacrifice the health or beauty of their woods in order to get it. Charlie's way of logging recommends itself to such people; he does not need to advertise. As we were driving away from his house on the morning of our second day, one of the neighbors waved us to a stop. This man makes his living selling firewood, and he had learned of two people who wanted their woodlands logged by a horse logger. That is the way business comes to him, Charlie said. Like other horse loggers, he has all the work he can do, and more. It has been ten years since he has had to hunt for woodlots to log. He said, "Everybody else has buyers out running the roads, looking for timber." But he can't buy all that he is offered.

I don't know that I have ever met a man with more enthusiasms than Charlie Fisher. I have mentioned already his abounding interest in his family, in forestry, and in working and pulling horses, but I have neglected to say that he is also a coon hunter. This seems to me a most revealing detail. Here is a man who makes his living by walking the woods all day, and who then entertains himself by walking the woods at night.

He told me that he had a list of several things he had planned to do when he retired, but that now, at sixty-six, he is busier than ever.

"Well," I said, "you seem to be enjoying it."

"Oh," he said, "I *love* it!"

A Talent for Necessity

(1980)

꒳

I N THE DAYS when the Southdown ram was king of the sheep pastures and the show ring, Henry Besuden of Vinewood Farm in Clark
County, Kentucky, was perhaps the premier breeder and showman of
Southdown sheep in the United States. The list of his winnings at major
shows would be too long to put down here, but the character of his
achievement can be indicated by his success in showing carload lots of
fat lambs in the Chicago International Livestock Exposition. Starting in
1946, he sent eighteen carloads to the International, and won the competition twelve times. "I had 'em fat," he says, remembering. "I had 'em
good." Such was the esteem and demand for his stock among fellow
breeders that in 1954 he sold a yearling ram for $1,200, then a record
price for a Southdown.

One would imagine that such accomplishments must have rested
on the very best of Bluegrass farmland. But the truth, nearly opposite
to that, is much more interesting. "If I'd inherited good land," Henry
Besuden says, "I'd probably have been just another Bluegrass farmer."

What he inherited, in fact, was 632 acres of rolling land, fairly steep
in places, thin soiled even originally, and by the time he got it, worn-out,

"corned to death." His grandfather would rent the land out to corn, two hundred acres at a time, and not even get up to see where it would be planted—even though "it was understood to be the rule that renters ruined the land." By the time Henry Besuden was eight years old both his mother and father were dead, and the land was farmed by tenants under the trusteeship of a Cincinnati bank. When the farm came to him in 1927, it was heavily encumbered by debt and covered with gullies, some of which were deep enough to hide a standing man.

And so Mr. Besuden began his life as a farmer with the odds against him. But his predicament became his education and, finally, his triumph. "I was lucky," he told Grant Cannon of *The Farm Quarterly* in 1951. "I found that I had some talent for doing the things I *had* to do. I *had* to improve the farm or starve to death; and I *had* to go into the sheep business because sheep were the only animals that could have lived off the farm."

Now seventy-six years old and not in the best of health, Mr. Besuden has not owned a sheep for several years, but he speaks of them with exact remembrance and exacting intelligence; he is one of the best talkers I have had the luck to listen to. How did he get started with sheep? "I was told they'd eat weeds and briars," he says, looking sideways through pipesmoke to see if I get the connection, for the connection between sheep and land is the critical one for him. The history of his sheep and the history of his farm are one history, and it is his own.

Having only talent and necessity—and unusual energy and determination—Mr. Besuden set about the restoration of his ravaged fields. There was no Soil Conservation Service then, but a young man in his predicament was bound to get plenty of advice. To check erosion he first tried building rock dams across the gullies. That wasn't satisfactory; the dams did catch some dirt, but then the fields were marred by half-buried rock walls that interfered with work. He tried huge windrows of weeds and brush to the same purpose, but that was not satisfactory either.

Some of the worst gullies he eventually had to fill with a bulldozer. But his main erosion-stopping tool turned out, strangely enough, to be the plow, the tool that in the wrong hands had nearly ruined the farm, in the right hands healed it. Starting at the edge of a gulley he would run a backfurrow up one side and down the other, continuing to plow until he had completed a sizable land. And then he would start at the gulley again, turning the furrows inward as before. He repeated this process until what had been a ditch had become a saucer, so that the runoff, rather than concentrating its force in an abrasive torrent, would be shallowly dispersed over as wide an area as possible. This, as he knew, had been the method of the renters to prepare the gullied land for yet another crop of corn. For them, it had been a temporary remedy; he made it a permanent one.

Nowadays Kentucky fescue 31 would be the grass to sow on such places, but fescue was not available then. Mr. Besuden used small grains, timothy, sweet clover, Korean lespedeza. He used mulches, and he did not overlook the usefulness of what he knew for certain would grow on his land—weeds: "Briars are a good thing for a little hollow." In places he planted thickets of black locust—a native leguminous tree that would serve four purposes: hold the land, encourage grass to grow, provide shade for livestock, and produce posts. But his highest praise is given to the sweet clover which he calls "the best land builder I've ever run into. It'll open up clay, and throw a lot of nitrogen into the ground." The grass would come then, and the real healing would start.

Once the land was in grass, his policy generally was to leave it in grass. Only the best-laying, least vulnerable land was broken for tobacco, the region's major money crop then as now. Even today, I noticed, he sees that his fields are plowed very conservatively. The plowlands are small and carefully placed, leaving out thin places and waterways.

The basic work of restoration continued for twenty-three years. By 1950 the scars were grassed over, and the land was supporting one of the great Southdown flocks of the time. But it was not healed. What was there is gone, and Henry Besuden knows that it will be a long time building back. "'Tain't in good shape, yet," he told an interviewer in 1978.

And so if Mr. Besuden built a reputation as one of the best of livestock showmen, the focus of his interest was nevertheless not the show ring but the farm. It would be true, it seems, to say that he became a master sheepman and shepherd as one of the ways of becoming a master farmer. For this reason, his standards of quality were never frivolous or freakish, as show-ring standards have sometimes been accused of being, but insistently practical. He never forgot that the purpose of a sheep is to produce a living for the farmer and to put good meat on the table: "When they asked me, 'What do you consider a perfect lamb?' I said, 'One a farmer can make money on!' The foundation has to be the commercial flock." And he wrote in praise of the Southdown ram that "he paid his rent."

But it was perhaps even more characteristic of him to write in 1945 that "one very important thing is that sheep are land builders," and to plead for their continued inclusion in farm livestock programs. He had seen the handwriting on the wall: the new emphasis on row cropping and "production" which in the years after World War II would radically alter the balance of crops and animals on farms, and which, as he feared, would help to destroy the sheep business in his own state. (In 1947, Mr. Besuden's county of Clark had twenty-four breeding flocks of Southdowns, and 30,000 head of grade ewes. That is more than remain now in the whole state of Kentucky.) What he called for instead—and events are rapidly proving him right—was "a long-time program of land building" by which he meant a way of farming based on grass and forage crops, which would build up and maintain reserves of fertility. And in that kind of farming, he was prepared to insist, because he knew, sheep would have an important place.

"I think," he wrote in his series of columns, "Sheep Sense," published in *The Sheepman* in 1945 and 1946, "the fertilizing effect of sheep on the farm has never received the attention it deserves. As one who has had to farm poor land where the least amount of fertilizer shows up plainly, I have noticed that on land often thought too poor for cattle the sheep do well and in time benefit the crops and grass to such an extent that other stock can then be carried. I have seldom seen sheep bed down for the night on anything but high land, and their droppings are evenly scattered on the pasture while grazing, so that no vegetation is killed."

What he wanted was "a way of farming compatible with nature"; this was the constant theme of his work, and he followed it faithfully, both in his pleasure in the lives and events of nature and in his practical solutions to the problems of farming and soil husbandry. He was never too busy to appreciate, and to praise, the spiritual by-products, as he called them, of farm life. Nor was he too busy to attend to the smallest needs of his land. At one time, for example, he built "two small houses on skids," each of which would hold twenty-five bales of hay. These could be pulled to places where the soil was thin, where the hay would be fed out, and then moved on to other such places. (In the spring they could be used to raise chickens.)

"It's good to have Nature working for you," he says. "She works for a minimum wage." But in reading his "Sheep Sense" columns, one realizes that he not only did not separate the spiritual from the practical, but insisted that they cannot be separated: "This thing of soil conservation involves more than laying out a few terraces and diversion ditches and sowing to grass and legumes, it also involves the heart of the man managing the land. If he loves his soil he will save it." Once, he says, he thought of numbering his fields, but decided against it—"That didn't seem fair to them"—for each has its own character and potential.

As a rule, he would have 400 head of ewes in two flocks—a flock of registered Southdowns and a flock of "Western" commercial ewes. After lambing, he would be running something in the neighborhood of 1,000 head. To handle so many sheep on a diversified farm required a great deal of care, and Mr. Besuden's system of management, worked out with thorough understanding and attention to detail, is worth the interest and reflection of any raiser of livestock.

It was a system intended, first of all, to get the maximum use of forage. This rested on what he understands to be a sound principle of livestock farming and soil conservation, but it was forced upon him by the poor quality of his land. He had to keep row cropping to a minimum, and if that meant buying grain, then he would buy it. But he did not buy much. He usually fed, he told me, one pound of corn per ewe per day for sixty days. But in "Sheep Sense" for December 1945, he wrote: "One-half pound grain with three pounds legume hay should do the job, starting with the hay and adding the grain later." He creep-fed his early lambs, but took them off grain as soon as pasture was available. In "Sheep Sense," March 1946, he stated flatly that "creep-feeding after good grass arrives does not pay."

Grain, then, he considered not a diet, but a supplement, almost an emergency ration, to ensure health and growth in the flock during the time when he had no pasture. It must be remembered that he was talking about a kind of sheep bred to make efficient use of pasture and hay, and that the market then favored that kind. In the decades following World War II, cheap energy and cheap grain allowed interest to shift to the larger breeds of sheep and larger slaughter lambs that must be grain-fed. But now with the cost of energy rising, pushing up the cost of grain, and the human consumption of grain rising with the increase of population, Henry Besuden's sentence of a generation ago resounds with good sense: "Due to the shortage of grain throughout the world, the sheep farmer needs to study the possibilities of grass fattening."

Those, anyhow, were the possibilities that *he* was studying. And the management of pasture, the management of sheep *on* pasture, was his art.

In the fall he would select certain pastures close to the barn to be used for late grazing. This is what is now called "stockpiling"—which, he points out, is only a new word for old common sense. It was sometimes possible, in favorable years, to keep the ewes on grass all through December, feeding "very little hay" and "a small amount of grain." Sometimes he sowed rye early to provide late fall pasture and so extend the grazing season.

His ewes were bred to lamb in January and February. He fed good clover or alfalfa hay, and from about the middle of January to about the middle of March he gave the ewes their sixty daily rations of grain. In mid-March the grain-feeding ended, and ewes and lambs went out on early pasture of rye which had been sown as a cover crop on the last year's tobacco patches. "A sack of Balboa rye sown in the early fall," he wrote, "is worth several sacks of feed fed in the spring and is much cheaper." From the rye they went to the clover fields where tobacco had grown two years before. From the clover they were moved onto the grass pastures. The market lambs were sold straight off the pastures, at eighty to eighty-five pounds, starting the first of May.

After fescue became available, Mr. Besuden made extensive use of it in his pastures. But he feels that this grass, though an excellent land conserver, is not nutritious or palatable enough to make the best sheep pasture, and so he took pains to diversify his fescue stands with timothy and legumes. His favorite pasture legume is Korean lespedeza, though he joins in the fairly common complaint that it is less vigorous and productive now than it used to be. He has also used red clover, alsike, ladino, and birdsfoot trefoil. He says that he had trouble getting his ewes with lamb in the first heat when they were bred on clover pastures, but that he never had this trouble on lespedeza.

His pastures were regularly reseeded to legumes, usually in March, the sheep tramping in the seed, and he found this method of "renovation" to be as good as any. The pastures were clipped twice during the growing season, sometimes oftener, to keep the growth vigorous and uniform.

The key to efficient management of sheep on pasture is paying attention, and it was important to Mr. Besuden that he should be on horseback among his sheep in the early mornings. The sheep would be out of the shade then, grazing, and he could study their condition and the condition of the field. He speaks of the "bloom" of a pasture, referring to a certain freshness of appearance made by new, tender growth sprigging up through the old. When that bloom is gone, he thinks, the sheep should be moved. The move from a stale pasture to a fresh one can lengthen the grazing time by as much as two hours a day. He believes also that lambs do best when the flock is not too large. That is because sheep tend to bunch together when grazing, the least vigorous lambs coming last and having to feed on grass mouthed over and rejected by the others. He saw to it that his pastures were amply provided with shade, and he knew that the shade needed to be well placed: "I think the best lamb-growing pastures I have are the ones where the shade is close to the water. I have seen times during July and August when sheep would not leave the shade and go to water if the shade and water happened to be at opposite ends of a large field."

The crisis of the shepherd's year, of course, is lambing time. That is the time that the year's work stands or falls by. And because it usually takes place in cold weather, the success of lambing is almost as dependent on the shepherd's facilities as on his knowledge. The lambing barn at Vinewood is an instructive embodiment of Mr. Besuden's understanding of his work and his gift for order. He gives a good description of it himself in one of his columns:

> Practically all the lambing here at Vinewood in recent years has been in a barn especially made for the purpose, shiplap (tongue groove) boxing with a low loft and a window in each bent. The east end of the barn

[away from the prevailing winds] is rarely ever closed, a gate being used.
Often in extremely cold weather the temperature can be raised fifteen or
twenty degrees by the heat from the sheep. Some thirty feet out in the
front and extending the width of the barn [is] a heavy layer of rock. . . .
This prevents the muddy place that often appears at the barn door and . . .
pulls at the sheep as they walk through it, causing slipped lambs. Also at
the entrance . . . a locust post is half embedded across the door. This serves
as a protection in case of dogs trying to dig under the door or gate and
helps to hold the bedding in the barn as the sheep go out. Any kind of a
sill that is too high or causes the heavy-in-lamb ewes to jump or strain
to cross is too risky.

The barn is admirably laid out, with pens, chutes, and gates to permit the feeding, handling, sorting, and loading of a large number of sheep
with the least trouble. There were lambing pens for forty ewes. There
was also a small room with pens that could be heated by a stove. Above
each pen was a red wooden "button" that could be turned down to indicate that a ewe was near to lambing or for any other reason in need of
close attention. These were used when Mr. Besuden had an experienced
helper to share the nighttime duty with him. "They saved a lot of cold
midnight talk," he says.

But experienced help was not always available, and then he would
have to work through the days and nights of lambing alone. Staying awake
would get to be a problem. Sometimes, sitting beside one of the pens,
waiting for a ewe to lamb, he would tie a string from one of her hind legs
to his wrist. When her labor pains came and she began to shift around,
she would tug the string and he would wake up and tend to her.

And so the talent for what he "had to do" was in large measure the
ability to bear the good outcome in mind: to envision, in spite of rocks
and gullies, the good health of the fields; to foresee in the pregnant ewes
and the advancing seasons a good crop of lambs. And it was the ability to
carry in his head for nearly half a century the ideal character and pattern

147

of the Southdown, and to measure his animals relentlessly against it—an ability, rare enough, that marked him as a master stockman.

He told me a story that suggests very well the distinction and the effect of that ability. On one of his trips to the International he competed against a western sheepman who had selected his carload of fifty fat lambs out of ten thousand head.

After the Vinewood carload had won the class, this gentleman came up and asked: "How many did you pick yours from, Mr. Besuden?"

"About seventy-five."

"Well," the western breeder said, "I guess it's better to have the right seventy-five than the wrong ten thousand."

But the ability to recognize the right seventy-five is worthless by itself. Just as necessary is the ability to do the work and to pay attention. To pay attention, above all—that is another of the persistent themes of Mr. Besuden's talk and of his life. He is convinced that paying attention pays, and this sets him apart from the mechanized "modern" farmers who are pushed to accept more responsibility than they can properly meet, and to work at freeway speeds. He wrote in his column of the importance of "little things done on time." He said that they paid, but he knew that people did them for more than pay.

He told me also about a farmer who couldn't scrape the manure off his shoes until he came to a spot that was bare of grass. "That's what I mean," he said. "You have to keep it on your mind."

Elmer Lapp's Place

(1979)

༄

T HE THIRTY COWS come up from the pasture and go one by one
into the barn. Most of them are Guernseys, but there are also a few
red Holsteins and a couple of Jerseys. They go to their places and wait
while their neck chains are fastened. And then Elmer Lapp, his oldest
son, and his youngest daughter go about the work of feeding, washing,
and milking.

In the low, square room, lighted by a row of big windows, a radio
is quietly playing music. Several white cats sit around waiting for milk
to be poured out for them from the test cup. Two collie dogs rest by the
wall, out of the way. Several buff Cochin bantams are busily foraging for
whatever waste grain can be found in the bedding and in the gutters.
Overhead, fastened to the ceiling joists, are many barn swallow nests,
their mud cups empty now at the end of October. Two rusty-barreled
.22 rifles are propped in window frames, kept handy to shoot English
sparrows, and there are no sparrows to be seen. Outside the door a
bred heifer and a rather timeworn pet jenny are eating their suppers
out of feed boxes. Beyond, on the stream that runs through the pasture,

wild ducks are swimming. The shadows have grown long under the low-slanting amber light.

This is a farm of eighty-three acres that has been in the Lapp family since 1915, five years before Elmer Lapp was born, and he has been here all his life. Three years ago a new house was built for Mr. Lapp's oldest son, who is his farming partner, father and son doing all the carpentry themselves. Except for the four or five days a month that the son works off the farm, the two households take their living from this place, plus fourteen acres of rented pasture and forty acres of hay harvested on the shares on a farm some distance away. They are farming then, all told, 117 acres.

Because this farm is in Lancaster County, Pennsylvania, in an enclave of Amish and Mennonite farms that has become a "tourist attraction," the Lapps are able to supplement their agricultural income by selling farm tours, chicken barbecue, and homemade ice cream to busloads of schoolchildren and tourists. But as profitable a sideline as this undoubt-edly is, it should not distract from the economic and ecological good health of the farm operation itself. At a time when so many small farms are struggling or failing, it may be easy to suspect that this farm survives by dependence on the tourist industry. I do not think so. Here, at least, the opposite would seem to be true: The sideline succeeds because the main enterprise is a success.

Standing in the stanchion barn while the cows are being milked, I am impressed by how quietly the work is done. No voice is raised. There is never a sudden or violent motion. Although the work is quickly done, no one rushes. And finally comes the realization that the room is quiet because it is orderly: All the creatures there, people and animals alike, are at rest within a pattern deeply familiar to them all. That evening and the day following, as I extend my acquaintance with the farm and with Elmer Lapp's understanding of it, I see that quiet chore time as a nucleus or gathering point in a pattern that includes the whole farm. The farm is thriving because what I would call its structural problems have been sat-isfactorily solved. The patterns necessary to its life have been perceived and worked out.

THE COMMERCIAL PATTERN

IN ITS COMMERCIAL aspect, this is a livestock farm. Its crops are not grown to sell, but to feed animals. The main enterprises are the thirty-cow dairy, and eleven Belgian brood mares.

Mr. Lapp's dairy herd is made up mainly of Guernseys because, he says, "Big cows eat too much." And the richer milk of the Guernseys brings a premium price. His few Holsteins are red ones, because their milk is richer than that of the blacks. Their milk "tests with the Guernseys'," Mr. Lapp says.

He now sells manufacturing milk to the people who make Hershey chocolate. He used to ship Grade A, but quit, he says, because "The Grade A guys got under my hide. You could never satisfy them. They always wanted something else." At several points in our conversation Mr. Lapp showed this sort of independence. He is not a man to put up long with anything he does not like. And this, again, I take as an indication of his success as a farmer. He is independent because he can afford to be.

At present, in addition to the thirty milking cows, he has twelve heifers, six of which he has just started on the bucket. He likes to have a couple of heifers coming fresh each year. He sells his bull calves as babies. His heifer calves are started on milk replacer, which he considers better for the purpose than milk. They are given two quarts at a feeding.

When I ask Mr. Lapp what a farmer could expect to make from a farm of this size, managed as this one is, he replies by saying that he sells $20,000 to $30,000 worth of milk each year. Last year his dairy grossed $25,000.

I ask him how much of that was net.

He can't tell me exactly, he says. He bought $5,000 worth of supplements, but that included extra feed for his chickens, horses, and calves. And, of course, some of the expense was offset by the sale of bull calves and heifers. Aside from this information, he describes his income by saying "I pay taxes."

Mr. Lapp offers no information about his income from his horses. But the market for draft horses is booming, and one must suppose that the Lapp farm is sharing in the payoff. Last year Mr. Lapp sold nine head. This past season he has bred eleven mares. He also has an income from his stallion who serves, he says, "all the outside mares I can handle." Besides the brood mares and the stallion, he presently has on hand a two-year-old filly, two yearling fillies, two yearling stud colts, and two foals.

He prefers the draftier type of Belgians, but wants them long-legged enough to walk fast, and because he works his horses he is attentive to the need for good feet. Along with those practical virtues, he likes his horses to show a good deal of refinement, and in selecting breeding stock pays particular attention to heads and necks. Among his mares are several that are half or full sisters, and this gives his horses a very noticeable uniformity of both color and conformation.

Because for some reason his land will not produce oats of satisfactory quality, Mr. Lapp grows barley for his horses. If barley was good enough horse feed for King Solomon, he says, it is good enough for him. He crimps or grinds the barley and adds molasses.

Unlike many horsemen, Mr. Lapp has no elaborate lore or procedure for breeding mares. He serves a mare only once, on whatever day he notices that she is in heat. And he sees no sense in pregnancy tests or examinations. Even so, he says, he has no trouble getting mares to conceive—or cows either, except with artificial insemination.

But just because his major income is from dairy cows and brood mares, Mr. Lapp does not shut his eyes to other opportunities. "You stay awake," he says. He knows what will sell, and so far as his place and time allow he has it for sale. He feeds three hundred guineas at a time in a small loft. He raises and sells collie pups. He sells his surplus of eggs and honey. Even the barn cats contribute their share of income, for when he gets too many he sells the surplus at the local sale barn.

THE PATTERN OF SUBSISTENCE

T HOUGH THE LAPP farm is commercially profitable its balance sheet would fall far short of accounting for the life of the place, or even for its economy.

Elmer Lapp is eminently a traditional farmer in the sense that his farm is his home, his life, and his way of life—not just his "work place" or his "job." For that reason, though his farm produces a cash income, that is not all it produces, and some of what it produces cannot be valued in cash.

In obedience to traditional principle, the Lapps take their subsistence from the farm, and they are as attentive to the production of what they eat as to the production of what they sell. The farm is expected to make a profit, but it must make sense too, and a part of that sense is that it must feed the farmers. And so a pattern of subsistence joins, and at certain points overlaps, the commercial pattern.

For instance, the Lapps drink their own milk. I know that a lot of dairying families buy their milk at the grocery store, and so I ask Mr. Lapp why he doesn't buy milk for his own household.

He answers unhesitatingly: "I don't like that slop."

He also grows a garden. He has an orchard of apple, peach, and plum trees for fruit, and for blossoms for his bees. He is feeding four hogs, bought cheaply because they were runts, to slaughter for home use. He slaughters his own beef, and produces his own poultry, eggs, and honey.

He is also aware that the pattern of subsistence is a community pattern. He says, for instance, that he deals with the little country stores rather than the supermarkets in the city. The little country stores support the life of the community, whereas the supermarkets support "the economy" at the expense of communities.

THE PATTERNS OF SOIL HUSBANDRY

U NDERLYING THE PATTERNS of the farm's productivity is a stewardship of the soil at all points knowledgeable, disciplined, and responsible. And this stewardship, necessarily, has evolved its own appropriate patterns.

In any year, Mr. Lapp will have twenty-two acres in corn (twelve for silage, ten to husk), twenty-five acres in clover or alfalfa, ten acres in barley or rye, and the rest in permanent pasture. The rotation is, mainly, as follows:

First year: Corn for husking.

Second year: Silage corn.

Third year: Barley, planted in preceding fall, with clover and timothy sowed broadcast onto frozen ground in spring. After the barley is harvested, the field produces one cutting of hay.

Fourth year: Clover and timothy (two cuttings).

Fifth year: Back to corn.

This pattern is varied in two ways. Where alfalfa is sowed instead of clover, the field is left in sod for three or four years instead of two. And when rye is sowed instead of barley, the rye is flail-chopped in the bloom and baled for bedding, and the land is returned to silage corn the same year.

The whole farm is covered with manure each year, at a rate, Mr. Lapp figures, of about eight tons per acre. And care is taken to get the manure on at the right time. I ask if this use of manure did not reduce the need for commercial fertilizer. "I don't buy any fertilizer," Mr. Lapp says. (He does use an herbicide on his cornfields, but only because the time when corn needs cultivation is also the time when he is busiest with tours.)

The present system of rotation and fertilization has been in use on this farm, Mr. Lapp says, "as long as I remember." But he himself, with the county agent's help, laid the farm off in three-acre strips to help control runoff and erosion. Yet even though soil conservation can to a considerable extent be formalized in set patterns of layout and rotation, there is still a need for vigilance and intelligent improvisation. This fall, for instance, the barley is coming on too late to provide good winter protection. As a remedy, Mr. Lapp says, he will cover the barley fields with strawy manure on the first morning the ground is frozen. That will protect the fields through the winter without smothering the barley.

One of the best ways to measure the quality of soil husbandry and the richness of soil on a farm is to look at its first-year hayfields. How quickly will clover and grass make a sod after the land has been row cropped? How healthy and productive is it? The height, density, color, and uniformity of the plants all have a tale to tell. Mr. Lapp leads the way up past his garden to a four-acre hayfield that is good in all respects. It was sowed in the spring to red clover, timothy, and a little alsike for the bees. The barley was taken off in July. And then in early October the field was mowed for hay, yielding 400 bales. Next year, it may reasonably be expected to yield 800–1,000 bales on the first cutting, and 500–600 on the second.

Two Kinds of Horsepower

WHEN ELMER LAPP was still just a boy, his father, recognizing a gift in him, gave him the colts to work.

"Made you a little proud?" I say.

He grins and nods. "I guess it did a little bit."

Because he is a capable horseman and likes horses, he has never quit using them—although he has certain uses for a tractor as well. "I'd rather drive horses than a tractor," he says. "I have them here, they're eating, so

I might as well use them. I'm doing my work while I'm having pleasure. If I didn't enjoy it I wouldn't do it."

He uses a tractor for what a tractor does best, and horses for what they do best, keeping in mind always the scale of his operation. "On a small farm," he says, "you don't need expensive equipment." And he seems immune to the horsepower intoxication that leads so many small farmers to buy larger tractors then they need. He paid $2,000 for a John Deere 60 twenty years ago, and is still using it. It will pull a three-bottom plow. When he needs a tractor for an occasional heavier job, such as silo filling, he hires a larger one. He does all his plowing and hay baling with his tractor, and uses it to load manure. He uses his horses to spread manure, plant corn, clip pasture, rake and haul hay. If he is "not pushed too hard," he uses them also in seedbed preparation. He is sure that he gets this work done cheaper with horses than with a tractor—even setting aside the value of their colts.

He says that rubber-tired equipment is far easier on horses than the steel-tired, because the tires absorb much of the shock when working over rough ground. And he dislikes wide hitches largely because they too are hard on horses. On an eight-foot tandem disk he will hitch two in front and three behind—or, if the footing is solid and the going relatively easy, he will work as many as four abreast. He says that he sees far too much mistreatment of horses through ignorance and indifference—something he resents and tries, so far as he can, to correct.

The use of the horses, whose feed is grown on the farm, greatly extends Mr. Lapp's dependence on solar energy, and greatly reduces his dependence on increasingly expensive fossil fuel energy. The tractor is used to supplement the energy already available on the farm.

In addition to the two varieties of horsepower, the farm makes a small use of waterpower. The stream is dammed and the impounded water used to turn a small water wheel which, in turn, works a water pump.

It is another manifestation of this farm's thriftiness. Mr. Lapp looks at the escaping water with some regret: "That's all going to waste."

A WELL-PLANNED BARN

THE LAPPS ARE just completing a small barn that is a good example of the care and the sense of order that have gone into the making of their farm.

This is a "bank barn" with a drive-in loft, approximately thirty by forty-eight feet. The lower story is a feeding area that will accommodate five hundred guineas in the summer and twelve heifers and perhaps as many young horses in the winter. It is divided across the middle by a feed bunk which extends out into a lot.

The upper story will have a corn crib across each end, eight feet wide by fourteen deep. The area in the center will be for storage of hay and equipment. The cribs are to be ventilated by lattices along the lower part of the outside walls. Outside, these lattices will be sheltered by awnings, four feet wide on one end, but on the other end ten feet wide to provide yet more shelter for equipment.

All possibilities of site, shape, and use have been considered.

THE ECOLOGICAL PATTERN

CONCERNED AS HE is that the usable be put to use, that there be no waste, still there is nothing utilitarian or mechanistic about Mr. Lapp's farm—or his mind. His aim, it seems, is not that the place should be put to the fullest use, but that it should have the most abundant life. The best farmers, Sir Albert Howard said, imitate nature, not least in the love of variety. Elmer Lapp answers to that definition as fully as any farmer I have encountered. Like nature herself, he and his family seem preoccupied with the filling of niches.

Driving into the place, one is aware before anything else that wherever flowers can be grown flowers are growing; beds and borders are everywhere. The barn swallow nests in the milking barn are not there just by happenstance; little wooden steps have been nailed to the joists to encourage them to nest there. Elmer Lapp has defended them against milk inspectors—"If those barn swallows go, I'm going somewhere else with my milk"—and against the cats, which he pens up during the nesting season, "if they get nasty."

Among the wild creatures, he seems especially partial to birds. Wild waterfowl make themselves peacefully at home along his pasture stream, and he speaks of his failure to attract martins with obvious grief. One can justify the existence of birds by "insect control," but one can also like them. Elmer Lapp likes them. His one acknowledged regret about his place is that it doesn't have a woodlot. He could use the firewood; he would also like the wild creatures it would attract. Above his row of beehives is a border of sudan grass that he has let go to seed for the birds.

He likes too the buff Cochin bantams that live in the milking barn and the stable—they scatter the manure piles and so keep flies from hatching—and the goldfish who live in the drinking trough and keep the water clean. Walking around the place, I keep being surprised by some other creature that has found room and board there, and is contributing a little something—maybe only pleasure—in return: peafowl, wild turkeys, pigeons, a pair of bobwhites.

For a man giftedly practical, Mr. Lapp justifies what he has and does remarkably often by his *likes*. One finally realizes that on the Lapp farm one is surrounded by an abounding variety of lives that are there, and are thriving there, because Elmer Lapp *likes* them. And from that it is only a step to the realization that the commercial enterprises of the farm are likewise there, and thriving, because he likes them too. The Belgians and the Guernseys are profitable, in large part, because they were liked *before* they were profitable. Mr. Lapp is as fine a farmer as he is because liking has joined his intelligence intricately to his place.

And that is why the place makes sense. All the patterns of the farm are finally gathered into an ecological pattern; it is one "household," its various parts joined to each other and the whole joined to nature, to the world, by liking, by delighted and affectionate understanding. The ecological pattern is a pattern of pleasure.

ON *The Soil and Health*

(2006)

꜅

I N 1964 MY wife Tanya and I bought a rough and neglected little farm on which we intended to grow as much of our own food as we could. My editor at the time was Dan Wickenden who was an organic gardener and whose father, Leonard Wickenden, had written a practical and inspiring book, *Gardening with Nature*, which I bought and read. Tanya and I wanted to raise our own food because we liked the idea of being independent to that extent, and because we did not like the toxicity, expensiveness, and wastefulness of "modern" food production. *Gardening with Nature* was written for people like us, and it helped us to see that what we wanted to do was possible. I asked Dan where his father's ideas had come from, and he gave me the name of Sir Albert Howard. My reading of Howard, which began at that time, has never stopped, for I have returned again and again to his work and his thought. I have been aware of his influence in virtually everything I have done, and I don't expect to graduate from it. That is because his way of dealing with the subject of agriculture is also a way of dealing with the subject of life in this world. His thought is systematic, coherent, and inexhaustible.

161

Sir Albert Howard published several books and also many articles in journals of agricultural science. The two of his books that are best known were addressed both to general readers and to his fellow scientists: *An Agricultural Testament* and *The Soil and Health*. He was born in 1873 to a farming family in Shropshire, and he died in 1947.

An Agricultural Testament and *The Soil and Health* are products of Howard's many years as a government scientist in India, during which he conceived, and set upon a sound scientific footing, the kind of agriculture to which his followers have applied the term "organic." But by 1940, when the first of these books was published, the industrialization of agriculture had already begun. By 1947, when *The Soil and Health* was published, World War II had proved the effectiveness of the mechanical and chemical technology that in the coming decades would radically alter both the practice of agriculture and its underlying assumptions.

This "revolution" marginalized Howard's work and the kind of agriculture he advocated. So-called organic agriculture survived only on the margin. It was practiced by some farmers of admirable independence and good sense and also by some authentic nuts. In the hands of the better practitioners, it was proven to be a healthful, productive, and economical way of farming. But while millions of their clients spent themselves into bankruptcy on industrial supplies, the evangelists of industrial agriculture in government and the universities ignored the example of the successful organic farmers, just as they ignored the equally successful example of Amish farming.

Meanwhile, Howard's thought, as manifested by the "organic movement," was seriously oversimplified. As it was understood and prescribed, organic agriculture improved the health of crops by building humus in the soil, and it abstained from the use of toxic chemicals. There is nothing objectionable about this kind of agriculture, so far as it goes, but it does not go far enough. It does not conceive of farms in terms of their biological and economic structure, because it does not connect farming

162

with its ecological and social contexts. Under the current and now of-
ficial definition of organic farming, it is possible to have a huge "organic"
farm that grows only one or two crops, has no animals or pastures, is
entirely dependent on industrial technology and economics, and imports
all its fertility and energy. It was precisely this sort of specialization and
oversimplification that Sir Albert Howard worked and wrote against all
his life.

At present this movement (if we can still apply that term to an effort that is many-branched, multicentered, and always in flux) in at least
some of its manifestations appears to be working decisively against such
oversimplification and the industrial gigantism that oversimplification allows. Some food companies as well as some consumers now understand
that only the smaller family farms, such as those of the Amish, permit the
diversity and the careful attention that Howard's standards require.

HOWARD'S FUNDAMENTAL ASSUMPTION was that the processes of agriculture, if they are to endure, have to be analogous to the processes of nature. If one is farming in a place previously forested, then the farm must
be a systematic analogue of the forest, and the farmer must be a student
of the forest. Howard stated his premise as a little allegory:

> The main characteristic of Nature's farming can ... be summed up in a
> few words. Mother earth never attempts to farm without live stock; she
> always raises mixed crops; great pains are taken to preserve the soil and
> to prevent erosion; the mixed vegetable and animal wastes are converted
> into humus; there is no waste; the processes of growth and the processes
> of decay balance one another; ample provision is made to maintain large
> reserves of fertility; the greatest care is taken to store the rainfall; both
> plants and animals are left to protect themselves against disease.[1]

Nature is the ultimate value of the practical or economic world. We
cannot escape either it or our dependence on it. It is, so to speak, its
own context, whereas the context of agriculture is, first, nature and then

the human economy. Harmony between agriculture and its natural and human contexts would be health, and health was the invariable standard of Howard's work. His aim always was to treat "the whole problem of health in soil, plant, animal, and man as one great subject."[2] And Louise Howard spells this out in *Sir Albert Howard in India*:

> *A fertile soil, that is, a soil teeming with healthy life in the shape of abundant microflora and microfauna, will bear healthy plants, and these, when consumed by animals and man, will confer health on animals and man. But an infertile soil, that is, one lacking sufficient microbial, fungous, and other life, will pass on some form of deficiency to the plant, and such plant, in turn, will pass on some form of deficiency to animal and man.[3]*

This was Howard's "master idea" and he understood that it implied a long-term research agenda, calling for "a boldly revised point of view and entirely fresh investigations."[4]

His premise, then, was that the human economy, which is inescapably a land-using economy, must be constructed as an analogue of the organic world, which is inescapably its practical context. And so he was fundamentally at odds with the industrial economy, which sees creatures, including humans, as machines, and agriculture, like ultimately the entire human economy, as an analogue of an industrial system. This was, and is, the inevitable and characteristic product of the dead-end materialism that is the premise of both industrialism and the science that supports it.

Howard understood that such reductionism could not work for agriculture:

> *But the growing of crops and the raising of live stock belong to biology, a domain where everything is alive and which is poles asunder from chemistry and physics. Many of the things that matter on the land, such as soil fertility, tilth, soil management, the quality of produce, the bloom and health of animals, the general management of live stock, the*

164

working relations between master and man, the esprit de corps of the farm as a whole, cannot be weighed or measured. Nevertheless their presence is everything: their absence spells failure.[5]

This understanding has a scientific basis, as it should have, for Howard was an able and conscientious scientist. But I think it comes also from intuition, and probably could not have come otherwise. Howard's intuition was that of a man who was a farmer by birth and heritage and who was a sympathetic as well as a scientific observer of the lives of plants, animals, and farmers.

IF THE FARM is to last—if it is to be "sustainable," as we now say—then it must waste nothing. It must obey in all its processes what Howard called "the law of return." Under this law, agriculture produces no waste; what is taken from the soil is returned to it. Growth must be balanced by decay: "In this breaking down of organic matter we see in operation the reverse of the building-up process which takes place in the leaf."[6]

The balance between growth and decay is the sole principle of stability in nature and in agriculture. And this balance is never static, never finally achieved, for it is dependent upon a cycle, which in nature, and within the limits of nature, is self-sustaining, but which in agriculture must be made continuous by purpose and by correct methods. "This cycle," Howard wrote, "is constituted of the successive and repeated processes of birth, growth, maturity, death, and decay."[7]

The interaction, the interdependence, of life and death, which in nature is the source of an inexhaustible fecundity, is the basis of a set of analogies, to which agriculture and the rest of the human economy must conform in order to endure, and which is ultimately religious, as Howard knew: "An eastern religion calls this cycle the Wheel of Life . . . Death supersedes life and life rises again from what is dead and decayed."[8]

The maintenance of this cycle is the practical basis of good farming and its moral basis as well:

> *[T]he correct relation between the processes of growth and the processes*
> *of decay is the first principle of successful farming. Agriculture must al-*
> *ways be balanced. If we speed up growth we must accelerate decay. If, on*
> *the other hand, the soil's reserves are squandered, crop production ceases*
> *to be good farming: it becomes something very different. The farmer is*
> *transformed into a bandit.*[9]

IT SEEMS TO me that Howard's originating force, innate in his character and refined in his work, was his sense of context. This made him eminent and effective in his own day, and it makes his work urgently relevant to our own. He lacked completely the specialist impulse, so prominent among the scientists and intellectuals of the present-day university, to see things in isolation.

He himself began as a specialist, a mycologist, but he soon saw that this made him "a laboratory hermit," and he felt that this was fundamentally wrong:

> *I was an investigator of plant diseases, but I had myself no crops on*
> *which I could try out the remedies I advocated: I could not take my own*
> *advice before offering it to other people. It was borne in on me that there*
> *was a wide chasm between science in the laboratory and practice in the*
> *field, and I began to suspect that unless this gap could be bridged no*
> *real progress could be made in the control of plant diseases: research and*
> *practice would remain apart: mycological work threatened to degenerate*
> *into little more than a convenient agency by which—provided I issued*
> *a sufficient supply of learned reports fortified by a judicious mixture of*
> *scientific jargon—practical difficulties could be side-tracked.*[10]

The theme of his life's work was his effort to bridge this gap. The way to do it was simply to refuse to see anything in isolation. Everything, as he saw it, existed within a context, outside of which it was unintelligible. Moreover, every problem existed within a context, outside of which it was unsolvable. Agriculture, thus, cannot be understood or its problems solved without respect to context. The same applied even to an individual plant or crop. And this respect for context properly set the standard and determined the methodology of agricultural science:

The basis of research was obviously to be investigation directed to the whole existence of a selected crop, namely, "the plant itself in relation to the soil in which it grows, to the conditions of village agriculture under which it is cultivated, and with reference to the economic uses of the product"; in other words research was to be integral, never fragmented.[11]

If nothing exists in isolation, then all problems are circumstantial; no problem resides, or can be solved, in anybody's department. A disease was, thus, a symptom of a larger disorder. The following passage shows as well as any the way his mind worked:

I found when I took up land in India and learned what the people of the country know, that the diseases of plants and animals were very useful agents for keeping me in order, and for teaching me agriculture. I have learnt more from the diseases of plants and animals than I have from all the professors of Cambridge, Rothamsted and other places who gave me my preliminary training. I argued the matter in this way. If diseases attacked my crops, it was because I was doing something wrong. I therefore used diseases to teach me. In this way I really learnt agriculture—from my father and from my relatives and from the professors I only obtained a mass of preliminary information. Diseases taught me to understand agriculture. I think if we used diseases more instead of running to sprays and killing off pests, and if we let diseases rip and then found out what is wrong and then tried to put it right, we should get much deeper into agricultural problems than we shall do by calling in all these artificial aids. After all, the destruction of a pest is the evasion of, rather than the solution of, all agricultural problems.[12]

The implied approach to the problem of disease is illustrated by the way Howard and his first wife, Gabrielle, dealt with the problem of indigo wilt:

> *In fifteen years £54,207 had been spent on research, at that time a large sum. Yet the Imperial Entomologist could find no insect, the Imperial Mycologist no fungus, and the Imperial Bacteriologist no virus to account for the plague.*
>
> *The Howards proceeded differently. Their start was to grow the crop on a field scale and in the best possible way, taking note of local methods. Their observation was directed to the whole plant, above and below ground; they followed the crop throughout its life history; they looked at all the surrounding circumstances, soil, moisture, temperature. But they looked for no virus, no fungus, and no insect.*[13]

And it was the Howards who solved the problem. The plants were wilting, they found, primarily because the soils were becoming waterlogged during the monsoon, killing the roots; the plants were wilting and dying from starvation. It was a problem of management, and it was solved by changes in management. But it could not have been solved except by studying the whole plant in its whole context.

Because he refused to accept the academic fragmentation that had become conventional by his time, Howard, of course, was "accused of invading fields not his own,"[14] and this he had done intentionally and in accordance with "the guiding principle of the closest contact between research and those to be served."[15]

AGRICULTURE IS PRACTICED inescapably in a context, and its context must not be specialized or simplified. Its context, first of all, is the nature of the place in which it is practiced, but it is also the society and the economy of those who practice it. And just as there are penalties for ignoring the natural context, so there are penalties for ignoring the human one. As Howard saw it, the agricultural industrialists' apparent belief that food production could be harmlessly divorced from the economic interest of farmers needlessly repeats a historical failure:

> *Judged by the ordinary standards of achievement the agricultural his-*
> *tory of the Roman Empire ended in failure due to inability to realize*
> *the fundamental principle that the maintenance of soil fertility coupled*
> *with the legitimate claims of the agricultural population should never*
> *have been allowed to come in conflict with the operations of the capital-*
> *ist. The most important possession of a country is its population. If this*
> *is maintained in health and vigour everything else will follow; if this is*
> *allowed to decline nothing, not even great riches, can save the country*
> *from eventual ruin.*[16]

The obligation of a country's agriculture, then, is to maintain its people in health, and this applies equally to the people who eat and to the people who produce the food.

Howard accepted this obligation unconditionally as the obligation also of his own work. He realized, moreover, that this obligation imposed strict limits both upon the work of farmers and upon his work as a scientist: First, neither farming nor experimentation should usurp the tolerances or violate the nature of the place where the work is done; and second, the work must respect and preserve the livelihoods of the local community. Before going to work, agricultural scientists are obliged to know both the place where their work is to be done and the people for whom they are working. It is remarkable that Howard came quietly, by thought and work, to these realizations a half century and more before they were forced upon us by the ecological and economic failures of industrial agriculture.

In India he used his training as a scientist and his ability to observe and think for himself, just as he would have been expected to do. But he also learned from the peasant farmers of the country, whom he respected as his "professors." He valued them for their knowledge of the land, for their industry, and for their "accuracy of eye."[17] He accepted also the economic and technological circumstances of those farmers as the limit within which he himself should do his work. He saw that it would be possible to ruin his clients by thoughtless or careless innovation:

> *Often improvements are possible but they are not economic. . . . In India the cultivators are mostly in debt and the holdings are small. Any capital required for developments has to be borrowed. A large number of possible improvements are barred by the fact that the extra return is not large enough to pay the high interest on the capital involved and also to yield a profit to the cultivator.*[18]

The reader may wish to contrast this way of thinking with that of the Green Revolution or with that of the headlong industrialization of American agriculture since World War II, in both of which the only recognized limit was technological, and in neither of which was there any concern for the ability of farmers or their communities to bear the costs.

Howard's solution to the problem was simply to do his work within the technological limits of the local farmers:

> *The existing system could not be radically changed, but it might be developed in useful ways. This must never exceed what the cultivator could afford, and, in a way, also what he was used to. This principle Sir Albert kept in mind to the very end . . . his standard seems to have been the possession of a yoke of oxen; when more power was needed, the presumption was that the second yoke could be borrowed from a neighbor. Thus the maximum draught contemplated was four animals.*[19]

By the observance of such limits, Howard was enfolded consciously and conscientiously within the natural and human communities that he endeavored to serve.

No university that I have heard of, land-grant or other, has yet attempted to establish its curriculum and its intellectual structure on Sir Albert Howard's "one great subject," or on his determination to serve respectfully and humbly the local population. But a university most

170

certainly could do so, and in doing so it could bring to bear all its disciplines and departments. In doing so, that is to say, it could become in truth a university.

At present our universities are not simply growing and expanding, according to the principle of "growth" universal in industrial societies, but they are at the same time disintegrating. They are a hodgepodge of unrelated parts. There is no unifying aim and no common critical standard that can serve equally well all the diverse parts or departments.

The fashion now is to think of universities as industries or businesses. University presidents, evidently thinking of themselves as CEOs, talk of "business plans" and "return on investment," as if the industrial economy could provide an aim and a critical standard appropriate either to education or to research.

But this is not possible. No economy, industrial or otherwise, can supply an appropriate aim or standard. Any economy must be either true or false to the world and to our life in it. If it is to be true, then it must be *made* true, according to a standard that is not economic.

To regard the economy as an end or as the measure of success is merely to reduce students, teachers, researchers, and all they know or learn to merchandise. It reduces knowledge to "property" and education to training for the "job market."

If, on the contrary, Howard was right in his belief that health is the "one great subject," then a unifying aim and a common critical standard are clearly implied. Health is at once quantitative and qualitative; it requires both sufficiency and goodness. It is comprehensive (it is synonymous with "wholeness"), for it must leave nothing out. And it is uncompromisingly local and particular; it has to do with the sustenance of particular places, creatures, human bodies, and human minds.

If a university began to assume responsibility for the health of its place and its local constituents, then all of its departments would have a common aim, and they would have to judge their place and themselves and one another by a common standard. They would need one another's knowledge. They would have to communicate with one another; the diversity of specialists would have to speak to one another in a common language. And here again Howard is exemplary, for he wrote, and presumably spoke, a plain, vigorous, forthright English—no jargon, no condescension, no ostentation, no fooling around.

NOTES

1. *An Agricultural Testament* (London: Oxford University Press, 1956), 4.

2. Sir Albert Howard, *The Soil and Health* (Lexington: University Press of Kentucky, 2006), 11.

3. Louise E. Howard, *Sir Albert Howard in India* (Emmaus, Pa.: Rodale Press, 1954), 162.

4. *The Soil and Health*, 11.

5. *An Agricultural Testament*, 196.

6. *The Soil and Health*, 22.

7. Ibid., 18.

8. Ibid.

9. *An Agricultural Testament*, 25.

10. *The Soil and Health*, 1–2.

11. *Sir Albert Howard in India*, 42.

12. Howard, as quoted in *Sir Albert Howard in India*, 190.

13. *Sir Albert Howard in India*, 170.

14. Ibid., 42.

15. Ibid., 44.

16. *An Agricultural Testament*, 9.

17. *Sir Albert Howard in India*, 222 and 228.

18. Howard, as quoted in *Sir Albert Howard in India*, 37–38.

19. *Sir Albert Howard in India*, 224.

Agriculture from the Roots Up

(2004)

ॐ

H ENRY DAVID THOREAU wrote somewhere that hundreds are hacking at the branches for every one who is striking at the root. He meant this as a metaphor, but it applies literally to modern agriculture and to the science of modern agriculture. As it has become more and more industrialized, agriculture increasingly has been understood as an enterprise established upon the surface of the ground. Most people nowadays lack even a superficial knowledge of agriculture, and most who do know something about it are paying little or no attention to what is happening under the surface.

The scientists at The Land Institute in Salina, Kansas, on the contrary, are striking at the root. Their study of the root and the roots of our agricultural problems has produced a radical criticism, leading to a proposed solution that is radical.

THEIR CRITICISM IS made radical by one crucial choice: the adoption of the natural ecosystem as the first standard of agricultural performance, having priority over the standard of productivity and certainly over the delusional and dangerous industrial standard of "efficiency." That single change makes a momentous difference, one that is historical and cultural as well as scientific.

By the standard of the natural or the healthy ecosystem, we see as if suddenly the shortcomings, not only of industrial agriculture but of agriculture itself, insofar as agriculture has consisted of annual monocultures. To those of us who are devoted to agriculture in any of its historical forms, such criticism is inevitably painful. And yet we may see its justice and accept it, understanding how much is at stake. To others, who have founded their careers or their businesses precisely upon the shortcomings of agriculture as we now have it, this criticism will perhaps be even more painful, and no doubt they will resist with all the great power we know they have.

Even so, this is a criticism for which the time is ripe. A rational denial of its justice is no longer possible. There are many reasons for this, but the main one, I think, is the virtual meltdown of the old boundaries of specialist thought in agriculture—a meltdown that I hope foretells the same fate for the boundaries of all specialist thought.

The justifying assumptions of the industrial agriculture that we now have are based on a reductive science working within strictly bounded specializations. This agriculture, an agglomeration of specialties, appeared perfectly rational and salutary so long as it was assumable that efficiency and productivity were adequate standards, that husbandry was safely reducible to science and fertility to chemistry, that organisms are merely machines, that agriculture is under no obligation to nature, that it has only agricultural results, and that it can be confidently based upon "cheap" fossil fuels.

The inventors of this agriculture assumed, in short, that the human will is sovereign in the universe, that the only laws are the laws of mechanics, and that the material world and its "natural resources" are without limit. These are the assumptions that, acknowledged or not, underlie the "war" by which we humans have undertaken to "conquer" nature, and which is the dominant myth of modern intellectual life.

IN THE DAYS of human darkness and ignorance, now supposedly past, we found ways to acknowledge the sanctity of nature and to honor her as the common mother of all creatures, including ourselves. We conducted our relations with her by prayer, propitiation, skilled work, thrift, caution, and care. Our concern about that relationship produced the concepts of usufruct and stewardship. A few lines from the "Two Cantos of Mutabilitie" that Edmund Spenser placed at the end of *The Faerie Queene* will suffice to give a sense of our ancient veneration:

> *Then forth issewed (great goddesse) great dame Nature,*
>
> *With goodly port and gracious Majesty;*
>
> *Being far greater and more tall of stature*
>
> *Than any of the gods or Powers on hie . . .*
>
> . . .
>
> *This great Grandmother of all creatures bred*
>
> *Great Nature, ever young yet full of eld,*
>
> *Still moving, yet unmoved from her sted;*
>
> *Unseen of any, yet of all beheld . . .*

Thus, though he was a Christian, Spenser still saw fit at the end of the sixteenth century to present Nature as the genius of the sublunary world, a figure of the greatest majesty, mystery, and power, the source of all earthly life. He addressed her, in addition, as the supreme judge of all her creatures, ruling by standards that we would now call ecological:

> *Who Right to all dost deal indifferently,*
>
> *Damning all Wrong and tortious Injurie,*
>
> *Which any of thy creatures do to other*
>
> *(Oppressing them with power, unequally)*

Sith of them all thou art the equall mother,

And knittest each to each, as brother unto brother.

And then, at about Spenser's time or a little after, we set forth in our "war against nature" with the purpose of conquering her and wringing her powerful and lucrative secrets from her by various forms of "tortious Injurie." This we have thought of as our "enlightenment" and as "progress." But in the event this war, like most wars, has turned out to be a trickier business than we expected. We must now face two shocking surprises. The first surprise is that if we say and believe that we are at war with nature, then we are in the fullest sense at war: That is, we are both opposing and being opposed, and the costs to both sides are extremely high.

The second surprise is that we are not winning. On the evidence now available, we have to conclude that we are losing—and, moreover, that there was never a chance that we could win. Despite the immense power and violence that we have deployed against her, nature is handing us one defeat after another. Even in our most grievous offenses against her—as in the present epidemic of habitat destruction and species extinction—we are being defeated, for in the long run we can less afford the losses than nature can. And we have to look upon soil erosion and the spread of exotic diseases, weeds, and pests as nature's direct reprisals for our violations of her laws. Sometimes she seems terrifyingly serene in her triumphs over us, as when, simply by refusing to absorb our pollutants, she forces us to live in our mess.

Thus she has forced us to recognize that the context of American agriculture is not merely fields and farms or the free market or the economy, but it is also the polluted Mississippi River, the hypoxic zone in the Gulf of Mexico, all the small towns whose drinking water contains pesticides and nitrates, the pumped-down aquifers and the no-longer-flowing rivers, and all the lands that we have scalped, gouged, poisoned, or destroyed utterly for "cheap" fuels and raw materials.

Thus she is forcing us to believe what the great teachers and prophets have always told us and what the ecologists are telling us again: All things are connected; the context of everything is everything else. By now, many of us know, and more are learning, that if you want to evaluate the agriculture of a region, you must begin not with a balance sheet, but with the local water. How continuously do the small streams flow? How clear is the water? How much sediment and how many pollutants are carried in the runoff? Are the ponds and creeks and rivers fit for swimming? Can you eat the fish?

We know, or we are learning, that from the questions about water we go naturally to questions about the soil. Is it staying in place? What is its water-holding capacity? Does it drain well? How much humus is in it? What of its biological health? How often and for how long is it exposed to the weather? How deep in it do the roots go?

SUCH ARE THE questions that trouble and urge and inspire the scientists at The Land Institute, for everything depends upon the answers. The answers, as these scientists know, will reveal not only the state of the health of the landscape, but also the state of the culture of the people who inhabit and use the landscape. Is it a culture of respect, thrift, and seemly skills, or a culture of indifference and mechanical force? A culture of life, or a culture of death?

And beyond those questions are questions insistently practical and economic, questions of accounting. What is the worth, to us humans with our now insupportable health care industry, of ecological health? Is our health in any way separable from the health of our economic landscapes? Must not the health of water and soil be accounted an economic asset? Will not this greater health support, sustain, and in the long run cheapen the productivity of our farms?

If our war against nature destroys the health of water and soil, and thus inevitably the health of agriculture and our own health, and can only lead to our economic ruin, then we need to try another possibility. And there is only one: If we cannot establish an enduring or even a humanly bearable economy by our attempt to defeat nature, then we will have to try living in harmony and cooperation with her.

By its adoption of the healthy ecosystem as the appropriate standard of agricultural performance, The Land Institute has rejected competition as the fundamental principle of economics, and therefore of the applied sciences, and has replaced it with the principle of harmony. In doing so, it has placed its work within a lineage and tradition that predate both industrialism and modern science. The theme of a human and even an economic harmony with nature goes back many hundreds of years in the literary record. Its age in the prehistoric cultures can only be conjec-tured, but we may confidently assume that it is ancient, probably as old as the human race. In the early twentieth century this theme was applied explicitly to agriculture by writers such as F. H. King, Liberty Hyde Bailey, J. Russell Smith, Sir Albert Howard, and Aldo Leopold, Howard being the one who gave it the soundest and most elaborate scientific underpinning. This modern lineage was interrupted by the juggernaut of industrial agriculture following World War II. But, in the 1970s, when Wes Jackson began thinking about the Kansas prairie as a standard and model for Kansas farming, he took up the old theme at about where Howard had left it, doing so remarkably without previous knowledge of Howard.

And so, in espousing the principle and the goal of harmony, The Land Institute acquired an old and honorable ancestry. It acquired at the same time, in the same way, a working principle also old and honorable: that of art as imitation of nature. The initiating question was this: If, so to speak, you place a Kansas wheatfield beside a surviving patch of the native Kansas prairie, what is the difference?

Well, the primary difference, obvious to any observer, is that, whereas the wheatfield is a monoculture of annuals, the plant community

178

of the prairie is highly diverse and perennial. There are many implications in that difference, not all of which are agricultural, but five of which are of immediate and urgent agricultural interest: The prairie's loss of soil to erosion is minimal; it is highly efficient in its ability to absorb, store, and use water; it makes the maximum use of every year's sunlight; it builds and preserves its own fertility; and it protects itself against pests and diseases.

The next question, the practical one, follows logically and naturally from the first: How might we contrive, let us say, a Kansas farm in imitation of a Kansas prairie, acquiring for agriculture the several ecological services of the prairie along with the economic benefit of a sufficient harvest of edible seeds? And so we come to the great project of The Land Institute.

I lack the technical proficiency to comment at much length on this work. I would like to end simply by saying how I believe the science now in practice at The Land Institute differs from the science of industrial agriculture.

WE ARE LIVING in an age of technological innovation. Our preoccupation with invention and novelty has begun, by this late day, to look rather absurd, especially in our strict avoidance of cost accounting. What invention, after all, has done more net good or given more net pleasure than soap? And who invented soap? It is all too easy, under the circumstances, to imagine a media publicist snatching at The Land Institute's project as "innovation on an epic scale" or "the next revolution in agriculture" or "the new scientific frontier."

But these scientists are contemplating no such thing. Their vision and their work do not arise from or lead to any mechanical or chemical breakthrough; they do not depend on any newly discovered fuel. The innovation they have in mind is something old under the sun: a better adaptation of the human organism to its natural habitat. They are not seeking to implement a technological revolution or a revolution of any kind. They are interested merely in improving our fundamental relationship to the earth, changing the kind of roots we put down and deepening the depth we put them down to. This is not revolutionary, because it is merely a part of a long job that we have not finished, that we have tried for a little while to finish in the wrong way, but one that we will never finish if we do it the right way. Harmony between our human economy and the natural world—local adaptation—is a perfection we will never finally achieve but must continuously try for. There is never a finality to it because it involves living creatures who change. The soil has living creatures in it. It has live roots in it, perennial roots if it is lucky. If it is the soil of the right kind of farm, it has a farm family growing out of it. The work of adaptation must go on because the world changes; our places change and we change; we change our places and our places change us. The science of adaptation, then, is unending. Anybody who undertakes to adapt agriculture to a place—or, in J. Russell Smith's words, to fit the farming to the farm—will never run out of problems or want for intellectual stimulation.

The science of The Land Institute promptly exposes the weakness of the annual thought of agricultural industrialism because it measures its work by the standard of the natural ecosystem, which gives pride of place to perennials. It exposes also the weakness of the top-down thought of technological innovation by proceeding from the roots up, and by aiming not at universality and uniformity, but at local adaptation. It would deepen the formal limits of agricultural practice many feet below the roots of the annual grain crops, but it would draw in the limits of concern to the local watershed, ecosystem, farm, and field. This is by definition a science of place, operating within a world of acknowledged limits—of space, time, energy, soil, water, and human intelligence. It is a science facing, in the most local and intimate terms, a world of daunting formal complexity and of an ultimately impenetrable mystery—exactly the world that the reductive sciences of industrial agriculture have sought to oversimplify and thus ignore. This new science, in its ancient quest, demands the acceptance of human ignorance as the ever-present starting point of human work, and it requires the use of all the intelligence we have.

PART III
FOOD

AUTHOR'S NOTE

P ART III CALLS for a few words of explanation. The publisher's idea was to show in this gathering of writings the connections that make one subject of farming, farms, farmers, and food. I agreed, thinking the idea was a good one. But if we limited the contents of our book to essays, as at first we thought we would do, we were going to come up short on food. Though I have written many essays on farming, farms, and farmers, I have written only one specifically on food. I am by no means a chef, and as a cook I am limited to frying and scorching.

And so we decided to include in Part III, in addition to the lone essay, "The Pleasures of Eating," a selection from my fiction of passages in which people eat. This is a good idea also, I think, because it unspecializes the idea of food. All the episodes from my stories and novels are not about food only, but about *meals*. You can eat food by yourself. A meal, according to my understanding anyhow, is a communal event, bringing together family members, neighbors, even strangers. At its most ordinary, it involves hospitality, giving, receiving, and gratitude. It pleases me that in these fictional passages food is placed in its circumstances of history, work, and companionship.

I have provided notes to accompany these episodes, to say when they took place, and to give some sense of the stories they belong to.

But I need to say, furthermore, something about the part of the women in these episodes. The effort of justice to women, in addition to the substantial good it has done and is doing, has attached a sense of belittlement to "women's work." I know that there are reasons for this. But understandable as it may be, it is unjust when it extends to traditional farm housewifery.

People and their domestic arrangements are imperfect, of course. Abuses no doubt can be found in the customs and usages of any time, no matter how enlightened or liberated. But the women in the episodes that follow, as I think is obvious, are not the "little women" of the liberationist stereotype, and are related distantly if at all to the housewives of the modern suburbs. They are not consumers. They are not openers of cans or heaters of frozen dinners or stirrers of "mixes."

On the contrary, they are, with their menfolk, managers of domestic economies that are complex, practically and culturally. These economies unite household and farm. They are as dependent on old knowledge and immediate intelligence as on the land. In accordance with tradition, these women do the cooking, but this is a cooking that is only a part of an intricate seasonal procedure that includes the cultivation of plants and the nurturing of animals, harvesting and bringing in, slaughtering and butchering, preserving and canning and storing for the winter. How all this work was (and sometimes still is) divided between the sexes would vary, according to preferences and abilities, from one household and marriage to another. But both men and women participated and were associated in the work.

Justice to these women requires recognition of the entirely admirable knowledge, intelligence, and skill that they applied to their "women's work." Moreover, many of these women were perfectly capable also of "men's work." The reader will notice, in the passage from *The Memory of Old Jack*, that Mary Penn is helping to prepare a harvest dinner, but also that she is wearing work clothes. After the women have eaten (with the men fed and gone, this will be a leisurely, quietly sociable meal that the women have) and after they have washed the dishes and set the kitchen to rights, Mary will go to the field to work with the men. Hannah would be going too if she were not pregnant.

from *That Distant Land*

ॐ

Here is a glimpse of an old way of family life and hospitality before the twentieth century, and its invariable resort to war and industrial destruction, changed everything. These paragraphs are from the short story "Turn Back the Bed."

OLD ANT'NY WAS a provider, and he did provide. He saw to it that twelve hogs were slaughtered for his own use every fall— and twenty-four hams and twenty-four shoulders and twenty-four middlings were hung in his smokehouse. And his wife, Maw Proudfoot, kept a flock of turkeys and a flock of geese and a flock of guineas, and her henhouse was as populous as a county seat. And long after he was "too old to farm," Old Ant'ny grew a garden as big as some people's crop. He picked and dug and fetched, and Maw Proudfoot canned and preserved and pickled and cured as if they had an army to feed—which they more or less did, for there were not only the announced family gatherings but always somebody or some few happening by, and always somebody to give something to.

The Proudfoot family gatherings were famous. As feasts, as collections and concentrations of good things, they were unequaled. Especially in summer there was nothing like them, for then there would be old ham and fried chicken and gravy, and two or three kinds of fish, and hot biscuits and three kinds of cornbread, and potatoes and beans and roasting ears and carrots and beets and onions, and corn pudding and corn creamed and fried, and cabbage boiled and scalloped, and tomatoes stewed and sliced, and fresh cucumbers soaked in vinegar, and three or four kinds of pickles, and if it was late enough in the summer there would be watermelons and muskmelons, and there would be pies and cakes and cobblers and dumplings, and milk and coffee by the gallon. And there would be, too, half a dozen or so gallon or half-gallon stone jugs making their way from one adult male to another as surreptitious as moles. For in those days the Proudfoot homeplace, with its broad cornfields in the creek bottom, was famous also for the excellence of its whiskey.

So of course these affairs were numerously attended. When the word went out to family and in-laws it was bound to be overheard, and people came in whose veins Proudfoot blood ran extremely thin, if at all. And there would be babble and uproar all day, for every door stood open, and the old house was not ceiled; the upstairs floorboards were simply nailed to the naked joists, leaving cracks that you could not only hear through but in places see through. Whatever happened anywhere could be heard everywhere.

The storm of feet and voices would continue unabated from not long after sunup until after sundown when the voice of Old Ant'ny would rise abruptly over the multitude: "Well, Maw, turn back the bed. These folks want to be gettin' on home." And then, as if at the bidding of some Heavenly sign, the family sorted itself into its branches. Children and shoes and hats were found, identified, and claimed; horses were hitched; and the tribes of the children of Old Ant'ny Proudfoot set out in their various directions in the twilight.

3⌐

The following passage also is from a short story, "The Solemn Boy." Going home at noon with a load of corn on a bitter cold day between Thanksgiving and Christmas, 1934, Tol Proudfoot gives a ride to a man and his young son. These are people clearly displaced by the Depression. Because he understands this, and has seen how poorly dressed they are for the weather and how cold, and because kindness is anyhow his rule, Tol insists that the two strangers come to his house for dinner—the big meal, that is to say, that the country people ate at noon. He sends them to the house while he drives on to the barn to care for his horses.

T OL SPOKE TO his team and drove on into the barn lot. He positioned the wagon in front of the corncrib, so he could scoop the load off after dinner, and then he unhitched the horses. He watered them, led them to their stalls, and fed them.

"Eat, boys, eat," he said.

And then he started to the house. As he walked along he opened his hand, and the old dog put his head under it.

THE MAN AND boy evidently had done as he had told them, for they were not in sight. Tol already knew how Miss Minnie would have greeted them.

"Well, come on in!" she would have said, opening the door and seeing the little boy. "Looks like we're having company for dinner! Come in here, honey, and get warm!"

He knew how the sight of that little shivering boy would have called the heart right out of her. Tol and Miss Minnie had married late, and time had gone by, and no child of their own had come. Now they were stricken in age, and it had long ceased to be with Miss Minnie after the manner of women.

He told the old dog to lie down on the porch, opened the kitchen door, and stepped inside. The room was warm, well lit from the two big windows in the opposite wall, and filled with the smells of things cooking. They had killed hogs only a week or so before, and the kitchen was full of the smell of frying sausage. Tol could hear it sizzling in the skillet.

He stood just inside the door, unbuttoning his coat and looking around. The boy was sitting close to the stove, a little sleepy looking now in the warmth, some color coming into his face. The man was standing near the boy, looking out the window—feeling himself a stranger, poor fellow, and trying to pretend he was somewhere else.

Tol took off his outdoor clothes and hung them up. He nodded to Miss Minnie, who gave him a smile. She was rolling out the dough for an extra pan of biscuits. Aside from that, the preparations looked about as usual. Miss Minnie ordinarily cooked enough at dinner so that there would be leftovers to warm up or eat cold for supper. There would be plenty. The presence of the two strangers made Tol newly aware of the abundance, fragrance, and warmth of that kitchen.

"Cold out," Miss Minnie said. "This boy was nearly frozen."

Tol saw that she had had no luck either in learning who their guests were. "Yes," he said. "Pretty cold."

He turned to the little washstand beside the door, dipped water from the bucket into the wash pan, warmed it with water from the tea-kettle on the stove. He washed his hands, splashed his face, groped for the towel.

As soon as Tol quit looking at his guests, they began to look at him. Only now that they saw him standing up could they have seen how big he was. He was broad and wide and tall. All his movements had about them an air of casualness or indifference as if he were not conscious of his whole strength. He wore his clothes with the same carelessness, evidently not having thought of them since he put them on. And though the little boy had not smiled, at least not where Tol or Miss Minnie could see him, he must at least have wanted to smile at the way Tol's stiff gray hair stuck out hither and yon after Tol combed it, as indifferent to the comb as if the comb had been merely fingers or a stick. But when Tol turned away from the washstand, the man looked back to the window and the boy looked down at his knee.

"It's ready," Miss Minnie said to Tol, as she took a pan of biscuits from the oven and slid another in.

Tol went to the chair at the end of the table farthest from the stove. He gestured to the two chairs on either side of the table. "Make yourself at home, now," he said to the man and the boy. "Sit down, sit down."

He sat down himself and the two guests sat down.

"We're mightily obliged," the man said.

"Don't wait on me," Miss Minnie said. "I'll be there in just a minute."

"My boy, reach for that sausage," Tol said. "Take two and pass 'em.

"Have biscuits," he said to the man. "Naw, that ain't enough. Take two or three. There's plenty of 'em."

There was plenty of everything: a platter of sausage, and more already in the skillet on the stove; biscuits brown and light, and more in the oven; a big bowl of navy beans, and more in the kettle on the stove, a big bowl of applesauce and one of mashed potatoes. There was a pitcher of milk and one of buttermilk.

Tol heaped his plate, and saw to it that his guests heaped theirs. "Eat till it's gone," he said, "and don't ask for nothing you don't see."

Miss Minnie sat down presently, and they all ate. Now and again Tol and Miss Minnie glanced at each other, each wanting to be sure the other saw how their guests applied themselves to the food. For the man and the boy ate hungrily without looking up, as though to avoid acknowledging that others saw how hungry they were. And Tol thought, "No breakfast." In his concern for the little boy, he forgot his curiosity about where the two had come from and where they were going.

Miss Minnie helped the boy to more sausage and more beans, and she buttered two more biscuits and put them on his plate. Tol saw how her hand hovered above the boy's shoulder, wanting to touch him. He was a nice-looking little boy, but he never smiled. Tol passed the boy the potatoes and refilled his glass with milk.

191

"Why, he eats so much it makes him poor to carry it," Tol said. "That boy can put it away!"

The boy looked up, but he did not smile or say anything. Neither Tol nor Miss Minnie had heard one peep out of him. Tol passed everything to the man, who helped himself and did not look up.

"We surely are obliged," he said.

Tol said, "Why, I wish you would look. Every time that boy's elbow bends, his mouth flies open."

But the boy did not smile. He was a solemn boy, far too solemn for his age.

"Well, we know somebody else whose mouth's connected to his elbow, don't we?" Miss Minnie said to the boy, who did not look up and did not smile. "Honey, don't you want another biscuit?"

The men appeared to be finishing up now. She rose and brought to the table a pitcher of sorghum molasses, and she brought the second pan of biscuits, hot from the oven.

The two men buttered biscuits, and then, when the butter had melted, laid them open on their plates and covered them with molasses. And Miss Minnie did the same for the boy. She longed to see him smile, and so did Tol.

"Now, Miss Minnie," Tol said, "that boy will want to go easy on them biscuits from here on, for we ain't got but three or four hundred of 'em left."

But the boy only ate his biscuits and molasses and did not look at anybody.

And now the meal was ending, and what were they going to do? Tol and Miss Minnie yearned toward that nice, skinny, really pretty little boy, and the old kitchen filled with their yearning, and maybe there was to be no answer. Maybe that man and this little boy would just get up in their silence and say, "Much obliged," and go away, and leave nothing of themselves at all.

"My boy," Tol said—he had his glass half-full of buttermilk in his hand, and was holding it up. "My boy, when you drink buttermilk, always remember to drink from the near side of the glass—like this." Tol tilted his glass and took a sip from the near side. "For drinking from the far side, as you'll find out, don't work anything like so well." And then—and perhaps to his own surprise—he applied the far side of the glass to his lips, turned it up, and poured the rest of the buttermilk right down the front of his shirt. And then he looked at Miss Minnie with an expression of absolute astonishment.

For several seconds nobody made a sound. They all were looking at Tol, and Tol, with his hair asserting itself in all directions and buttermilk on his chin and his shirt and alarm and wonder in his eyes, was looking at Miss Minnie.

And then Miss Minnie said quietly, "Mr. Proudfoot, you are the limit."

And then they heard the boy. At first it sounded like he had an obstruction in his throat that he worked at with a sort of strangling. And then he laughed.

He laughed with a free, strong laugh that seemed to open his throat as wide as a stovepipe. It was the laugh of a boy who was completely tickled. It transformed everything. Miss Minnie smiled. And then Tol laughed his big hollering laugh. And then Miss Minnie laughed. And then the boy's father laughed. The man and the boy looked up, they all looked full into one another's eyes, and they laughed.

They laughed until Miss Minnie had to wipe her eyes with the hem of her apron.

"Lord," she said, getting up, "what's next?" She went to get Tol a clean shirt.

"Let's have some more biscuits," Tol said. And they all buttered more biscuits and passed the molasses again.

FROM *Hannah Coulter*

☙

Christmas 1941, the Christmas after Pearl Harbor, came not long after Hannah, who is speaking here, married Virgil Feltner. Soon after that Christmas Virgil will be drafted into the Army, as they have expected. Because the war has so unsettled the future, Hannah and Virgil are living with his parents, Margaret and Mat Feltner.

I T WAS THE Christmas season, and we made the most of it. Virgil and I cut a cedar tree that filled a corner of the parlor, reached to the ceiling, and gave its fragrance to the whole room. We hung its branches with ornaments and lights, and wrapped our presents and put them underneath. One evening Virgil called up the Catlett children, pretending to be Santa Claus, and wound them up so that Bess and Wheeler nearly never got them to bed. We cooked for a week—Nettie Banion, the Feltners' cook, and Mrs. Feltner and I. We made cookies and candy, some for ourselves, some to give away. We made a fruit cake, a pecan cake, and a jam cake. Mr. Feltner went to the smokehouse and brought in an old ham, which we boiled and then baked. We made criss-crosses in the fat on top, finished it off with a glaze, and then put one clove exactly in the center of each square. We talked no end, of course, and joked and laughed. And I couldn't help going often to the pantry to look at what we had done and admire it, for these Christmas doings ran far ahead of any I had known before.

Each of us knew that the others were dealing nearly all the time with the thought of the war, but that thought we kept in the secret quiet of our own minds. Maybe we were thinking too of the sky opening over the shepherds who were abiding in the field, keeping watch over their flocks, and the light of Heaven falling over them, and the angel announcing peace. I was thinking of that, and also of the sufferers in the Bethlehem stable, as I never had before. There was an ache that from time to time seemed to fall entirely through me like a misting rain. The war was a bodily presence. It was in all of us, and nobody said a word.

Virgil and I brought Grandmam over from Shagbark on Christmas Eve. She was wearing her Sunday black and her silver earrings and broach. To keep from embarrassing me, as I understood, she had bought a nice winter coat and a little suitcase. She had presents for the Feltners and for Virgil and me in a shopping bag that she refused to let Virgil carry. I had worried that she would feel out of place at the Feltners, but I need not have. Mr. and Mrs. Feltner were at the door to welcome her, and she thanked them with honest pleasure and with grace.

On Christmas morning Nettie Banion's mother-in-law, Aunt Fanny, came up to the house with Nettie to resume for the day her old command of the kitchen. Joe Banion soon followed them under Aunt Fanny's orders to be on hand if needed.

And then the others came. Bess and Wheeler were first. Their boys flew through the front door, leaving it open, waving two new pearl-handled cap pistols apiece, followed by their little sisters with their Christmas dolls, followed by Bess and Wheeler with their arms full of wrapped presents. We all gathered around, smiling and talking and hugging and laughing. The boys were noisy as a crowd until Virgil said, "Now, Andy and Henry, you remember our rule—I get half of what you get, and you get half of what I get." And then they got noisier, Henry offering

Virgil one of his pistols, Andy backing up to keep both of his. And then all three of them went to the kitchen to smell the cooking and show their pistols to Nettie and Aunt Fanny.

Hearing the commotion, Ernest Finley came down from his room. Ernest had been wounded in the First World War and walked on crutches. He was a woodworker and a carpenter, a thoughtful, quiet-speaking man who usually worked alone. The Catlett boys loved him because of his work and his tools and his neat shop and the long bedtime stories he told them when they came to visit.

Miss Ora came, still alert to see that I called her "Auntie," with Aunt Lizzie and Uncle Homer Lord, who had come down to Hargrave the day before from Indianapolis. The Lords weren't kin to the Feltners at all, except that Aunt Lizzie and Mrs. Feltner had been best friends when they were girls—which, Aunt Lizzie said, was as close kin as you could get.

And then Virgil and I and the boys with their pistols drove out the Bird's Branch road to Uncle Jack Beechum's place—where he had been "batching it," as he said, since the death of his wife—and brought him to our house. He was the much younger brother of Mr. Feltner's mother, Nancy Beechum Feltner. Mr. Feltner's father, Ben, had been a father and a friend to Uncle Jack, who now was in a way the head of the family, though he never claimed such authority. Everybody looked up to him and loved him and, as sometimes was necessary, put up with him.

Uncle Jack didn't try to have dignity, he just had it. A man of great strength in his day, he walked now with a cane, bent a little at the hips but still straight-backed. He was a big man, work-brittle, and there was no foolishness about him.

You would have thought Henry would not have dared to do it, but as we were going from the car to the house he ran in front of Uncle Jack and shot at him with his pistols. I didn't think Uncle Jack would see anything funny in that, but he did. He gave a great snort of delight. He said, "*That boy'll put the cat in the churn.*"

And so we all were there.

To get the children calmed down before dinner and so the little girls could have a nap afterwards, we opened the presents right away. The old parlor was crowded with the tree and the people and the presents and the pretty wrapping papers flying about. Nettie Banion and Joe and Aunt Fanny sat in the doorway, waiting to receive the presents everybody had brought for them. The boys sat beside Virgil, who was making a big to-do over their presents, in which he was still claiming half-interest. The boys were a little unsure about this, but they loved his carrying on, and they sat as close to him as they could get.

There were sixteen of us around the long table in the dining room. The table was so beautiful when we came in that it seemed almost a shame not to just stand and look at it. Mrs. Feltner had put on her best tablecloth and her good dishes and silverware that she never used except for company. And on the table at last, after our long preparations, were our ham, our turkey and dressing, and our scalloped oysters under their brown crust. There was a cut glass bowl of cranberry sauce. There were mashed potatoes and gravy, green beans and butter beans, corn pudding, and hot rolls. On the sideboard were our lovely cakes on cake stands and a big pitcher of custard that would be served with whipped cream.

It looked too good to touch, let alone eat, and yet of course we ate. Grandmam sat at Mr. Feltner's right hand at his end of the table, and Uncle Jack sat at Mrs. Feltner's right hand at her end. Virgil and I sat opposite Bess and Wheeler at the center. And the children in their chairs and high chairs were portioned out among the grownups, no two together.

Every meal at the Feltners was good, for Mrs. Feltner and Nettie Banion both were fine cooks, but this one was extra good, and there were many compliments. Of all the compliments Uncle Jack's were the best, though he only increased the compliments of other people. He ate with great hunger and relish, and it was a joy to watch him. When somebody would say, "That is a wonderful ham" or "This dressing is perfect," Uncle Jack would solemnly shake his head and say, "Ay Lord, it is that!" And his words fell upon the table like a blessing.

Beyond that, he said little, and Grandmam too had little to say, but whatever they said was gracious. To have the two of them there, at opposite corners of the table, with their long endurance in their faces, and their present affection and pleasure, was a blessing of another kind.

FROM *Andy Catlett*

&

Now Andy Catlett is speaking as an aging man looking back to the Christmastime of 1943 when he first traveled away from his parents alone. He went by bus ten miles to visit, first, his grandma and grandpa Catlett who lived on the Bird's Branch road near Port William, and then his granny and granddaddy Feltner who lived on one of the outer edges of Port William itself. This passage and the two that follow are from Andy Catlett: Early Travels. *Here he has just arrived and is visiting with Grandma Catlett in her kitchen.*

RURAL ELECTRIFICATION WAS on its way, I suppose, for it would soon arrive, but it had not arrived yet. On the back porch there was a large icebox that, when ice was available, preserved leftovers and cooled the milk in the summer. That and the battery-powered radio and the telephone were the only modern devices in the house. Its old economy of the farm household was still intact. The supply lines ran to the kitchen from the henhouse and garden, cellar and smokehouse, cropland and pasture. On the kitchen table were two quart jars of green beans, a quart jar of applesauce, and a pint jar of what I knew to be the wild black raspberries that abounded in the thickets and woods edges of that time. I thought, "Pie!"

"Are you going to make a pie?" I asked.

"Hmh!" she said. "Maybe. Would you like to have a pie?"

And I said, with my best manners, "Yes, mam."

She was soon done with the potatoes. She shut the draft on the stove, taming the fire, changed the water on the potatoes, clapped a lid onto the pot, and set it on the stove to boil. She got out another pot, emptied the beans into it, added salt, some pepper, and a fine piece of fat pork. She was talking at large, commenting on her work, telling what she had learned from relatives' letters and Christmas cards and from listening in on the party line. I was up and following her around by then, to make sure I got the benefit of everything.

She washed her hands at the washstand by the back door and dried them. I followed her into the cool pantry and watched as she measured out flour and lard and the other ingredients and began making the dough for a pie crust. She rolled out the dough to the right thickness, pressed it into a pie pan, and, holding the pan on the fingertips of her left hand, passed a knife around its edge to carve off the surplus dough.

. . .

As she went about her preparations for dinner, she was commenting to herself, with grunts of determination or approval, on her progress. I knew even then that it was a wonder to see her at her work, and I know it more completely now. Her kitchen would be counted a poor thing by modern standards. There was of course no electrical equipment at all. The cooking utensils, excepting the invincible iron skillet and griddle, were chipped or dented or patched. The kitchen knives were worn lean with sharpening. Everything was signed with the wear of a lifetime or more. She was a fine cook. She did not do much in the way of exact measurement. She seasoned to taste. She mixed by experience and to the right consistency. The dough for a pie crust or biscuits, for instance, had to be neither too flabby nor too stiff; it was right when it felt right. She did not own a cookbook or a written recipe.

Meanwhile, she had prepared the raspberries, adding flour and sugar to the juice and heating it in a saucepan. Now she poured berries and juice into the dough-lined pan. She balled up the surplus dough, worked it briskly with her hands on the broken marble dresser top that she used for such work, sprinkled flour over it, rolled it flat, and then she sliced it rapidly into strips, which she laid in a beautiful lattice over the filling. As a final touch she sprinkled over the top a thin layer of sugar that in the heat of the oven would turn crisp and brown. And then she slid the pie into the oven.

She was being extravagant with the sugar for my sake, as I was more or less aware, and as I took for granted. But knowledge grows with age, and gratitude grows with knowledge. Now I am as grateful to her as I should have been then, and I am troubled with love for her, knowing how she was wrung all her life between her cherished resentments and her fierce affections. A peculiar sorrow hovered about her, and not only for the inevitable losses and griefs of her years; it came also from her settled conviction of the tendency of things to be unsatisfactory, to fail to live up to expectation, to fall short. She was haunted, I think, by the suspicion of a comedown always lurking behind the best appearances. I wonder now if she had ever read *Paradise Lost*. That poem, with its cosmos of Heaven and Hell and Paradise and the Fallen World, was a presence felt by most of her generation, if only by way of preachers who had read it. Whether or not she had read it for herself, the lostness of Paradise was the prime fact of her world, and she felt it keenly.

Once the pie was out of the way, she went ahead and made biscuit dough, flattened it with her rolling pin, cut out the biscuits, and laid them into the pans ready for the oven when the time would come.

She had cooked breakfast, strained the morning milk, made the beds, set the house to rights, washed the breakfast dishes, and cleaned up the kitchen before I got there. Now she let me help her, and we carried the crocks of morning milk from the back porch down into the cellar, and brought the crocks of last night's milk up from the cellar to the kitchen for skimming.

༄

Now it is noon of the same day. Andy has brought in the newspaper from the mailbox out at the road.

I WENT AROUND the house and in at the kitchen door, pried off my over-shoes, handed the paper to Grandma, took off my wraps, and washed my hands.

"Try combing that hair of yours," Grandma said. "Nobody ever saw the like. It's a regular straw stack."

Knowing it would do no good, I took the comb from the shelf where the water bucket sat and passed it several times through my hair.

Grandma watched me, and then she laughed. "You *are* the limit!" Her laugh was affectionate and indulgent, and yet it was a laugh with a history, conveying her perfected assurance that some things were hopeless. "Well, give up," she finally said. "Come and eat."

She had made a splendid dinner, a feast, little affected by wartime stringencies, which, except for the rationing of coffee and sugar, were little felt in such households. It hadn't been long since hog-killing, and so there was not only a platter of fresh sausage but also a bowl of souse soaking in vinegar. There was a bowl of sausage gravy, another of mashed potatoes, another of green beans, another of apple sauce. There was a pan of hot biscuits, to be buttered or gravied, and another in the oven. There was a handsome cake of freshly churned butter, the top marked in squares neatly carved with the edge of the butter paddle. There was a pitcher of buttermilk and one of sweet milk. And finally there was the pie, still warm, the top crust crisp and sugary and brown.

Oh, I ate as one eats who has not eaten for days, as if my legs were hollow, as if I were bigger inside than outside, and Grandma urged me on as if I were her champion in a tournament of eating.

Grandpa began the meal protesting that he was not hungry, but he ate, as Grandma said, "with a coming appetite," and when it came it came in force. Before my time he had ridden horseback the five miles to Smallwood where his friend the atheist doctor Gib Holston had pulled all his teeth, but he "gummed it" as fast as I could chew with teeth, and he had more capacity.

We ate and said little, for all of us were hungry. The food, as I see now but did not then, looked beautiful laid out before us on the table. And never then did I know that it was laid out in such profusion in honor of me. It was offered to me out of the loneliness of Grandma's life, out of her disappointments, her craving for small comforts and pleasures beyond her reach, to which Grandpa was indifferent. When I had washed down the last bite of my second piece of pie with a final swallow of milk, my stomach was as tight as a tick. I am sure I said "That was good." I may even have said "Thank you," for I was ever conscious that I was traveling alone and therefore in need of my manners. But time has taught me greater thanks.

‿ꝫ‿

And here Andy is visiting his mother's parents, Granny and Granddaddy Feltner, in Port William.

GRANDDADDY HAD GONE down into town after breakfast, I didn't know what for. But I knew he was on the bank board and was trusted, and people depended on him for things. When he got back to the house, he came on to the dining room door and looked in.

"Come on, son. Time to go to work."

I knew he wanted me to go with him, and I sort of wanted to, but I knew too that it was a bitter morning outside, and mostly I didn't want to go. The weather made it lovely to imagine a whole morning snug in the house, listening to the sounds of housekeeping and cooking and the women talking.

"Well," I said, "I think I'd rather just stay here."

I have reason to believe that he would not have accepted that reply from my mother or Uncle Virgil when they were young. But I was different. I was his grandson, more my parents' responsibility than his, and, after all, still a boy.

He just laughed a little to himself and said, "Well. All right." I heard him go through the house and out the back door.

But it was not long until Granny came in. She said in her gentle way, "Andy, your granddaddy has some work that he needs you to help him with," and I knew I had to go.

She had a promptitude of goodness that could be just fierce. She knew in an instant when I was dishonest or thoughtless or wrong. Much of my growing up, it seems to me now, was quietly required of me by her. She would correct me—"Listen to Granny. I expected something better from you"—and it would be as if in my mind a pawl had dropped into a notch; there was to be no going back.

I went and got my outdoor things, put them on, and went out the back door. It was cold, and to make things worse a few freezing rain-drops were coming down in a slant along the raw wind. I walked through the chicken yard where a few of Granddaddy's old hens were standing around with their tails drooped, looking miserable. They looked like I felt. I was full of reluctance and embarrassment and shrunken in my clothes from the cold. Where Granddaddy was I had no idea, for I had not asked. I went through the gate on the far end of the chicken yard and into the field behind the barn, listening all the time.

And then I heard Joe Banion speak in the driveway of the barn: "Come up." And he came out, standing on a hay wagon drawn by his team of mules, old Mary and old Jim. "Whoa-ho!" he said when he saw me. "I reckon you just as well get on."

"I reckon I just as well," I said, and I got on.

Joe drove up to the tobacco barn on the highest part of the ridge. When we came even with the front of the barn Joe stopped the team again. "They inside," he told me. I jumped down and he drove on.

I didn't know who "they" would be, but when I went through the front door, standing wide open to let in the light, I saw that they were Granddaddy and Burley Coulter.

The Coulters, Burley and his brother, Jarrat, had housed tobacco in that barn, but now they had emptied it. What Granddaddy and Burley were doing that morning was preparing the barn for the lambing that was due to begin in just a few days. Because they had used the barn, this was partly the Coulters' responsibility, and Burley had come to help. I was still feeling ashamed and a little odd because of my refusal, and so when I had stepped through the door I just stopped.

There was a large rick of baled alfalfa in one corner of the barn, put there to be handy to feed the lambing ewes. Granddaddy and Burley were building a low partition around it to keep the ewes from ruining it before they could eat it. Granddaddy was starting to nail up a board, and Burley was sorting through a stack of old lumber.

The first to notice me was Granddaddy. He said, "Hello, son."

And then Burley turned to look and said, "Well! If it ain't Andy!"

It was a moment not possible to forget. Tom Coulter, who not long ago had been killed in the fighting in Italy, was Burley's nephew. Part of the blood that had been shed in that bad year of 1943 had been Tom Coulter's. I had not seen Burley since the news of Tom's death had come. I didn't have grown-up manners, and I didn't know what to say. When

207

Burley spoke to me, it was as if he was not just greeting or welcoming me, but receiving me into his tenderness for Tom. It put a lump in my throat. He came over, taking off his right glove, and shook my hand.

He said, "How you making it, old boy?"

I just nodded, afraid if I said "Fine" I would cry.

Granddaddy said, "Andy, pick up the other end of this board, honey."

I picked it up and held it while he nailed his end. And then he came over and nailed my end. We did the same with the next board. And so I was helping. All through the morning they kept finding ways for me to help. They let me belong there at work with them. They kept me busy. And I experienced a beautiful change that was still new to me then but is old and familiar now. I went from reluctance and dread to interest in what we were doing, and then to pleasure in it. I got warm.

We finished the barrier around the hay rick. We picked up everything that was out of place or in the way. We made the barn neat. Joe returned with a load of straw from the straw stack. And then we bedded the barn, carrying forkloads of straw from the wagon and shaking it out level and deep over the whole floor, replacing the old fragrance of tobacco with the new fragrance of clean straw. Granddaddy had some long panels that would be used, as soon as needed, to portion the barn between the ewes with lambs and those still to lamb. We repaired the panels and propped them against the walls where they would be handy. We unstacked the mangers and lined them up in a row down the center of the driveway. Along one wall we set up the four-by-four-foot lambing pens where the ewes with new lambs would be confined and watched over until the lambs were well started and strong—"the maternity ward," Granddaddy called it.

The men were letting me help sometimes even when I could see I was slowing them down. We transformed the barn from a tobacco barn recalling last summer's crop to a sheep barn expecting next year's lambs.

In our work we could feel the new year coming, the days lengthening, the time of birth and growth returning, and this seemed to bring a happiness to everybody, in spite of the war and people's griefs and fears. The last thing we did was clean up the stripping room. It would be a sort of hospital, where Granddaddy, when he would be watching in the cold nights, could build a fire and help with a difficult birth, or pen a ewe with weak lambs until the lambs had sucked and were well dried, or keep orphan lambs until they got a good start.

When we were done at last, Granddaddy looked at his watch and then at me. "Well," he said, "could you eat a little something?"

The whole morning had gone by already, and I had not thought of hunger, but now when I thought of it I was hungry. I said, "I could eat a *lot* of something."

We laughed, and Burley said, "His belly thinks his throat's been cut."

"Burley," Granddaddy said, "won't you come have a bite of dinner with us?"

And Burley said, "Naw, Mat. Thank you. I left some dinner on the stove at home. I better go see about it."

Joe took the team and wagon back to the feed barn then, and I went with Granddaddy to drive Burley out to his house.

By the time we got back and washed, everybody was in the kitchen. Nettie was finishing up at the stove and Granny and Hannah were putting the food on the table. The smell of it seemed fairly to hollow me out inside. We had sausage and gravy and mashed potatoes, just like at Grandma's. Granny's sausage was seasoned differently but was just as good. And we had, besides, hominy and creamed butter beans and, instead of biscuits, hoecake—one already on the table, sliced, another on the griddle—a pitcher of fresh milk, coffee for the grown-ups, and again all the Christmas desserts, and again, for me, ice cream.

"Save room," Granny said again.

209

And I said, "I'm going to have plenty of room."

I had more room even than I thought.

Hannah said, "Do you think he'll leave us anything to eat tomorrow?"

"I don't know," Granddaddy said. "We may have to skip a day or two."

FROM "Misery"

⟡

Here again Andy Catlett is speaking in old age, again remembering his Catlett grandparents, but this is from a short story. The time is 1945.

THE HOUSEHOLD EMBODIED and was sustained by an agricultural order, resting upon the order of time and nature, that was at once demanding and consoling. Because this order was the order of the house, a child could be happy in it.

But the time was coming, was already arriving, when that order would be disvalued and taken apart piece by piece. I had come along just in time to glimpse the old order when it was still somewhat intact. I had played or idled in blacksmith shops while the smiths shod horses or mules, and built from raw iron and wood many of the simple farming tools still in use. I had gone along with the crews of neighbors as they followed the binder in the grainfields, gathering the bound sheaves into shocks, stopping to catch the young rabbits that ran from the still-standing wheat or barley. I had watched as they fed load after load of sheaves into the threshing machine and sacked and hauled away the grain. And I had been on hand when the sweated crews washed on the back porch and sat down to harvest meals equal to Christmas dinners, even in wartime with no sugar for the iced tea, to eat big and tell stories and laugh.

And then there came a day when Grandma, old and ill and without help, was not up to the task of cooking for a threshing crew, and my father could see that she was not. He had taken time off from his law office to splice out Grandpa, who also was not equal to the day.

"It's all right," my father said, comforting Grandma. "I'll take care of it."

And he did take care of it, for he was a man who refused to be at a loss, and he was capable. He went and bought a great pile of ground beef and sacks full of packaged buns. He fired up the kitchen stove and, overpowering Grandma's attempts to help, fried hamburgers enough, and more than enough, to feed the crew of hungry men and their retinue of hungry boys. It was adequate. It was even admirable, in its way, I could see that. But I could see also that something old and good was turning, or had turned, profoundly wrong. An old propriety that I knew was not mine had been offended. I could not have said this at the time, but I felt it; I felt it entirely. There was my father in the kitchen, cooking, not like any cook I had ever seen, but like himself, all concentration and haste, going at a big job that had to be done, nothing lovely about it. And there was the crew sitting down, not to a proper harvest meal, but to hamburgers that I knew they associated, as I did, with town life, with hamburger joints.

Grandma and Grandpa had achieved their threescore years and ten and more; their strength had become labor and sorrow. The life they had lived, the old season-governed life of the country, was passing away as they watched. No threshing machine or threshing crew would come to their place again, and there would be no more big straw stacks for a boy to climb up and slide down. The combines had arrived, their service to be purchased by mere money.

FROM *The Memory of Old Jack*

⁊

It is September 1952, during the tobacco cutting on the Feltner place. The tradition of work-swapping has continued until now, as it will continue, slowly raveling out, for another thirty or so years. The men have gathered to harvest the crop and the women to feed them dinner. Margaret Feltner is getting on in years and Hannah—who, after Virgil Feltner's death in World War II, married Nathan Coulter—is pregnant. But Mary Penn, as soon as dinner is over and the dishes done, will go out to work the rest of the day with the men. At the start of this passage Hannah has found Old Jack Beechum in the barbershop, where he has been sleeping and dreaming, and she is bringing him to the Feltner house for dinner.

THEY WALK SLOWLY up the street toward Mat's, Hannah holding to the old man's arm as if to be helped, but in reality helping him. And yet she knows that, by taking that arm so graciously bent at her service, she *is* being helped. She is sturdily accompanied by his knowledge, in which she knows that she is whole. In his gaze she feels herself to be not just physically but historically a woman, one among generations, bearing into mystery the dark seed. She feels herself completed by that as she could not be completed by the desire of a younger man. As they walk, she tells him such news as there is: how they all are, where they are working, what they have got done, what they have left to do. From time to time she stops, as if to give all her attention to her story, to allow him a moment of rest. But she is glad to prolong the walk. She is moved by him, pleased to stand in his sight, whose final knowledge is womanly, who knows that all human labor passes into mystery, who has been faithful unto death to the life of his fields to no end that he will know in this world. As for Old Jack, he listens to the sound of her voice, strong and full of hope, knowing and near to joy, that pleases him and tells him what he wants to know. He nods and smiles, encouraging her to go on. Occasionally he praises her, in that tone of final judgment old age has given him. "You're a fine woman. You're all right," he says. And his tone implies: Believe it of yourself forever.

They are crossing Mat's yard now, and suddenly Old Jack can smell dinner. It is strong, and it stirs him. It changes his mind. He steps faster. He is leaving the world of his old age and entering a stronger, younger world. He is going into the very heart of that world where labor's hunger is fed with its increase. That is the order that he knows, and knows only and finally: that complexity of returns between work and hunger.

They turn the corner of the house into sight of the back porch, and there are all the men just come in. Two washpans and two kettles of hot water have been brought out and set down. Little Margaret stands nearby, holding a towel. Lightning and Mat's grandson, Andy Catlett, are washing at the edge of the porch, leaning over the pans. Mat is sitting in a willow rocking chair on the porch with Mattie on his lap. The others—Burley, Jarrat, Nathan, Elton—stand or squat in the yard beyond the porch, smoking, waiting their turns. Their shirts are wet with sweat. Their hands and the fronts of their clothes are dark with tobacco gum. They smell of sweat and tobacco and the earth of the field. In the stance of all of them there is relish of the stillness that comes after heavy labor. They have come to rest, and their stillness now, because of the long afternoon's work yet ahead of them, is more intense, more deeply felt, more carefully enjoyed, than that which will come at the day's end. Even Mat, who ordinarily would be carrying on some sort of play with Mattie, is sitting still, his hands at rest on the chair arms. Mattie is leaning against his shoulder, nearly asleep. Only Burley is talking, though he keeps otherwise as carefully still as the others. He is directing a mixture of banter and praise at Lightning's back. It is a bill of goods designed, as the rest of them well know, to keep Lightning on hand. Under the burden of such a stretch of hard work his customary bragging has given way to periods of sulkiness.

"Why, look at the *arm* on him," Burley is saying. "Look at the *muscle* the fellow's got. Damn, he can barely get his sleeve rolled up over it. No wonder I can't stay with him."

The others grin and wink. The fact is that, left to himself, Lightning is slow. But all week Burley has been working constantly at his heel, bragging on him, threatening to pass him, never quite doing it—and has succeeded in driving him almost up with Elton and Nathan, who are the best of them.

Lightning straightens from his washing and dries hands and face on the towel that Little Margaret holds out to him. He is doing his best to stay aloof from Burley's talk, but it gets to him, and he touches lovingly the muscle of his right arm.

"He put it on me this morning, Uncle Jack," Burley says, seeing the old man coming around the house. "I tried him, but I couldn't shake him."

"Go on and wash," he says to Jarrat. "I got to finish my smoke." He stands bent forward a little at the hips, hand on the small of his back. He seems to be hurting a little. He probably is, but he is playing on it too, parodying an aged and a beaten man. He looks afar, soliloquizing about his defeat. "Nawsir! Couldn't handle him! Too few biscuits and too many years have done made the difference."

"Ay Lord, he's a good one!" Old Jack says, seeing the point. He knows where that Lightning would be if somebody was not crowding him all the time. Somewhere asleep. But he shakes his head in approbation of Burley's praise. "He's got the right look about him."

215

"You're right, old scout," Burley says. "He's the pride of Landing Branch, and no doubt about it. But I believe I smell a biscuit in the wind, and maybe a ham, and that may make a difference this afternoon. When I go back out there I aim to be properly fed. Oh, I may not get ahead of him, but I'll be where he can hear me coming. Ham and biscuits!" he says. And he sings:

How many biscuits can you eat?
Forty-nine and a ham of meat
This mornin'.

Lightning is at work now with a comb, putting the finishing touches to his wave and ducktail, a sculpture not destined to survive the next motion of his head. There is an arrogance in his eye and jaw and the line of his mouth, based not upon any excellence of his own but upon his contempt for excellence: If he is not the best man in the field, then he is nevertheless equal to the best man by the perfection of his scorn, for the best man and for the possibility that is incarnate in him. Old Jack studies Lightning's face—he recognizes it; he has known other men who have worn it, too many—and then he grunts, "*Hunh!*" and looks away.

Jarrat and Elton finish washing and Burley and Nathan take their places. Hannah picks up Mattie, who has fallen asleep in Mat's lap, and takes him in to his napping place on the parlor floor. Little Margaret has wandered off to play.

Now Mat gets up and he and Old Jack wash. When they have finished with the towel, Mat hangs it on the back of the rocking chair.

"Let's go eat it," he says. He holds open the kitchen door and they file in past him, Old Jack first and the others following. There is a general exchange of greetings between the men and the three women.

Old Jack takes his place at the head of the table. "Sit down, boys," he says, and they pull out their chairs and sit down. Mat is at the foot of the table. At the sides, to Old Jack's right, are Elton and Lightning and Andy and, to his left, Burley and Nathan and Jarrat. They pass various loaded platters and bowls, filling their plates.

They fall silent now, eating with the concentration of hunger. The women keep the dishes moving around the table as necessary and keep the glasses filled with iced tea.

"Lay it away, boys," Old Jack says. "It's fine and there's plenty of it."

Following his lead, the others praise the food, the ones whose wives have cooked being careful to praise the cooking of the other women.

In the presence of that hunger and that eager filling, Old Jack eats well himself. But his thoughts go to the other men, and he watches them. He watches the older ones—Mat and Jarrat and Burley—sensing their weariness and their will to endure, troubling about them and admiring them. He watches the five proven men, whom he loves with the satisfaction of thorough knowledge and long trust, praising and blessing them in his mind. He watches them with pleasure so keen it is almost pain.

And he watches the boy, Andy, whom he loves out of kinship and because he is not afraid of work and because of his good, promising mind, but with uneasiness also because he has so little meat on his bones and has a lot to go through, a lot to make up his mind about.

And he watches Lightning, whom he does not love. That one, he thinks, will be hard put to be worth what he will eat. For he is one who believes in a way out. As long as he has two choices, or thinks he has, he will never do his best or think of the possibility of the best.

Old Jack shakes his head. "See that that Andy gets plenty to eat," he tells Mat.

"Don't you worry. I'm going to take care of this boy," Mat says. And he gives Andy a squeeze and a pat on the shoulder.

"We going to miss old Andy when he's gone," Burley says.

The edge is off their hunger now, and they give attention to Andy, for whom this is the summer's last workday. Tomorrow he will be leaving to begin his first year of college.

"We'll be looking around here for the old boy," Burley says, "and he'll done be gone. They'll say, 'Where's the old long boy that could load the wagon so good? Where's that one that used to house the top tiers?' And we'll say, 'Old Andy ain't here no more. He's up there to the university, studying his books.'"

"Studying the girls," Nathan says, grinning and winking at Hannah.

"He'll be all right with the girls if he wants to be," Hannah says. "I'm a better judge of that than you."

"You do all right with Kirby, don't you, Andy, hon?" Mary Penn says.

"Yeah, if old Kirby's going to have any say-so, he *better* keep his mind on his books while he's up there," Burley says. "He don't, she'll kick over the beehive, I expect."

"You keep your mind on your books anyhow, Andy," Jarrat says, looking gravely across the table at the boy, his gaze ponderous and straight under thick brows. "Mind your books, and amount to something."

"Andy," Elton says, "you'll get full of book learning and fine ways up there, and you won't have any more time for us here at all."

Andy, who has been grinning at this commentary on his departure, now flushes with embarrassment. "Yes I will," he says, though he knows the inadequacy of such an avowal. The faith that Elton has called for, though he spoke in jest, will have to be proved.

They all know it. Andy has not yet chosen among his choices.

And then Mat says, "Well, he's learned some things here with us that he couldn't have learned in a school. A lot of his teachers there won't know them. And if he's the boy I think he is, he won't forget them."

"Yessir!" Old Jack says. "By God, that's right!"

Now all the plates are empty. The women gather them and stack them by the sink. They replace them with dishes of blackberry cobbler, still warm from the oven, covered with cold whipped cream.

"You all can thank Andy for this," Hannah says. "I made it for him because it's his favorite."

"*Thank* him!" Nathan says. "I'm mad as hell about it. When are you going to fix me something because it's *my* favorite?"

Hannah grins. "Your time is coming," she says, "*junior.*"

The others laugh. The iced tea glasses are filled again. They take their time over the cobbler, talking idly now of the past, of other crops.

The afternoon's work is near them, not to be put off much longer. Old Jack can feel it around him in the air, that dread of the heat and heaviness of the afternoon that even the strongest and the best man will suffer. But not for him anymore the going back to the field. No more for him the breaking sweat under the sun's blaze, the delight of skill and strength, and the pride.

FROM *Jayber Crow*

꒛

Jayber himself is speaking. From 1937 until 1969 he was the barber in Port William, living in the single room over his shop. Health regulations requiring hot running water put him out of business there. Now he is living, and still barbering, in a remote camp house on the river. Not much is said here about food, though the occasion is partly a meal. But maybe the real subject is the free exchanging of affection and help that makes what Burley Coulter calls "the membership" of Port William.

To get my own hair cut, I had continued to go down to Hargrave. When I lived in Port William, this was easy enough to arrange. I would hear that somebody was going and would speak for a ride. From the house on the river, it was not so easy. Sometimes it would come to hitchhiking, which could take half a day. I happened to mention this to Danny.

He said, "Why, Jayber, you don't need to go to Hargrave to get your hair cut. Lyda can cut it."

It was evening. He had finished running his lines and was going home. "Come on," he said.

So we went up to his truck and I rode home with him.

"Lyda," he said, "Jayber here needs to get his hair cut."

221

She said, "Well, he'll have to eat his supper first. I can't stop now."

I said, "Oh, now, I hate to put you to the trouble."

"One more mouth won't make any difference here," she said.

"Naw, Jayber," Burley called from the porch swing, "it won't be any trouble. Come on up. I'll have supper on the table in a few minutes."

Lyda took a swipe at his shoulder with the rag she had in her hand. "*You'll* have it on the table! *That'll* be a fair fine day in Hell!"

"That's where they've got something cooking all the time," Burley said. "Come on up, Jayber."

By then all the children and dogs knew there was a stranger on the place, and they had come to look. They all crowded around me as if maybe I had my pockets full of candy.

"Get back! Get back!" Danny said. "Give a man room to walk!" He made a parting motion with his hands.

Children and dogs fell back to each side like the waters of the Red Sea, leaving a sort of aisle that Danny and I walked through to the washstand by the rain barrel at the corner of the porch. Danny picked up the wash pan, smote the surface of the water in the barrel with the bottom of the pan to drive the wigglers down, dipped the pan half full of water, set it down on the washstand, and stepped aside, gesturing welcome with his hand. "There's soap and a towel if you'd like to wash up," he said to me, and then to the children and dogs who had clustered around again, "Get back!"

The children and dogs fell back, never ceasing to watch me. I washed up, threw the water out, dipped the pan for Danny, and made my way amongst the children and dogs up onto the porch. "Sit down, Jayber," Burley said, and I sat down.

When he had washed, Danny refilled the pan and stood there watching while the children washed, the bigger ones seeing to the littler ones, who wanted to splash more than wash. Danny said, "Keep your hands off of them dogs, now, till after supper."

You might think that so many young children would make a considerable uproar at a meal, but when Lyda called us in to supper those
children (from Will, who was fourteen, right down to Rosie, who was
four) went in and sat down in their places and never made a peep. I
thought at first that that probably was because I was there, but in fact it
was pretty much according to rule. But this wasn't spiritlessness: It was
discipline. Out from under Lyda's gaze, the children were noisy enough.
When Reuben and the two girls were little, they talked all the time, all at
the same time, in high chirps, like a tree full of sparrows.

When the meal was over, the children scraped and stacked the
dishes, which Burley then washed and Will dried and put away.

There was a running joke between Burley and Lyda about Burley's
reluctance and incompetence at housework, but of course Burley had
lived alone for a long time before Danny and Lyda came, and he could
do all the household work, if not to Lyda's taste at least well enough.
When they came, since it was his house, he might have treated them
as the beneficiaries of his hospitality, but instead he made himself their
guest. They responded, as maybe they didn't have to do, by being hos-
pitable to him. He was, I think, a good guest, helping especially Lyda in
every way he could. She caught his trick of dealing with this arrangement and their large affection for each other as an endlessly branch-
ing joke, in which they said the opposite of what they meant. If Burley
complained that he was behind in his housework because she was always
underfoot and in the way, he meant that she was anything but in the way
and he was thankful to have her there. If Lyda said that it would have
been a mercy if she had married one husband instead of two bachelors,
that meant that she loved them both more than enough to put up with
them. And so on.

While Burley and Will did the dishes and Danny and Royal and
Coulter and Fount went out to feed the dogs and do a few last chores
(the children having milked and fed before supper), Lyda gave me my

haircut. The sight of their mother cutting a stranger's hair was so shocking that Rachel and Rosie whispered and giggled throughout the operation, and Reuben could bear to watch only from under the table.

FROM *Hannah Coulter*

༷

These two paragraphs return us to Hannah Coulter. It is the year 2000. Her sec-
ond husband, Nathan, has died. Her grandson Virgie—son of Margaret, daughter
of Hannah and her first husband, Virgil Feltner—has taken to disillusion and
drugs, and has disappeared. Caleb is Hannah and Nathan's son. He is a scientist,
a professor of agriculture in a university some distance away. Alice is his wife.

EVEN OLD, YOUR husband is the young man you remember now.
Even dead, he is the man you remember, not as he was but as he
is, alive still in your love. Death is a sort of lens, though I used to think
of it as a wall or a shut door. It changes things and makes them clear.
Maybe it is the truest way of knowing this dream, this brief and timeless
life. Sometimes when I try to remember Nathan, I can't see him exactly
enough. Other times, when I haven't thought of him, he comes to me
unbidden, and I see him more clearly, I think, than ever I did. Am I awake
then, or there, or here?

It is the fall of the year. We have had Thanksgiving. Caleb and Alice
were here. And Margaret came, reconciled by now maybe to Virgie's absence, but not one of us spoke of Virgie. I fixed a big dinner, enough to
keep us all in leftovers for a while: a young gobbler that Coulter Branch
shot and gave to me, dressing and gravy, mashed potatoes, green beans,

corn pudding, hot rolls, a cushaw pie. We sat down to it, the four of us, like stray pieces of several puzzles. Nathan would have asked the blessing, and I should have, I tried to, but that turned out to be a silence I could not speak in. I only sat with my head down, while the others waited for me to say something out loud. And then, to change the subject, I said, "Caleb, take a roll and pass 'em."

The Pleasures of Eating

(1989)

⸜

M ANY TIMES, AFTER I have finished a lecture on the decline of
American farming and rural life, someone in the audience has
asked, "What can city people do?"

"Eat responsibly," I have usually answered. Of course, I have tried to
explain what I meant by that, but afterwards I have invariably felt that
there was more to be said than I had been able to say. Now I would like
to attempt a better explanation.

I begin with the proposition that eating is an agricultural act. Eating
ends the annual drama of the food economy that begins with planting
and birth. Most eaters, however, are no longer aware that this is true.
They think of food as an agricultural product, perhaps, but they do not
think of themselves as "consumers." If they think beyond that, they recognize that they are passive consumers. They buy what they want—or
what they have been persuaded to want—within the limits of what they
can get. They pay, mostly without protest, what they are charged. And
they mostly ignore certain critical questions about the quality and the
cost of what they are sold: How fresh is it? How pure or clean is it, how
free of dangerous chemicals? How far was it transported, and what did

transportation add to the cost? How much did manufacturing or pack-aging or advertising add to the cost? When the food product has been manufactured or "processed" or "precooked," how has that affected its quality or price or nutritional value?

Most urban shoppers would tell you that food is produced on farms. But most of them do not know what farms, or what kinds of farms, or where the farms are, or what knowledge or skills are involved in farming. They apparently have little doubt that farms will continue to produce, but they do not know how or over what obstacles. For them, then, food is pretty much an abstract idea—something they do not know or imag-ine—until it appears on the grocery shelf or on the table.

The specialization of production induces specialization of consump-tion. Patrons of the entertainment industry, for example, entertain them-selves less and less and have become more and more passively dependent on commercial suppliers. This is certainly true also of patrons of the food industry, who have tended more and more to be *mere* consumers—passive, uncritical, and dependent. Indeed, this sort of consumption may be said to be one of the chief goals of industrial production. The food in-dustrialists have by now persuaded millions of consumers to prefer food that is already prepared. They will grow, deliver, and cook your food for you and (just like your mother) beg you to eat it. That they do not yet offer to insert it, prechewed, into your mouth is only because they have found no profitable way to do so. We may rest assured that they would be glad to find such a way. The ideal industrial food consumer would be strapped to a table with a tube running from the food factory directly into his or her stomach.

Perhaps I exaggerate, but not by much. The industrial eater is, in fact, one who does not know that eating is an agricultural act, who no longer knows or imagines the connections between eating and the land, and who is therefore necessarily passive and uncritical—in short, a victim. When food, in the minds of eaters, is no longer associated with farming and with the land, then the eaters are suffering a kind of cultural amnesia that is misleading and dangerous. The current version of the "dream home" of the future involves "effortless" shopping from a list of available goods on a television monitor and heating precooked food by remote control. Of course, this implies and depends on a perfect ignorance of the history of the food that is consumed. It requires that the citizenry should give up their hereditary and sensible aversion to buying a pig in a poke. It wishes to make the selling of pigs in pokes an honorable and glamorous activity. The dreamer in this dream home will perforce know nothing about the kind or quality of this food, or where it came from, or how it was produced and prepared, or what ingredients, additives, and residues it contains—unless, that is, the dreamer undertakes a close and constant study of the food industry, in which case he or she might as well wake up and play an active and responsible part in the economy of food.

There is, then, a politics of food that, like any politics, involves our freedom. We still (sometimes) remember that we cannot be free if our minds and voices are controlled by someone else. But we have neglected to understand that we cannot be free if our food and its sources are controlled by someone else. The condition of the passive consumer of food is not a democratic condition. One reason to eat responsibly is to live free.

But if there is a food politics, there are also a food esthetics and a food ethics, neither of which is dissociated from politics. Like industrial sex, industrial eating has become a degraded, poor, and paltry thing. Our kitchens and other eating places more and more resemble filling stations, as our homes more and more resemble motels. "Life is not very interesting," we seem to have decided. "Let its satisfactions be minimal, perfunctory, and fast." We hurry through our meals to go to work and hurry through our work in order to "recreate" ourselves in the evenings and on weekends and vacations. And then we hurry, with the greatest possible speed and noise and violence, through our recreation—for what? To eat the billionth hamburger at some fast-food joint hellbent on increasing the "quality" of our life? And all this is carried out in a remarkable obliviousness to the causes and effects, the possibilities and the purposes, of the life of the body in this world.

One will find this obliviousness represented in virgin purity in the advertisements of the food industry, in which food wears as much makeup as the actors. If one gained one's whole knowledge of food from these advertisements (as some presumably do), one would not know that the various edibles were ever living creatures, or that they all come from the soil, or that they were produced by work. The passive American consumer, sitting down to a meal of pre-prepared or fast food, confronts a platter covered with inert, anonymous substances that have been processed, dyed, breaded, sauced, gravied, ground, pulped, strained, blended, prettified, and sanitized beyond resemblance to any part of any creature that ever lived. The products of nature and agriculture have been made, to all appearances, the products of industry. Both eater and eaten are thus in exile from biological reality. And the result is a kind of solitude, unprecedented in human experience, in which the eater may think of eating as, first, a purely commercial transaction between him and a supplier and then as a purely appetitive transaction between him and his food.

And this peculiar specialization of the act of eating is, again, of obvious benefit to the food industry, which has good reasons to obscure the connection between food and farming. It would not do for the consumer to know that the hamburger she is eating came from a steer who spent much of his life standing deep in his own excrement in a feedlot, helping to pollute the local streams, or that the calf that yielded the veal cutlet on her plate spent its life in a box in which it did not have room to turn around. And, though her sympathy for the slaw might be less tender, she should not be encouraged to meditate on the hygienic and biological implications of mile-square fields of cabbage, for vegetables grown in huge monocultures are dependent on toxic chemicals—just as animals in close confinement are dependent on antibiotics and other drugs.

The consumer, that is to say, must be kept from discovering that, in the food industry—as in any other industry—the overriding concerns are not quality and health, but volume and price. For decades now the entire industrial food economy, from the large farms and feedlots to the chains of supermarkets and fast-food restaurants, has been obsessed with volume. It has relentlessly increased scale in order to increase volume in order (presumably) to reduce costs. But as scale increases, diversity declines; as diversity declines, so does health; as health declines, the dependence on drugs and chemicals necessarily increases. As capital replaces labor, it does so by substituting machines, drugs, and chemicals for human workers and for the natural health and fertility of the soil. The food is produced by any means or any shortcut that will increase profits. And the business of the cosmeticians of advertising is to persuade the consumer that food so produced is good, tasty, healthful, and a guarantee of marital fidelity and long life.

It is possible, then, to be liberated from the husbandry and wifery of the old household food economy. But one can be thus liberated only by entering a trap (unless one sees ignorance and helplessness as the signs of privilege, as many people apparently do). The trap is the ideal of industrialism: a walled city surrounded by valves that let merchandise in but no consciousness out. How does one escape this trap? Only voluntarily, the same way that one went in: by restoring one's consciousness of what is involved in eating, by reclaiming responsibility for one's own part in the food economy. One might begin with the illuminating principle of Sir Albert Howard's *The Soil and Health*, that we should understand "the whole problem of health in soil, plant, animal, and man as one great subject." Eaters, that is, must understand that eating takes place inescapably in the world, that it is inescapably an agricultural act, and that how we eat determines, to a considerable extent, how the world is used. This is a simple way of describing a relationship that is inexpressibly complex. To eat responsibly is to understand and enact, so far as one can, this complex relationship. What can one do? Here is a list, probably not definitive:

1. Participate in food production to the extent that you can. If you have a yard or even just a porch box or a pot in a sunny window, grow something to eat in it. Make a little compost of your kitchen scraps and use it for fertilizer. Only by growing some food for yourself can you become acquainted with the beautiful energy cycle that revolves from soil to seed to flower to fruit to food to offal to decay, and around again. You will be fully responsible for any food that you grow for yourself, and you will know all about it. You will appreciate it fully, having known it all its life.

2. Prepare your own food. This means reviving in your own mind and life the arts of kitchen and household. This should enable you to eat more cheaply, and it will give you a measure of "quality control": You will have some reliable knowledge of what has been added to the food you eat.

3. Learn the origins of the food you buy, and buy the food that is produced closest to your home. The idea that every locality should be, as much as possible, the source of its own food makes several kinds of sense. The locally produced food supply is the most secure, the freshest, and the easiest for local consumers to know about and to influence.

4. Whenever possible, deal directly with a local farmer, gardener, or orchardist. All the reasons listed for the previous suggestion apply here. In addition, by such dealing you eliminate the whole pack of merchants, transporters, processors, packagers, and advertisers who thrive at the expense of both producers and consumers.

5. Learn, in self-defense, as much as you can of the economy and technology of industrial food production. What is added to food that is not food, and what do you pay for these additions?

6. Learn what is involved in the *best* farming and gardening.

7. Learn as much as you can, by direct observation and experience if possible, of the life histories of the food species.

The last suggestion seems particularly important to me. Many people are now as much estranged from the lives of domestic plants and animals (except for flowers and dogs and cats) as they are from the lives of the wild ones. This is regrettable, for these domestic creatures are in diverse ways attractive; there is much pleasure in knowing them. And farming, animal husbandry, horticulture, and gardening, at their best, are complex and comely arts; there is much pleasure in knowing them, too.

It follows that there is great *dis*pleasure in knowing about a food economy that degrades and abuses those arts and those plants and animals and the soil from which they come. For anyone who does know something of the modern history of food, eating away from home can be a chore. My own inclination is to eat seafood instead of red meat or poultry when I am traveling. Though I am by no means a vegetarian, I dislike the thought that some animal has been made miserable in order to feed me. If I am going to eat meat, I want it to be from an animal that has lived a pleasant, uncrowded life outdoors, on bountiful pasture, with good water nearby and trees for shade. And I am getting almost as fussy about food plants. I like to eat vegetables and fruits that I know have lived happily and healthily in good soil, not the products of the huge, bechemicaled factory-fields that I have seen, for example, in the Central Valley of California. The industrial farm is said to have been patterned on the factory production line. In practice, it looks more like a concentration camp.

The pleasure of eating should be an *extensive* pleasure, not that of the mere gourmet. People who know the garden in which their vegetables have grown and know that the garden is healthy will remember the beauty of the growing plants, perhaps in the dewy first light of morning when gardens are at their best. Such a memory involves itself with the food and is one of the pleasures of eating. The knowledge of the good health of the garden relieves and frees and comforts the eater. The same goes for eating meat. The thought of the good pasture and of the calf contentedly grazing flavors the steak. Some, I know, will think it blood-thirsty or worse to eat a fellow creature you have known all its life. On the contrary, I think it means that you eat with understanding and with gratitude. A significant part of the pleasure of eating is one's accurate consciousness of the lives and the world from which food comes. The pleasure of eating, then, may be the best available standard of our health. And this pleasure, I think, is pretty fully available to the urban consumer who will make the necessary effort.

I mentioned earlier the politics, esthetics, and ethics of food. But to speak of the pleasure of eating is to go beyond those categories. Eating with the fullest pleasure—pleasure, that is, that does not depend on ig-norance—is perhaps the profoundest enactment of our connection with the world. In this pleasure we experience and celebrate our dependence and our gratitude, for we are living from mystery, from creatures we did not make and powers we cannot comprehend. When I think of the mean-ing of food, I always remember these lines by the poet William Carlos Williams, which seem to me merely honest:

> There is nothing to eat,
>   seek it where you will,
>   but of the body of the Lord.
> The blessed plants
>   and the sea, yield it
>   to the imagination
> intact.

About the Author

Author of fifty books of fiction, poetry, and essays, Wendell Berry has farmed a hillside in his native Henry County, Kentucky, with his wife Tanya for over forty years. He has received numerous awards for his work, including the T.S. Eliot Award, the Aiken Taylor Award for poetry, the John Hay Award of the Orion Society, and recently the Cleanth Brooks Medal for Excellence in Southern Letters and the Louis Bromfield Society Award.